THE STARLIGHT RITE

Cherise Sinclair

VanScoy Publishing Group

The Starlight Rite

Copyright © 2010 by Cherise Sinclair
Print Edition
ISBN 978-0-9913222-6-8
Published by VanScoy Publishing Group
Cover Art: The Killion Group
~ Reprint ~

Author's Note

To *my readers,*

The books I write are fiction, not reality, and as in most romantic fiction, the romance is compressed into a very, very short time period.

You, my darlings, live in the real world, and I want you to take a little more time in your relationships. Good Doms don't grow on trees, and there are some strange people out there. So while you're looking for that special Dom, please, be careful.

When you find him, realize he can't read your mind. Yes, frightening as it might be, you're going to have to open up and talk to him. And you listen to him, in return. Share your hopes and fears, what you want from him, what scares you spitless. Okay, he may try to push your boundaries a little—he's a Dom, after all—but you will have your safe word. You will have a safe word, am I clear? Use protection. Have a back-up person. Communicate.

Remember: safe, sane, and consensual.

Know that I'm hoping you find that special, loving person who will understand your needs and hold you close.

And while you're looking or even if you have already found your dearheart, come and hang out with the dominant kinlines on Nexus.

Love,
Cherise
Cherise@CheriseSinclair.com

Chapter One

*D*AMN HIM. THE fat, overly jeweled Nexan she'd chosen as her target had picked up two companions in the fancy men's club. If he'd left by himself, she'd have managed him easily enough, considering how drunk he was. But two more?

Grinding her teeth in frustration, Armelina Archer settled lower in the small space between the two solacars and watched the fat man stagger out of reach, taking with him the jewelry that would have bought her next few meals and provided some money toward a ticket off-planet.

That just isn't fair. She huffed a bitter laugh. Nothing had been fair recently, not since she'd landed on this horrible planet.

Why had she ever come here? But she couldn't have known what would happen. Couldn't have known that her husband—someone she'd thought she loved—could be so evil. *A monster.*

She closed her eyes, hearing again the ear-cracking booms as the ship exploded in the dock, taking with it the bodies of the crew she'd come to love. The monster had paid to have her murdered, and they had died instead.

She swallowed hard. Cap and Johnnie and Pard—*my fault that they died.* "I'm sorry," she whispered, "so, so sorry."

Tears slid down her cheeks. Night after night, old Cap had sat with her in the tiny lounge, a comforting companion as the stars streamed by. Now he was gone... *No, don't start again.* She scrubbed her face with dirty hands and grimaced as grit abraded her chapped skin. She hadn't had a shower since the night of the explosion over three weeks ago.

Stranded on a strange planet. No friends. No money. Of anywhere in the galaxy to end up flat broke, the frontier planet Nexus was the worst.

As the evening air chilled, Mella waited. Another customer left the club, but an attendant drove his horse and carriage up to the door. A *horse.* How could a space-faring people still use such antiquated transportation? Why didn't they stick to solacars?

The club door opened again. Music spilled out, her own voice singing a love song filled with joy. *Oh Prophet.* Mella wrapped her arms around herself and breathed hard against the wrenching pain. Her voice. Her song—written before her parents and sister were taken from her in a fiery hovercar accident. She hadn't written or sung a note since. All her joy and creativity had dried up like an unwatered, unloved plant. *Mama, Daddy, Kalie… Why did you leave me? I miss you all so much.*

She shoved away the growing ache and concentrated on the goal. The air slowly chilled, and the low chirps of sleepy avians stilled. She'd grown stiff by the time another man finally emerged from the club. Leaning on a cane, he limped down the steps and—*oh yes!*—actually continued across the manicured purple grass that served as a walkway. Maybe…maybe…

Mella edged out from her hiding spot as he headed toward the car lot. Empty street, disabled guy. She squinted. With only one moon in the sky, she couldn't determine his age. His long black cape disguised his build, but he was tall—very tall—with broad shoulders. Still…*crippled.* She could just knock him down, grab his totepurse, and run really, really fast.

Pretty dangerous.

Pretty despicable. To steal and maybe even hurt someone. But did she have a choice? Damn this planet that had no charities or help for the penniless. They put the indigent up for auction to the highest bidder and would do the same to her if she got caught. She'd end up working her indenture off in the mines, pulling weeds on a farm…or servicing men in a brothel. A brothel. This terrifyingly immoral world allowed sex not just for reproduction, but for…for recreation. She could be forced to couple with strangers.

Her fingers trembled. She needed money to eat. And to return to Earth before Nathan discovered she was still alive.

Pulling out her tiny knife, she kicked off her shoes. Her bare feet soundless, she ran after the man. As he leaned on the cane, she came up behind him and slammed into him with her shoulder.

He went down like a toppled tree, landing with a low *oomph*.

She ripped his coat open, grabbed the totepurse, and slashed the strings. *Success*! One step back and suddenly a hard hand closed around her ankle. She tried to yank away, but his grip only tightened.

"Let me go!" She kicked at him with her free foot.

She had time to think *mistake*! before he yanked the leg supporting her weight right out from under her. Her shoulder and side slammed into the ground, and for a second, she couldn't get a breath. *Run.* Gasping, she elbowed herself upward, and he came down on top of her, pressing her flat on her back with his heavy, muscular body. Her fingers curled into claws, and she tried to scratch him.

A viselike grip caught her wrists, and he pinned her hands over her head.

Face-to-face. *Oh Prophet, he isn't old at all.* In the glimmer of the parking-lot lights, she saw dark eyes in a lean, hard face. He was probably around forty Earth years. A man in his prime. *A major mistake.*

"Stop struggling, or I will hurt you," he said. "Badly." His voice was deep. Authoritative.

She couldn't quit. But he didn't even seem to notice her furious thrashing as he secured the grip on her wrists with one hand and his iron-hard legs pinned hers.

With his free hand, he grasped her chin, turning her head from side to side, despite her attempts to jerk away. "Quite the dirty little thief, aren't you," he mused as if he were lounging idly at home rather than lying on a frantically struggling person. "I don't usually see female thieves."

She pulled at her arms. Trying to throw him off, she jerked her hips up…and froze as the hard ridge of an erection pressed against her mound.

Her breath stopped. Nexans had no rules about sex. He could… Terror clamped bands around her chest, and she yanked at her trapped wrists. "Don't touch me."

"Ah, an Earther. Interesting." His hand left her face to stroke her breast, his touch disconcertingly gentle. Warm even through her clothing. "You're a lush little thing. Not at all like our Nexan females."

No one had ever touched her like that. Not even Nathan when they coupled. Her heart hammered as she realized he could easily take her right here. He was strong—too strong for her weakened state. "Let me go," she said, realizing her words had sounded like a plea.

"Ah, *laria*, I cannot. The law is clear on this." With a flash of white teeth, he sat back and flipped her over. Pinning her in place with a knee in the small of her back, he lashed her hands together, using, of all things, the cord she'd cut from his totepurse. "You'll be in front of a judge before the sun rises."

HE HAD THE little thief to thank for adding some interest to a boring evening, Dain mused, but the excitement had come at a price. The gods knew he'd rather be scorched on Ekatae's sands than continue on medical leave for another Neman mooncycle. He shifted in the hard chair and rubbed his leg, trying to ease the pain from the fall and subsequent wrestling bout. Comfort was sorely lacking in the small judgment room where he and the judge waited. Used for trials without publicity, the stark white room held only the judge's chair at one end and several chairs for witnesses.

And a restraint pen for the accused by the door. Unlike the back-country, Port City had all the amenities.

The judge noticed him massaging his leg, and her lips compressed. "Did you reinjure your knee in the altercation? Did the doctor look at it?"

"It's fine—" Dain stopped as Srinda raised her eyebrows. *Scorch all truth-reading judges.* And his cousin from the Minerind kinline had less patience for evasion than most. "Yes, the doctor checked my leg."

"And he said…" Srinda prompted.

"Another three weeks of leave, more x-scans in a week," Dain growled, knowing she'd look up the information on the infodisc if he didn't tell her. By the gods, he hated to add the crime of *injury* to the little thief's transgressions—no matter how embarrassing it was that she'd managed to take him by surprise.

The door opened, and a burly enforcer pushed the thief into the room and into the restraint pen. He activated the controls as he stepped back, and red force lines sprang up around the young woman. A sizzling *zap* and a sharp cry showed the thief hadn't been in an r-pen before or else she'd have known not to touch the field.

Leaning back, Dain studied the criminal. Not a youth, maybe in her late twenties. About five feet five. The long braid appeared light colored, but she was too dirty to tell. Same with the skin. Her big eyes were a startling green color. And that body… Even her baggy men's attire couldn't hide the lushness of her figure.

His fingers remembered the heaviness of her breast and tingled to touch her again. This time without clothing in the way. It had been a long while since he'd felt so intrigued—so aroused. Not since he and Kritadona had backed away from contracting.

As he watched the thief, she composed herself and looked around the room. When her gaze met his, she blinked in surprise.

"We will begin now," Srinda said. "Recording on. Records, display the infractions."

The list of offenses appeared on the wall, rendered in Trade language so the prisoner could read it. The little thief was lucky the truth-reader had no reason to dig further. Considering her dexterity at cutting his totepurse, she'd obviously done it before.

Srinda tilted her head at the young woman. "You gave your name as simply *Mella* and carried no ID. It makes no difference; we consider the names of criminals to be unimportant. These are the offenses you are charged with. Is this list accurate, or are there any you wish to dispute?"

Hands clasped in front of her, the girl read the list. *Assault on a citizen, attempted theft from a citizen, infliction of injury on a citizen.* The green eyes widened. "Injury?" She looked at Dain and bit her lip, her sense of shame as obvious to him as when he caught his nephew teasing his nieces. "I…"

After a hard breath that jostled her lovely breasts, she frowned. "Would claiming mitigating circumstances gain me any leniency?"

Dain's eyebrows rose at the clever question. The little Earther was more educated than he'd thought. *Interesting.*

Srinda shook her head. "I've heard about your planet and the convoluted laws you use for justice. Here, the law is simple. If you committed the offense—for whatever reason—you pay the penalty. In addition, on Nexus, a convicted criminal's commitments, whether social, moral, or financial, are severed during the indenture period. That means job obligations, spousal contracts, or social duties are all null and void." She paused.

The thief nodded slowly.

"So." Srinda leaned forward. "You are assessed four hundred royals for these crimes."

In spite of the dirt, the Earther's face paled at the sum of her debt.

"Two hundred of that will be paid to Nexus for the cost of your trial and auction." The judge gestured toward Dain. "Two hundred goes to the victim, *Kinae* Dain of the Zarain clan."

The woman's hands clenched.

Srinda took no notice. "You had fifteen royals on your person and said that is the extent of your resources. With fifteen credited, you owe three hundred and eighty-five. The indenture period is calculated for a set ten royals per day, regardless of the selling price, so you will serve for thirty-nine days in whatever capacity brings the most return to Nexus. Since you inflicted physical damage on a citizen, your indenture is unrestricted, meaning the purchaser of your contract may use you in any way he sees fit, as long as your body is not permanently damaged."

Srinda paused, but the girl didn't respond, although her eyes had widened, and she appeared close to hyperventilating.

"You will be tested and prepared per regulations, and your contract will be auctioned off in the Port City plaza tomorrow morning. No matter your selling price, you will serve the full thirty-nine days; however, you will receive half of any amount over the three hundred and eighty-five upon the fulfillment of your indenture period."

The thief stood silent in the r-pen, and Dain felt a moment of pity. A lot of leeway existed between comfort and irreparable damage, and many owners went as far as they could.

"Is any part of what I have explained unclear to you?" Srinda asked.

The thief shook her head. Her lower lip quivered before she pressed her lips together.

Brave little criminal. Intelligent, courageous, proud. Beautiful? A man had to wonder what she would look like all cleaned up. Dain steepled his fingers and considered.

Perhaps he'd pay a visit to the market in the morning.

Now what? The next morning, Mella sat on the tiny cot. Her arms wrapped around her legs, she rested her chin on her knees. Exhaustion weighted her limbs, and her eyes felt gritty from lack of sleep. Even after she'd managed to doze off, nightmares of blood and knives and explosions had roused her over and over.

At least the jailers hadn't treated her badly, although they showed her no more respect than a stray dog. They'd brought her breakfast—nothing fancy, but any decent food tasted wonderful these days. She hadn't minded the hard bed, considering the night before her arrest, she'd curled under a bush to stay warm.

The cell was tidy enough, but the odor of fear and sweat overwhelmed the lingering scent of an astringent cleaning solution. The stench of her own terror likely added to the mix. They were going to *sell* her.

Stop. No panicking. Maybe her indenture period wouldn't be so bad. She snorted. It was going to be bad. They auctioned off indentured slaves in the Port City plaza. Naked. Handled by the potential buyers. After one glimpse two weeks ago, she'd never returned to that side of the plaza.

Now *she'd* stand up there on an auction stage.

What kind of person would buy her? Her stomach clenched. After breakfast, they'd brought in a testing infounit to discover her salable skills. Sitting at the archaic machine, she'd selected *cook* and quickly learned the unit would verify any skill she claimed to have. When she couldn't give the ingredients for a common meat pie, the program deleted *cook* from her list.

She did possess a talent—singing—and a pity she couldn't claim it. Not if she wanted to live. Too many people recognized her voice, even on this antiquated planet. If rumors started, the monster would learn she'd survived the explosion.

And yet... She stared at the gray walls around her. No skills meant hard labor...or a sex slave. Hard-labor slaves tended to have short life spans. But to serve as a sex slave—an *unshuline?*

She'd always behaved properly. If she'd had a few fantasies as a girl... Well, undoubtedly so had others. Mella shook her head. Over the past few weeks, she'd learned her fantasies had been very, very tame. Her tour of the rediscovered planets in the galaxy had revealed more than she'd wanted to know about sex. On Maliden, citizens actually held hands in public, right out on the streets! She'd even seen one couple kiss.

On Earth, the shepherds would have arrested them. Whipped them.

On Krador, men and women stood on special stands to sell their scantily clad bodies. *Prostitutes,* she'd learned from the hotel concierge. Earth didn't have whores, at least none that Mella knew about. Whorehouses had been burned during the Moral Wars forty years ago.

Only married couples had sex and only for reproduction. Decadent, sensual indulgence was a route straight to hell.

The vid in her hotel room on Delgato had shown people in bed—coupling. And even kissing and touching while coupling. She'd shut the vid off—eventually—but the images had burned into her memory. The man had put his hands on...

She huffed out a breath. And of course, she had had to end up on the most depraved planet of all. Only Nexans indentured people for sex. Only Nexans had parties where people coupled in public, and with more than one partner. Only Nexans married more than one person. Their culture seemed very rigid, but not about intercourse.

She shuddered at the thought of coupling. Of being touched. Laughter and song had died with her family, and the world had turned as gray as these walls. She stayed encased in ice, avoiding any touch, even Nathan's. She wanted it that way; no pain could get through the frozen wasteland.

Only, it could... Something had cracked with the captain's death. And Johnnie's and Pard's. *Oh Prophet.* Tears pooled, and she blinked hard. Their friendship had been so precious. She swallowed against the wrenching grief. She could still hear the enforcers talking—*laughing*—as they had placed explosives around her ship. She remembered the horror when she had realized she was going to die. Die like her newfound friends. "*I don't want to die,*" she'd whispered.

She wanted to live. Whether it was gray or not, she wasn't ready to leave the world. Not yet.

But to couple with a stranger?

She thought of the man last night—the way he had stroked her breast, his dark eyes on her—and shivered as embarrassment and...warmth...rolled through her. He'd touched her more intimately in those few seconds than Nathan ever had in their five years of marriage.

Marriage. She bit her lip. According to that judge, during the indenture, she wasn't married. After that? *No, I refuse to be married to that monster.* On Delgato, she'd learned their marriage could end with just the declaration of intent stated three times. She pulled in a breath.

"Nathan, I divorce you, I divorce you, I divorce you." Maybe only a rodent or two heard her, but inside, she knew the truth, and a knot of tension loosened in her chest.

At least they hadn't had children. When he'd called her barren, it had hurt, but now she found it a relief. Nexus didn't permit birth control.

Footsteps came briskly down the hall and stopped. Her heart thudded hard against her chest when a tall gaunt man clicked off the restraint field. "My title be Handler. You be Mella?"

Not me. She wanted to cling to the cot and refuse to leave, but her parents hadn't raised a coward. Shoving panic down, she rose to her feet and inclined her head. "I am Mella."

A flicker of a smile grazed his thin lips. "Earther. That be unusual." He fastened bright green metal bracelets around her wrists. "Green is for slave who have harmed someone and thus may be harmed in return. The bracelets will be removed in thirty-nine days."

Harmed in return? She shuddered and stared at the wide cuffs. They were lined with something soft, and each had a metal ring hanging from it. They made her feel like some sort of criminal. Her shoulders slumped. *I am a criminal.* "What happens if I run?"

"Added to indenture contract will be cost of locating you. And corporal punishment."

Like whipping? Forget running.

He headed for the door, paused, and frowned at her. "Come with."

Chapter Two

DOWN THE HALLWAY waited a line of men and women attired in red tunics with white trim. Handler beckoned to a stocky man a few years older than Mella. "Abelosh. This one prepare for auction today."

"Yes, Handler. Full prep?" The way Abelosh's full lips curved into a pleased smile made Mella's heart sink.

"No skills has she. Full prep."

The first room Abelosh took her to held a huge open shower. "Strip. Leave your clothing on the bench. Clean yourself." He leaned against the wall and crossed his arms.

He planned to watch her? Her hands went cold. "I can shower alone," she said, lifting her chin and giving him a frosty look. "Go outside."

"Doesn't work that way, girl," he said. "Get used to it, and fast."

She glared at him.

"You know why Handler picked me to process you?"

She shook her head, too angry and too scared to speak.

"Because the sooner you get used to a man's look—and touch—the better."

Even though she'd known something like this would happen, she felt the blood leaving her head. No one had seen her naked since she was a child.

"Strip and shower." He touched the three-foot metal rod hanging from his belt. "Next time you disobey, I'll use this." His eyes brightened, as if the thought of hitting her pleased him.

She had no choice. Mouth tight, she turned her back to him. After ensuring the monster's last message to her was safely buttoned in a pocket, she pulled her clothing off. Naked, she walked into the shower, and the spray came on. His gaze made her skin crawl. A dispenser slid out of the wall, and she used the unscented soap. Quickly. She ignored how good the warm water felt. Maybe if she stank, she'd go to the mines and not some whorehouse.

"Enough. This is just to get you clean for the doctor's exam." The man jerked his head toward a small cubicle. When she stepped in, warm air blew out of numerous jets, drying her body. Her wet hair tangled over her shoulders when he pulled her back out. Naked.

"Next stop, the doctor."

"What about my clothes?"

"You'll get them back after your indenture is up." He grinned, his gaze running up and down her body. "Slaves wear clothing provided by their owners. You have no owner yet, so no clothes."

But…the holocard. Her proof of Nathan's guilt. Her fingers twitched, and then she crossed her arms over her bare chest. Perhaps it would be safer here, locked away. Who knew what might happen to her belongings once someone bought her? "I understand." Resigned, she followed Abelosh down a long hallway.

As Mella stared at the stained wall, a female physician examined her, poking fingers into her mouth, checking her heart and lungs, and examining her private areas as if she were an animal. After using a small scanner, the doctor passed her back to Abelosh, saying, "No disease. Healthy and strong, if a bit undernourished. Not a virgin. No pregnancies. The report for the buyer will be ready in a few minutes."

And my teeth are fine.

Abelosh nodded, grasping Mella's upper arm. When his fingers brushed the side of her breast, she tried to step back. "Nope, don't bother, girl. Each time you flinch away, I'll touch you more." Still holding her arm, he ran his hand over her bare breasts.

Horror streaking through her, she gasped and hit him in the face as hard as she could. After yanking her arm from his grasp, she turned to run and got two steps.

His rod slapped against her leg.

Pain. Her muscles convulsed. Agony seared her body. She couldn't even scream. When he pulled the device away, she crumpled to the floor.

He dragged her to her feet and waited until her legs stopped shaking. Stabs of pain shot through her with every movement.

"The z-rod has a charge in it, and that was the lowest setting," he said. "Every person in processing and auctioning carries one." And then, as she stood stiffly, he ran his hands over her breasts again.

She didn't flinch, although her teeth gritted together so hard, she heard a grinding noise.

He patted her cheek. "Doncha worry, girl. Next time someone does this, you're going to beg for more."

He was wrong. He was totally wrong.

The next room contained attendants clustered by a round pool to the right. The left held more staff and several long tables with slaves lying on them. The people looked at her. When she moved her hands to cover herself, they laughed. Abelosh pushed her forward.

In the warm pool, attendants with soft brushes scoured Mella cleaner than the shower had. No wonder Abelosh hadn't cared how well she washed. They shampooed and conditioned her hair again, then dried it and brushed the snarls out until it flowed silky smooth down her back. The lotion they used bore the light, airy fragrance of Nexan flowers, one of their prime exports. At each stage, the attendants handled her indifferently, treating her body as if they'd never heard of privacy. Other women and men also were being cleansed in an assembly-line fashion.

When the attendants finished, Abelosh led her across the room to a table much like a doctor's exam table. "Sit here for a second."

She gave him a suspicious look. "What now?"

"A word to the wise, girl. Your future owner will punish you for speaking without permission."

An older man with dark brown eyes hurried over to them. Behind him followed a female attendant carrying a tray with a glass of fluid, a small jar, and some odd-looking machinelike things. Mella wrapped her arms around herself and stepped back. *Dear Prophet.* What were they planning to do now?

With a friendly smile, the female attendant handed her the drink.

"What's in it?" Mella asked, peering into the glass. "Some tranquilizer?"

Abelosh shook his head. "I promise there's no sedative or tranquilizer in there. It's fruit juice. You'll stay on the stage until someone buys you. The temperature is warm outside, and the Indenture Hall doesn't let their merchandise get dehydrated."

She eyed the glass. Her mouth felt like the Sahara in summer. With a sigh, she drank it. Sweet, almost like apple juice.

"Lie down, please," the old man said.

Naked, on that table? She scowled at him. "No way, I—"

Abelosh slapped the rod at his side.

She lay back, the leather cold against her bare skin. Her breath quickened when Abelosh pulled a wide strap across her biceps and chest. Another one went over her forearms and stomach, almost too tight, and she began to panic. She couldn't move. "Let me go." She struggled within the restraints, jerking from side to side to try to loosen the straps, but nothing gave.

Ignoring Mella's thrashing, the attendant helped Abelosh secure each of Mella's legs. Then to her horror, the lower part of the table separated, splitting her legs apart into a V shape. She strained against the straps, futilely trying to draw her thighs together. She subsided, panting. Cold air brushed her private areas and made her shiver.

After pulling a chair forward, the older man sat between her legs, and she felt something warm moving slowly across her outer lips, tingling slightly. A depilator, she realized. He was removing the hair from down there as if she were a man with a beard. This was so, so wrong. She shuddered uncontrollably as the thing moved over her.

Abelosh and the attendant pulled her buttocks apart, and the depilator worked farther down, closer to her ass.

"There," the man said. "All bare. She's quite pale skinned, isn't she? I like the pink coloration."

"Short and round and pale—very exotic. She'll bring a good price." Abelosh took a scoop of lotion and rubbed it onto her nipples.

The man patted her down below, and she jumped at the feel of his warm hand on her bare skin. "Very soft. Yes, she'll be popular. Give me the lotion." The man dipped his hand into the jar and spread the cool lotion all over the shaved area, rubbing it in thoroughly.

The sensation was so…different with no hair between his fingers and her skin. She tried to squirm against the sensations beginning to roll through her at his intimate touch but couldn't move.

"She's starting to feel it," he said to Abelosh and patted her bare leg. "Get her up onto the stage."

UNHINDERED BY THE dry desert air, the sun scorched Mella's skin as Abelosh led her outside into the noisy plaza. Stores lined three sides of the market area, and the far end held the colorful booths of the ship traders. Shouting and bargaining filled the edges of the square, and laughter came from children playing tag in the center near a fountain. The fragrances of spice, sweat, perfumes, and cooking food mingled in the air.

Outside the Indenture Hall stood the two auction stages, nearly filled with slaves, all tall and thin and dark. Typical Nexans. When the crowd around the wooden platforms turned to watch Mella, she flushed, all too aware of her nakedness and the way her full breasts jiggled with her walk. When she tried to hang back, Abelosh's grip on her arm tightened. He pulled her past the first platform crammed with muscular naked men and women.

"Good workers. Be able to work from dawn to dusk. Healthy specimens," the auctioneer on the stage yelled to the crowd.

Mella tried to stop Abelosh. "Put me up there. I want to be a worker."

He laughed. "You don't have the muscles to work the mines, and you wouldn't bring nearly the price as a worker as you will as an unshuline. Sorry, girl." He dragged her to a platform, which held tall, dark-haired women and one slender, pretty man—all Nexans. Two of the women stood quietly; two more had their arms chained overhead.

Chained and naked? Mella yanked against Abelosh's grip. "Let me go. You can't do this to me."

One of the market staff in the distinctive red tunic trotted over. Abelosh pushed her to him. "She's not cooperative. Don't leave her unchained."

"Thanks for the warning," the man said. His hand, twice as big as Abelosh's, wrapped firmly around her arm. "Come, little miss."

He pushed her up the stairs onto the stage, and she heard the customers laugh as she struggled. Terror like a cold wave rushed through her, and her skin went clammy, despite the heat. Another muscular staff member hurried forward, and ignoring her struggles, the two men lifted her hands, clipping the snap ring on her cuffs to chains dangling from a bar spanning the length of the stage. She glared at them, pleased to see she'd scratched one man's face. She tugged at the restraints. Nothing gave. *How can this be happening?*

To make everything worse, they knelt and cuffed her ankles too, pulling her legs wide open and fastening the cuffs to rings embedded in the stage floor. As they stood, one called, "Ready for viewing, Master Lucan."

The tall, emaciated auctioneer strolled over and walked around her as he consulted the infounit in his hand, touching the keys to check the information. "Thirty-nine days. Healthy. She'll bring a nice price." To her horror, he fondled her breasts, ran his hand down her stomach, pressed between her legs, and even stuck a finger inside her. "Wet already."

She felt herself quicken to his touch. Her hips uncontrollably tilted into his hand. "No," she whispered as her breasts tightened to hard nubs. Her whole body felt sensitive. Even the gentle breeze that brushed against her skin increased her arousal.

He grinned and tapped her cheek. "You can't fight it, little missy. We lace the drinks with an aphrodisiac, and the lotion on your skin contains something to make you very, very sensitive." To illustrate, he ran a finger around her nipple, and the feeling shot straight to her groin.

She clenched her teeth to contain a moan. Sweat beaded on her brow.

The auctioneer turned to the crowd. "The slaves are ready for your inspection, gentle sirs."

The stage filled with men and a few women, who walked around the slaves and examined them. A swarthy man in his sixties walked up to Mella. "Love the coloring," he said to the auctioneer. "Look at how pink her nipples are." He pinched one, and Mella squirmed as a craving for more filled her. "Ah, she's a hot one."

After a moment, never letting loose her nipple, he shook his head. "Too much energy for me. I prefer someone quieter." He moved toward one of the unchained women.

Engulfed in a haze of need that heightened with each intimate touch, Mella lost track of the men and women. Some stroked her breasts. Some touched the V between her legs so intimately that she pushed against their hands, whimpering. One made the attendants lower her chained hands and bend her forward so he could probe her rectum. "Not used there before, I see. I'd enjoy instructing her in the delights." He pressed a finger inside her, and she could only quiver with shock and hunger.

Returned to her standing position, she closed her eyes, wanting only to shut it all out. Yet her private areas throbbed, needing something so badly she could scream. A warm hand cupped her face, and she inhaled a familiar scent—light citrus, soap, and man. It was—

"Sleeping on the job, little thief?"

She opened her eyes to see Kinae Dain smiling at her, amusement in his gaze. Glaring at him, she snarled, "Go away. If you'd just let me go, I'd be free now. Not left here for brutes to maul."

"Ah. I am sworn to uphold the law. Setting you free would have forced me to break my oath, and that I will not do."

A man with honor? One who kept his promises? She found truth in his level gaze. He was no skulking coward like Nathan, but she hated the Nexans anyway. She tried to pull her face away, but he wouldn't release her.

"I haven't bought an indentured slave for several years, and never an unshuline. But looking at you..." His smile flashed white in the darkly tanned face, and crinkles appeared around his eyes, making him seem human, real, for the first time. "Looking at you, I'm thinking that I might enjoy your company."

"You just want a body to have intercourse with."

He tilted his head. "Well, yes, that is part of it. You have a lush body crying out to be savored." Holding her gaze, he slid his hand from her face, down her sensitive skin, past her collarbone. Lifting one of her heavy breasts, he cradled it in his palm and rubbed his thumb over her peaked nipple. A surge of pleasure washed through her, and her eyes half closed as he continued the sensual assault. His other hand touched her lower, hard fingers stroking through her wetness.

She moaned, pressing against his touch, and her wanton actions horrified her.

Hand still pressed between her legs, he moved close enough for her to feel the warmth of his body and see a thin white scar over his eyebrow, another on his chin. "You think about it, Mella. I don't whip my people or mistreat them. If you want to come home with me for your term, I'll buy your contract...but you will be an unshuline, and I'll expect you to uphold your part of the bargain."

"I'll rot in hell first," she hissed.

Shaking his head, he stepped back, and she almost cried at the removal of his touch. Her hips tilted forward involuntarily, and when he saw the movement, he only smiled. "I'll stay for a few minutes of the auction, in case you change your mind," he said gently. "If not, then I wish you well and that your service not prove too arduous."

Leaning on his cane, he limped off the stage, and a feeling of loss filled her, as if she'd driven away the only friend she had here. Only, he was no friend. But he'd said he didn't whip his slaves. Maybe she should have gone with—

Then the next man stepped up to her. He stood so close that the auctioneer didn't notice when he pinched Mella's nipple hard enough to bring tears to her eyes. She bit her lip to keep from screaming. The lust filling his eyes as he relished her pain made her feel sick to her stomach. And scared.

He gave a cruel laugh. "You will do nicely for what I have in mind. I'd have liked to hear you scream before buying you…but that can wait."

"Take your seats, please," the auctioneer yelled. "The bidding begins now."

RUBBING HIS KNEE, Dain shifted in his chair in front of the stage.

Thanks to a hefty bribe, the auctioneer started with Mella. "Here we have an Earther female, an exotic treat with lush breasts and fair coloring. She's indentured for thirty-nine days, beginning today. Certified by our physician as healthy, no pregnancies. A spirited female, she should give a man a nice ride. Starting bid is three hundred eighty-five royals."

A young man held up his hand, followed by a portly older man. Dain recognized the next bidder, a brothel owner near the port. The amount continued to grow. Not surprising. With her flame-colored hair and clear green eyes, she compelled a man's attention. And her shape… Well. He smothered a grin as he saw her glare at each man who bid on her.

Poor little thief. An article in the *Port City News* had contained information on recent Earth history and how the rise of the Divine Prophet had spawned an incredibly rigid moralistic society. If the reporter hadn't exaggerated, this Earther must be appalled at the indenture process.

"Five hundred," came from the back.

Dain turned and winced. Galtdon. The man took sadism to new levels. Several of the up-class brothels now refused him admittance after he'd brutally scarred their girls. By the four gods, could he live with himself if he let Galtdon buy the Earther?

The auctioneer called, "Any further bids?"

The little thief's face paled as she stared at Galtdon. Then she looked at Dain. Her lips moved. *Please.*

Well then. That settled the question. "Five twenty-five," Dain called.

The auctioneer grinned. "I have an offer of five hundred twenty-five royals from Kinae Dain. Will anyone give me more?"

"Five fifty," Galtdon growled.

"Five seventy-five," Dain said.

A chair screeched near the rear. Dain turned to keep Galtdon in his peripheral vision. Never good to have an enemy at your back. But Galtdon had given up, and he rudely pushed his way out of the crowd.

"The Earther's contract goes to Kinae Dain of the Zarain clan. Enjoy your thirty-nine days, sir," the auctioneer said. His assistants unchained the thief and led her to the accounting desk, where Dain scrawled his signature on a debit form.

"Very good, Kinae." The sharp-faced accountant pulled the paper back. "Here are her papers and doctor's report." He leaned forward to address Mella. "Unshuline, you have been sentenced to thirty-nine days of service starting today. You must obey your owner in all ways. Do you understand?"

Mella nodded, her hands in fists at her sides.

"Kinae," the accountant continued. "You must provide adequate food and fluids and may not inflict permanent damage on your indentured slave. Do you understand?"

Dain nodded.

"Finally, to discourage escape attempts, the Indenture Hall requires that an indentured slave who flees be punished with ten strikes of the cane with enough force to create welts. At least one other person must witness the discipline. Do I have your word on this, Kinae?"

"You do." Dain's voice came out clipped as he tried to suppress the loathing he felt at the idea of caning someone. He drew a slow breath in before looking down at the trembling little thief. She might have a temper, but she wasn't stupid. She wouldn't give him cause to cane her.

He tossed the accountant fifty bits to buy a long robe. No need to humiliate her further. When he put the dark green robe around her, she clenched it tightly and whispered, "Thank you, Kinae Dain."

"Call me Dain, and it was my pleasure," he said, running a finger down a pale cheek. Softer than Nexan women, but a thief nonetheless. He must be out of his mind.

He gave her an even look. "We have a deal. Is that correct?"

"Yes."

Chapter Three

HER BODY THROBBING with need, Mella tried to relax in the ground solacar. As he drove, Dain remained silent, his face expressionless. She couldn't take her gaze away from him. His tunic and trousers were an ominous black. The glittering embroidery over the cuffs, sleeves, and shoulders matched the silver that streaked his black hair. This was a man fully in his prime, not one she might manipulate.

His masculine scent filled the car and somehow increased her arousal. She gritted her teeth against the waves of lust. No one was touching her now, so why wouldn't her body quiet down?

What was going to happen now? Would he insist on coupling right away? She clasped the robe tighter around her, the movement netting her an amused look. The solacar hummed as Dain drove out of the city proper and followed a river road. The rolling countryside was dotted with what the Nexans called *enclaves*—several acres of land enclosed within eight-feet-tall adobe walls. Eventually, the car slowed and stopped at an iron post, where Dain punched in numbers. The heavy wood and metal gate rolled open.

Mella frowned at another sign of the primitive technology on this planet. Ground cars, mechanical gates. "You have vids in the hotels. Why not remote controls?"

"Solar storms fry fancy electronics and prevent remote communications. We use underground wiring. Even the vid system is connected that way." He drove into the enclave, down a fine gravel road, and past large, single-story adobe houses and well-tended gardens. The vibrant colors of the flowers and lush greenery eased her heart after the miles of dry scrubland outside the enclave.

Dain parked the solacar in a sunny spot behind the largest of the houses. As he helped her out, the dry heat enveloped her like a blanket, but the tiny grasses along the path felt cool under her bare feet. She bit her lip. Hopefully no one would notice her walking around in a dressing robe. Surely they didn't have shepherds wielding their whips here on decadent Nexus, did they?

"Let me show you to your room, and then you can relax," Dain said, urging her forward. The feel of his hand low on her back made her shiver with surging need.

The heat didn't penetrate the thick walls of the quiet house. A long, wide hallway ran down the length of the outer wall with the rooms to the inside. After turning a corner in the hall, Dain opened a wooden door with inlaid green tiles. "You'll stay here."

Fancy quarters for a slave, Mella thought as she stepped inside. After a glance at Dain, she explored the rooms. Decorated in rich blues and greens, the sitting area had glass doors that opened to a courtyard of flowers and fountains. There was a bath in deep blues with painted tiles. The bedroom had hardwood flooring with an obviously hand-loomed rug, a hand-carved armoire, and a tall king-size bed, not quite waist-high.

A bed. "The rooms are lovely," she murmured, backing up, trying to keep her mind on the decor. But her body still burned with need, enough that just his hand on her back raised her temperature.

He grasped her chin, tilted her face up. "Then I'll leave you for—"

When she trembled at the feeling of his firm fingers, his eyes narrowed. Slowly, ever so slowly, he stroked his hand down her neck.

Pressing her lips together, she tried not to moan.

"I'd forgotten. You received the Indenture Hall's aphrodisiac, didn't you?" When his lips quirked, she wanted to hit him. She nodded instead.

"Well then. You have two choices. You can satisfy yourself, or I can."

His blunt statement made her blush. "No. That is…wrong." Self-satisfaction was a moral crime.

"Mella, your arousal will continue until the drug is deactivated by the chemicals of release."

Her eyes widened. Feel like this forever? She almost groaned.

"There's a slight problem with doing it yourself," he continued. His voice was deep and strong, like the low French horns in the vids when a medieval king led his forces into war. She could listen to him for—

"The drug creates a need for something *inside* you to achieve true satisfaction. You can use your fingers, but to remove the drug that way takes longer and many more times."

Just his minimally descriptive words made her moisten and increased the burning in her body. She couldn't stand this. And she didn't even know how to go about achieving her own release. She'd never tried. Surely she could fumble through, but what if she didn't… And she wanted his hands on her. *Heavens*. His gaze was level, and she could see he hadn't lied to her. Dammit, she didn't want to couple with a stranger. But she did. How could this be happening to her?

He waited, his warm fingers curled around the nape of her neck. His thumb stroked the hollow under her ear, and a rushing wave of desire made her arguments crumble. "You," she whispered.

He nodded, his face not changing, although something flared deep in his eyes, something that made her legs go weak. When he leaned his cane against the wall, fear crawled up into her chest, and she moved back. Surely he wasn't planning to… During the daytime?

But he followed, his demeanor so intent that she kept retreating step-by-step until the backs of her thighs hit the edge of the bed. She stopped, torn between running and pulling him to her.

His lips curved. He grasped her robe, tugging it open. She pushed at his hands and then, with a sense of futility, let him slide the garment off her shoulders to pool on the floor.

Naked again. She lifted her hands to cover herself, and he shook his head, freezing her in place. Her heart rate increased, and her mind quailed. She needed to be touched so badly, yet she couldn't allow a stranger—or anyone—to couple with her.

"You have a beautiful body, little Earther." His hands skimmed her curves, wakening her to more sensation at each touch. She grabbed his wrists, but he didn't even notice her feeble efforts to make him stop. Her skin tingled everywhere he touched.

He pulled her closer. His erection lay long and hard against her bare stomach, and his hands on her bottom pressed her against it. He was going to…to put that…

With an exasperated sound, he kissed her, drawing it out, demanding a response from her. His lips felt firm, knowing, taking. No one had ever kissed her like this. His tongue took possession of her mouth and retreated, luring hers back. He sucked on her tongue lightly, and her legs shook as an uncontrollable trembling started inside her.

When he lifted his head, heat burned in his eyes. Smiling slightly, he pushed her back until she sat on the edge of the bed. Efficiently, he stripped his clothing off. The loose tunic had hidden his strength. Broad shoulders. Scars, white against the bronzed skin of his arm. Curly black hair across a muscle-packed chest. Thick ridges of abdominal muscle. His shaft…

Her mouth dropped open. His shaft was horribly long and thick. Surely much too big. Not that she'd ever coupled with Nathan with the lights on, but she knew he hadn't been that size. She blinked, glancing at the window. Heavens, the sun hadn't set. "We can't," she protested. "It's daytime. And that's not—"

With a snort of laughter, Dain grasped her around the waist and tossed her onto the center of the bed like she weighed no more than a doll. She bounced twice, and then he was on her, pressing her into the mattress with his weight. His hot skin against hers roused a new wave of sensation, heightening every nerve. The crisp hair on his chest rubbed her sensitive breasts.

She closed her hands on his biceps and shied away at the feel of his rock-hard muscles, the feel of his unclothed skin.

"You know, you have my permission to touch me, Iaria," he murmured, propping himself up on his forearms. He studied her with dark eyes, and his hard lips curved. "You're not just being a cautious slave, are you? You're shy. Even with the drug in you. Well, let's see if I can erase some of that shyness." He lowered his head and kissed the side of her neck. The feel of his lips and his teeth nibbling on her skin sent heat ribboning through her, making her very center ache.

Instinctively, her legs spread apart, and her hips pushed upward, grinding against his erection. She gasped, freezing completely. And a second later, her body took over and did it again, and the pressure of his shaft against the top of her private area made her head spin. Her center demanded more. She needed him to enter her so badly, she moaned.

He merely kissed her, his tongue tracing her lips.

Nathan would have pushed inside her long ago. That was what she needed now. Turning away, she reached down and grasped him. She'd show him and—

Chuckling, he removed her hand and flattened his hips onto hers so she couldn't reach him. "Not yet, little thief. This isn't something you'll steal from me."

What did he mean? She reached down again, trying to worm her fingers under his body. Why wasn't he putting it inside her?

With a grunt of exasperation, he pinned her face between his hands. She felt caught, vulnerable as he looked into her eyes as if searching for her soul. She tried to turn her head, but his strength easily kept her in place. "I'm going to take you—eventually." His deep voice sounded husky, almost a growl. "But I will enjoy myself first. And I prefer not to have to fight you off every moment, delightful as I find it."

Releasing her head, he reached down and caught her wrist. Weight fully on her, he grabbed her other wrist and pinned both over her head. A tiny *snick* sounded as he snapped her bracelets together, and a *click* as he fastened them to something—a chain—on the headboard.

"No!" Panic flared in her. She yanked at the restraints, struggling until her lungs heaved for air. "Why? I was cooperating."

"You were pushing." His grin flashed white in his tanned face. "The drug makes you demanding. Now you will stay in place until I've satisfied myself. Until I've tasted every inch of your skin." He slid down her body to nuzzle the side of her breast and run his chin across the top. When he licked between her breasts, she gasped at the hot feel and arched upward. Her breasts ached as if they wanted to be…touched.

Touch her breasts? Taste her? Nathan had never… This was all forbidden. She tried to move away, but the restraints and his weight held her pinned to the bed. "I changed my mind. Let me go," she demanded.

His eyes darkened as he watched her struggle. "There's something about the sight of a woman struggling and wanting at the same time… You will stay in place for the pleasure I will give you, laria." He toyed with her breast, circling, stroking gently—too gently—around the edge of the nipple. Every circle seemed to make her skin more sensitive.

She moved against him uncontrollably. "Please."

With a smile, he lowered his head. His hot, wet mouth closed on the peak, and pleasure rippled through her.

"Oh Prophet." Her breath turned ragged as he licked her breasts, then sucked. His tongue rubbed her nipple against his teeth, and pleasure-pain arced straight to her core. She tried to touch him, needing to hold him in place or even pull him closer, but her hands were restrained. He had all the control. Somehow knowing she couldn't stop him made her need all the greater.

When he raised his head, her swollen nipples stood out in a way she'd never seen. "Such abundance," he murmured, flicking one distended tip with his tongue, sending a sizzle through the pathways to her core that he'd created.

He moved lower, nibbling on her stomach, licking the crease between her hip and thigh. As his mouth got closer to her private area, everything in her tightened, as if her body knew what to expect.

"What are you doing?" she whispered.

His body stilled. Resting a forearm on her thigh, he studied her with narrowed eyes. Confused, she looked back. After a minute, he shook his head. "Little Earther, how many men have you been with?"

"One. Only one," she whispered. "You must know how wrong this is. Let me go."

"Laria, if I let you go, you'll go back on the auction stand. And by the time that happens, you'll beg any man who walks by to take you."

The appalling description sent a chill through her.

"You'd better stay here. Don't you think?" He waited.

Her body burned. When she nodded, he curled his hand around her upper thigh, pushing outward. Surely he wouldn't... And yet her hips pushed up, needy. "What are you going to do?" she repeated.

His chuckle was low and wicked. "Apparently I'm going to demonstrate a few things your lover neglected."

"But..."

He ignored her. With firm hands, he pushed her thighs apart, spreading her so she was completely open to him. As he lowered himself, his wide shoulders kept her legs parted. He didn't move for a moment, and she could almost feel his gaze heating her. In the light of day. Her private area. A hot flush of embarrassment seared her skin.

And then, with one finger, he touched her. The surprise made her jerk, and she inhaled sharply, her legs trying to close and ineffectually bumping against his shoulders. His finger slid through her wetness, the feeling indescribable, so satisfying, and yet it only increased the burning. He brushed something, a spot she knew was dreadfully forbidden, and her body strained upward for more.

"Your *somaline*. I believe you unpoetic Earthers call it a *clit*," he murmured and slid his finger over it again, and she whined at the intense sensation.

"Here, your *maline*"—he pressed his palm to the V between her legs, making her clench inside—"which you Earthers call a pussy." Again he stroked his finger over that tiny sensitive place, the nub in the center of her. He repeated the movement, sliding up and over the...*clit*...until her hips wiggled up every time he touched her there.

What was happening to her? She pulled at the cuffs on her wrists. "Please. I can't take this."

He never stopped. "Oh, you can, little thief. You will."

Her whole private place throbbed with need. As his finger kept circling, she felt her clit swell, becoming painfully tight. And then, to her disbelief, he leaned forward and touched her there with his tongue. Wet. Hot.

She froze. "You... No, you must not." She tried to close her legs, kick him away. He rested his forearms on her thighs, pinning her legs with his weight, and continued. The forbidden sensation felt so exquisite, and a moan escaped her.

He laughed, the vibrations transmitted to that spot, and she shivered. He flicked across her, tiny touches with his tongue, teasing until her center pulsed, and her world contracted to only that awareness. And then his tongue stroked across her, long and wet. Over and over.

Her whole body tightened, and her leg muscles quivered as her insides clenched harder and harder. She needed...something. She heard herself whimper.

"You taste so sweet," he murmured. "But perhaps I've tormented you long enough." His lips closed over her exquisitely sensitive clit, and—*oh Prophet*—he sucked hard.

She gasped, feeling everything tighten...tighten.

And then he plunged two fingers right inside her.

"Aaa...aaa...aaa..." Incredible pleasure ripped outward, splintering her world into pieces, and she arched, gasping for breath. Her hips jerked uncontrollably as he moved his fingers in and out, her insides spasming around him. Lightning flashed through her, sizzling right to her fingertips.

He licked over her, and another surge of ecstasy hit her.

The room wavered in her vision; she couldn't feel anything except him and his touch. Her heart pounded like a bass drum as she tried to control her gasping breaths. A moment passed...or more? She blinked at the strong face over hers.

His cheek creased as he smiled. "You still with me, little thief?"

She sighed, realizing every muscle in her body had gone limp. The horrible burning need had disappeared. "Thank you."

Except he'd chained her... She realized he'd freed her arms. Her hands rested on his wide shoulders, and she dug her fingers into the muscles as she remembered the rest of what he'd done. "That... You should never... You used your mouth..." The shepherds would have flogged him and driven him from the temple.

"Earther," he murmured. He rubbed his cheek against hers and then rolled on his back, placing her on top, smoothing her onto his chest like a blanket. His big hand cupped her head and urged it down into the hollow of his shoulder. "This is Nexus, and what I did is completely normal here. Expected." He chuckled and added, "Even demanded at times."

What he meant by that, she didn't know, but she was too comfortable to protest. With her cheek pillowed on his chest, she listened to the slow *thud* of his heart.

"Your first day as a sex slave is almost over. Only thirty-eight to go." When he rubbed her shoulder and slid his hand down her arm, she was so weak in character that she found his touch comforting.

"What a horrible day." All those men, touching her. And the way she'd responded, had to respond—that seemed even worse. She stiffened at a nasty thought. "You don't use that drug here, do you?"

"I don't use *aphrodica* for my pleasure, no. I prefer honest desire." He paused, stroking her hair gently. "Some people use it as a punishment."

She closed the hand that lay on his chest into a fist. "Punishment?"

"An alternative to beatings."

Mella shivered. How would she ever come to terms with someone having such control over her life? Thirty-eight more days. She'd have to make sure she never earned any punishment.

Her eyes drifted closed, and she lay still, trying not to notice how comfortable she felt. How safe after the trauma of her day.

And suddenly her body turned on as if someone had flipped a switch. Everywhere his hand touched her became sensitive. Her breasts burned at the heat of his skin. Her groin moved, rubbing against his thigh, and she stiffened. The drug's effects had returned. "No," she whispered. "Oh no."

"Ah." He slid his hand from her shoulder to her breast, and the nipple hardened in his palm. When he rolled it between his fingers, she arched uncontrollably.

"How long does this last?" Even as she asked, she slid her palms up his arms, savoring the granitelike muscles. She needed his hands on her skin. Needed... *No. Stop this. Don't give in.*

"It's different for each person. We'll have to...ride it out," he said and rolled on top of her.

She gasped at the thrilling sensation of his hard body against hers. "What are you...?"

He nudged her legs apart, and with one hand, he slid his shaft into her.

"Aaah!" The jolt of his entry reverberated through her body in pulsing pleasure. But then he continued to push into her, stretching her with his size. Too big, too full. "No," she gasped, shoving against his shoulders.

He stopped. Keeping most of his weight on his good knee, he propped himself up on one elbow. He used the other hand to tilt her chin up, capturing her gaze. "Easy, laria. Your body will adjust. Is your man so small, or has it been a long time?"

"A long time." A year of desolation and—

He considered her for a moment. "You will tell me more of this *long time* later. For now..." He moved into her farther, and she caught her breath at the feel of his erection bumping against her womb. She felt so invaded, as if he'd taken her whole body for his own. But he stopped and waited, his body over hers, his chest touching her breasts. The discomfort lessened, disappearing to be replaced by something else. Something urgent. She needed...

His eyes had never left hers, and now his lips curved into a faint smile. He withdrew, ever so slowly. As he did, he took her lips in a hard kiss. His tongue entered her even as he surged back into her. A moan escaped her. The feeling of his thick shaft sliding between her swollen tissues was indescribable, and her hands closed on his shoulders.

He didn't release into her as she expected. Instead he kept thrusting in a hard, fast rhythm with both tongue and shaft, until she was panting, hovering right on a pinnacle. Her thighs quivered as she tried to make him move faster, harder. More…more something. Her fingers dug into muscles as hard as hull plating.

He slowed, pulled back to lick her lips and whisper against them. "You feel like a man's finest dream. I would enjoy continuing all night, but you wouldn't be able to walk in the morning." Lifting his hips slightly, he reached down, stroking his hand through her wet folds and sliding his fingers over that place. Her clit.

Oh Prophet. Her head tipped back as sensations shot through her, as the whole center of her tightened around him with burning need.

Giving a low growl, he thrust into her hard and fast even as his fingers closed on her clit, pinching it gently. The noise she made disappeared in the roaring ecstasy that rushed through her as every nerve in her exploded at once like a ship entering subspace. Tremor after tremor shook her.

With a deep laugh, he pushed even farther inside her, and she felt his shaft jerking, the movements sending delirious spasms through her core.

After a moment, as the thundering in her ears eased and her shudders slowed, she managed to look at him.

He ran a finger across her cheek and then kissed her softly…sweetly. "Little thief, you have a body made for loving."

His words made her feel good and yet… Resentment mingled with her satisfaction, anger with pleasure. She didn't know what to say. He had been caring, even gentle in a way, but he'd had his own way in everything. He hadn't allowed any refusal.

He was studying her again with that concentrated gaze. As if he might read her thoughts by watching her. He couldn't, could he?

Amusement glinted in his eyes as he whispered in her ear, "And in the next thirty-eight days, I intend to use your body in every way possible. You will come screaming, again and again."

Oh Prophet.

Chapter Four

DAIN WOKE WITH the sunrise, realizing he'd slept through the night for the first time in years. No nightmares of blood. No visions of the despicable acts of violent men. No angry souls whose lives on this planet he'd cut short.

Looking down at the woman snuggled up against his side, he smiled. A comforting armful, apparently. Then again, the sex had been hot and wet and very satisfying. The scent of *shulin* still lingered in the room. Perhaps he'd just slept well because of the exercise.

He pushed a strand of her curly red hair away from her face and rubbed his knuckles against her cheek. So soft. He'd never seen anyone with such silky skin. Few of the other planets had women like this—so round and smooth. Everything a man might want, in a small package.

And the way she responded. He ran a hand over the gentle curve of her shoulder. Would she react the same way without aphrodica coursing through her system? Would she scream as she spasmed around him? Tremble at the touch of his tongue? He hardened, knowing he would definitely find out the answers to those questions.

But the sun had risen, and he had responsibilities. Rolling on top of the little Earther and taking her again would have to wait.

✦   ✦   ✦

MELLA WOKE UP to an empty room. She sat up, wincing as abused muscles and private areas made themselves known. Her breasts felt swollen. Her nipples were overly sensitive and still a shiny red.

Her cheeks heated as she remembered the events from yesterday. The Indenture Hall. The auction and the men. Here with Kinae Dain. How she'd begged him to take her, and he had, giving her satisfaction as she'd never known.

Arms over her head, she stretched, feeling strange. Like a healthy animal. Like… She winced in pain and pulled her arms down. Frowning, she stared at the faint bruising around her wrists. He'd cuffed her hands above her head. She had yanked against the restraints and discovered she didn't have any control over what happened to her.

And at the memory, heat washed through her and moisture gathered between her legs.

May the Prophet have mercy. What was wrong with her? Still sitting, she yanked the blankets off the bed and wrapped them around her. What was she thinking to stare at her own body? And thinking about coupling with that…that man. Might the drug still remain in her system?

Elbows on her knees, she dropped her head into her hands and shuddered. She had behaved…immodestly. No, worse, wantonly. On Earth, they'd call her before the church's tribunal and cast her out. The shepherds would whip her through the streets, and she'd be shunned by all moral people.

The thought of that punishment had always horrified her.

And suddenly seemed a little insane. All that for a night of pleasure? She rubbed her face. Truly, sometimes the Divine Prophet's laws seemed excessive. Rigid. Mama hadn't approved of the Prophet. She'd never said anything disparaging about the Blessed Holy One, but her face had chilled with any mention of his name. Of course, society and laws had been far different when Mama and Papa were growing up. Before the Moral Wars.

Once in a while they'd look at each other and then sneak into the back bedroom, away from the servants and Mella. She'd always wondered if they had been…coupling. Coupling for fun, and not just to make a child.

They weren't the only ones she wondered about. Some of her married friends would look at their husbands in a funny way. Or they'd touch…surreptitiously, as if the contact was accidental. Mella frowned, feeling stupid. She'd been blind, hadn't she? Or perhaps she hadn't wanted to see any of it.

She brushed her toes over the soft rug, the rich colors of the hand-woven landscape almost glowing in the morning light. So pretty. How long had passed since she'd looked at anything? Really looked? Her toes tapped on an outline of a mountain with darkness shrouding the base. Once upon a time, and oh, it seemed so long ago, she'd been a different person. Excited by the world, ignoring the rules. She'd actually kissed a boy in a hoverpark. A bubble of laughter rose in her and died. Back then, she'd still had hopes of finding someone who would love her. She'd wanted a husband who would sneak away with her like her father had with her mother.

Instead, giving in to societal pressure on single women, she'd married one of the elders from her local church. Nathan had been so sweet, so loving before they married. He'd probably had his eyes on her father's money all along.

The caring behavior had disappeared quickly enough. Hope after hope was ground away under his strict adherence to the Prophet's teachings. Before her marriage, she had wanted so much more. A bitter laugh escaped at the thought of how she'd spent the night. She'd certainly gotten more now, hadn't she?

And look, the Divine Prophet hadn't struck her—or anyone else on Nexus—dead. In fact, the people here appeared not only healthy, but happy in their immoral behavior. Had she lived all these years in a self-imposed prison?

She ran her foot over the aged carpet and set her toes where the mountain glowed with sunlight on the snowy peaks. What happened on Earth didn't matter, not right now. She was on Nexus, and she was an unshuline. For the next thirty-eight days, she wouldn't get to make any decisions, moral or otherwise.

After standing up, she tossed the covers on the bed and deliberately stretched again, letting the sensation of aching muscles and a satisfied body fill her mind. And tried to ignore the prudish compulsion to cover back up in the blankets.

So…she definitely needed a shower. The scent of sex clung to her, mingling with *his* scent: a masculine musk and a hint of cinnamon and something clean and fresh, like the wind off the Olympic Mountains. *Nice.*

Her mouth tightened. Nathan wore an overwhelming cologne with underlying bitter notes. Much like his personality. All friendly and good-natured on top, and cold, cold underneath.

Nathan would never have touched her…down there…with his lips. He'd never kissed her and used his tongue deep inside her mouth and… She shivered, remembering how Dain's tongue had invaded her mouth, how he'd teased her and…

She pressed her hand over her stomach. Dain had taken everything he wanted, yet given her pleasure too.

So who was the more moral of men—the murderer or the wanton?

After showering in the decadent bathroom and using the packaged toiletries apparently put there for a guest of the house, she braided her hair tightly, wishing for combs to secure it off her neck. Or a scarf. Since the armoire of beautifully carved dark wood and the ornately trimmed trunk held no apparel, she donned the ankle-length jewel green robe.

At least she had *something* to wear. The memory of walking naked across the plaza still made her queasy. She opened the door to the inner courtyard, smiling at how the tiny colorful birds darted so quickly through the miniature trees. No one out there. After a bit, she peeked out of her room into the hallway. He hadn't said what he'd require of her during the day. Were unshulines supposed to stay in bed, waiting for their masters to show up?

Or was she to serve as a maid or cook or something by day and a whore by night? Her stomach growled, urging her on. Dain didn't seem like the kind of person who starved his people, so maybe he wouldn't get angry if she left the room.

She wandered down the hallway, passing closed doors. Then the hallway turned to the right and reached the heart of the clanhome. The first wide arched doorway showed a huge living area, the next a dining room with a table that could easily sit twenty. Finally, the kitchen. The scents of spicy meat and toasted bread made her stomach rumble.

The big, brick-floored room held two people. A lean, older woman with pink cheeks and pinned-up graying hair chattered away in a laugh-filled voice to a young woman. Around seventeen in Earth years, the younger woman had purple-dyed hair in intricate knots and beads. Mella smiled. Apparently teenagers were the same everywhere.

"Hello," Mella said.

The older woman jumped, then laughed. "Himself did say he purchased a contract yesterday. What be your name, child?"

Child. If only she felt like one, but today she felt older than the woman before her. "Mella, ma'am."

"Ma'am?" The woman chuckled, poked the girl with her wooden spoon. "Hear you that, Blanesta? Respectful, as you should be."

Giggling, Blanesta crinkled her nose. "You're just old-fashioned like everybody from the backcountry."

Shaking her head, the older woman turned back to Mella. "I be Idesta of the Hermest kinline. Have you an appetite?"

"I'm starving." Mella bit her lip. What exactly was her status here? "I can make my own—"

"Make it you will not. We saved some sustenance for you." Idesta waved a hand at a black hotbox sitting on a counter. "Blani, bring Mella her food."

Following the woman's gesture, Mella seated herself at a round table in the corner. Blanesta brought out dishes containing what looked like eggs and some sort of meat. Cut-up fruit came from the coldbox. The youth poured an astringent drink like tea from a pot.

Mella stared at the riches in front of her and remembered her recent gratitude for a piece of stale bread. "Good heavens, there's enough for three people."

Idesta laughed again, the lines on her face speaking plainly that she'd spent her life smiling. Mella liked her already. "Eat what pleases you, child. Unsure we were of what an Earther would enjoy for firstmeal, and so we provided you with a variety. Eventually, as we learn your favorites, a better selection you will have."

They acted as if she was a guest. But Idesta had said she knew Dain had bought her contract. "Don't... I mean, I'm only here for thirty-eight more days." Her stomach growled and decided for her. She'd eat and then ask what her day duties entailed. She served herself a small sampling of everything and started on the food, smiling in delight. Idesta was a very good cook.

"And for those thirty-eight days you will have to eat, true?" Pleased with getting the last word, the cook beamed and returned to peeling a red-skinned vegetable.

A few minutes later, as Mella eyed a pink cherrylike fruit and wondered if it would fit in her full stomach, footsteps echoed in the hallway. In the doorway appeared a dignified woman in a white tunic with black embroidery, a loose golden skirt, and discreet pearl jewelry that blared *aristocrat*. Her dark hair was arranged in the latest swirling-braids fashion.

"Algraina," Idesta said with a slight bow of her head.

"Is my son in the kitchen? Yorest doesn't know where he has gone."

"He's not here, ma'am. In his office doing business, he had been."

"Not anymore, and I don't have time to wait. Please remind him of the Arewell clan festivities tomorrow." The woman turned to leave. Her gaze passed over Mella, then returned as if jerked by a leash. "You. Are you the unshuline whose contract my son purchased?" Her lips pursed at the word *unshuline* as if she'd tasted something rancid.

Darned if she'd stand and bow to this woman. Instead Mella inclined her head politely. "Yes."

Algraina's gaze traveled over Mella scornfully. "Most unusual coloring. But so short and fat. I cannot see how you attracted my son." Turning her head, she spoke to the cook. "Inform my son that his unshuline is not to leave the house."

As the woman exited the room, Mella placed her hands flat on the table to still the trembling. Humiliation created a nauseating feeling in her stomach, drowning out her anger. She'd been embarrassed at the auction yesterday, but somehow Algraina's contempt made her slavery even more real. Bending her head, she stared at the remains of her breakfast and blinked hard to hold back tears. *Please, someone, get me off this horrible planet and let me go home.*

"Mella, are you—"

The cook interrupted Blanesta. "Leave her be for a bit, young-un. Here, wash these taters from the bin."

The water in the sink was turned on.

The sound of footsteps came from the hallway again. Maybe Dain's mother had thought of another insult to add to Mella's store. Mella folded her hands, unwilling to look up and let the woman know how effective her verbal abuse had been. Because she did feel like trash. Stinking, foul trash. She was a thief. She'd been auctioned off naked in the plaza. She'd coupled with a stranger. She deserved every bit of the woman's scorn.

Forcing air in and out of her tight lungs, Mella stared at her hands. In a bit, she'd thank the kitchen staff for the food and go back to her room. With any luck, she could just hide there until her days were up.

After a minute, she realized the room had gone silent. A chair beside her scraped against the brick floor, and someone sat down. Black trousers and black boots appeared in her downcast vision. *Oh no.*

A hand wrapped around her arm, turning her firmly toward...him. Warm fingers cupped her chin, tilting her face up to meet a dark gray gaze. With his free hand, Dain brushed away the few tears she hadn't managed to contain.

"I'm sorry, Mella," he said. "My mother is overly judgmental, especially when it comes to unshulines. My father was neither discreet nor responsible when he was alive."

Pushing his hand away from her face, she forced a smile. "I didn't notice your mother being here. I'm merely weary."

Anger flared in his eyes.

Heavens, if he yelled at her, she really would cry. Shaking, she pushed her chair back, only to have two hard hands grip her shoulders, holding her in place.

"Mella," he said and stopped, waiting for her to look at him. When her eyes met his, he continued, "Nexans have no patience with lies, and I have no tolerance for them. I require honesty from the people around me."

She tried to pull away, but his fingers tightened. He leaned forward and spoke into her ear, his deeply timbered voice level. "In your case, honesty in bed and out, hiding neither your body nor your emotions from me."

The thought of being so open to anyone, especially this man, made her mind quail, and she cringed. His hands gentled. "Come, let us walk in the gardens." Hard muscles bunched in his forearms as he easily pulled her to her feet.

Glancing over her head, he told the cook, "Send for a seamstress. Set an appointment for tomorrow and have her drop off some ready-made clothing today, starting from the skin out. Can you make an estimate as to size?"

Idesta looked at Mella. "Yes, Kinae. Do you have a preference as to color or style?"

He stroked a hand down Mella's hair, and she stood rigid under his touch. "She has beautiful hair and coloring and a lush figure. Tell the seamstress to showcase those without being vulgar."

"Yes, sir."

HER SKIN WAS satin against his fingers, and Dain couldn't resist stroking her arm as they walked out the back door to the clan gardens. His jaw tightened when he thought of his mother's meddling. Although cool, she normally didn't descend into cruelty.

Mella didn't deserve such abuse. Odd how he felt such a need to protect the little thief.

He glanced down at the top of her head. Even now, she kept her gaze averted, not looking at him unless he forced the issue. His mother had undoubtedly contributed to her withdrawal, but there was more going on here. Was Mella shy? Or angry after his use of her last night? Or should he say, their use of each other? He had scratch marks down his back from her uninhibited response to his touch.

And just the memory of her screams of climax made him harden.

But this was not the time for shulin, not when she had drawn back into herself like an Earth turtle into its shell. As they reached the grassy path, he changed directions, heading toward the shade garden. "Did you have enough to eat in the kitchen?" he asked.

"Yes." At his silence, she obviously realized her answer had been less than polite. He watched her take a deep breath and straighten her shoulders before she looked up.

The bright daylight turned her eyes to a clear emerald. "You have a very talented cook...and a beautiful home. But Idesta said you were doing business this morning. What business?"

"Ah. Just estate dealing. As *clanae*, head of the Zarain clan, Grandsir does the majority of the work, but as *kinae*, head of our family line, I have various matters to tend to."

"So this place—the enclave—belongs to the clan? Who lives here?"

"Many of the kinlines that look to our clan reside here. Others prefer the farm enclave."

She slowed to look around, then nodded at the thick adobe wall. "Why the frontier-stockade look? Do you have wars here or something?"

"No wars. Our small population couldn't survive such needless waste." He touched her braid and watched the red strands glint gold in the sun. "The walls are to keep out the predators. During their migrations, very little else will stop them."

She glanced around uneasily. "Predators as in animals? Are they big?"

"*Regstal* are about seven feet or so, but they can't climb." He nodded up at the sky. "*Berstal* fly, and that's why our windows are small and the inner courtyard has a wire covering. The *agrustal* are four legged." He held his hand thigh-high. "Agrustal come from the sea during the rainy season and will eat anything in their path. Since our fields are not inside the enclaves, our warriors guard the new plantings until summer forces the creatures back into the ocean."

Her eyes widened. "They eat people?"

"People are just another form of meat." Although scars might excite some women, this one would probably flee if he showed her what a regstal's double rows of teeth could do to a man's leg.

"Dear Prophet."

Her reaction demonstrated why the so-civilized planet of Earth didn't understand the necessities of the frontier worlds. Time to change the subject. He guided her through the wide arch in the *larrien* bushes and past the small altar to Cernun, god of winter. "This is the shade garden." He smiled at the profusion of blue flowers climbing up the dark adobe walls. Thick purple grass covered the ground broken by tiny pools of water. The cool, moist air was filled with the sounds of a myriad of fountains and the chirping of *parogans*. The miniature yellow birds preferred to raise their young near water, and he'd spotted two nests in the last week.

"It's lovely." After a moment of stunned delight, Mella started down one of the narrow, winding paths. Dain dropped back a step, enjoying her obvious pleasure. Off-worlders rarely left Port City, so the beauty of the enclaves wasn't common knowledge.

Dain saw the ever-mischievous *felin* named Arala break out of cover and streak after a parogan.

Mella jerked to a stop. "What was that?"

"A felin. I believe they were called *cats* on Earth, but like everything else here, they have mutated."

"A *knee-high* cat?" She stared at the bushes. A second later, Arala padded back to her hiding place, sleek black tail twitching in annoyance. "It's huge."

"Big enough to bring down *deerlets*. The mountain kinlines hunt with them." He tugged on her braid lightly. "You know so little about my planet that I must wonder what brought you to Nexus."

Her gaze moved away from his. Was she planning to lie to him again? His jaw set. After twenty years in law enforcement, he had a profound dislike for being lied to. Although Nexans rarely lied, off-planet strangers had brought the filthy habit with them.

"I was traveling to see the sights."

Interesting. Not entirely a lie. "And did the sights include a stint as a thief?"

"Well, no," she said lightly, kneeling to touch a slender *violetta* flower with gentle fingers. "It happened I lost my money first, and your planet"—a hint of anger darkened her words—"doesn't have any help for the indigent."

"Actually, we do. There's an abundance of help for victims of crimes. Did you report the theft to the police?" He took her arm to assist her in rising.

"Ah, of course I did."

Lie. "Indeed. What did the thief look like? And where did this happen?"

She tried to pull away, and he kept his hand on her arm.

"Near the port," she said. "I didn't really see the man. Tall. His face was covered."

With his fingertips over her inner arm, he felt her pulse increase as lie piled upon lie. She'd probably stowed away on a ship, perhaps to evade arrest on her own or some other world, and then been discovered and tossed off on Nexus. Criminals did not knowingly come to Nexus.

Well, now he knew how much he could trust her—not at all. And the beginning of his pity had disappeared entirely.

Chapter Five

SINCE KINAE DAIN had ordered a supper tray delivered to his office, Mella ignored Idesta's hint she should join the Zarain family in their dining room and ate in the kitchen with the rest of the staff: Idesta and Blani, two housemaids, the butler, a gardener and his young apprentice, and three security men. Although everyone was polite, she saw the curiosity in less guarded eyes: *what crime had she committed?*

After helping the kitchen staff clean up, she returned to her rooms with a sense of relief. There she discovered several articles of clothing on the bed: a pale gold nightgown, a blue satin skirt with a silky cream blouse, and a stretchy breast undergarment. No panties or facsimile thereof. The lack sent a quiver through her.

After taking a hasty bath, fearing Dain's arrival, Mella donned the nightgown and gasped at how much it revealed. Not only was the fabric nearly transparent, but the bodice curved almost to her nipples. She started to take it off but heard footsteps in the isolated hallway. She had barely enough time to yank on her robe before the door opened.

Dain strolled into the room as if he owned it—well, yes, he did—but it was still her room for the duration. And she was his, she thought, her mouth tightening. He too wore a robe, and the black silk displayed the broadness of his shoulders and darkened his eyes. "Did you have supper?" he asked.

"I did. Did you get your business finished?" she asked politely in return. How could two people be in bedroom attire and conversing so stiffly?

He shook his head, moving steadily toward her, reminding her of a popular documentary that showed a lion stalking game across an open plain. "I have several full days in front of me." His smile creased his cheek. "But my nights are free."

At the smoldering look in his eyes, she stepped back, but he caught the lapels of her robe. "Your nights are free also, aren't they, little thief?" He raised an eyebrow, waiting for her answer.

"Apparently so," she said, bitterness searing her veins like acid.

"Ah. Back to being angry." He shook his head. "Then I will start from the beginning again."

What exactly did that mean? She tugged at his hands as he firmly pulled the front of her robe open. He looked at what the sheer nightgown revealed, and his eyes heated. *Oh Prophet.* She really, really didn't want to couple with him—nor with anyone. She tried to push his hands away.

He ran a finger over the top of the bodice, obviously enjoying himself, but all she felt was irritation and embarrassment. No drug controlled her now, and the cold had returned to her body.

His eyes narrowed. "Well, this is more than back to the beginning, isn't it, laria?" he asked softly. "I know you can feel passion."

She shrugged, wanting to look away, but caught in his steady gaze.

He cupped one breast and stroked his thumb over her nipple, watching her face. "Then again, a mind can overrule instincts. You don't want to feel anything, do you?"

His words touched her as intimately as his hand. She turned her head.

"No, you will look at me as we speak." He gripped her jaw, forcing her to meet his eyes.

His touch, his words scraped against her defenses; his hard eyes seemed to bore into her soul.

His thumb brushed over her lips. "Let's try this. Mella, if you will answer my questions honestly, then I will not insist on shulin tonight."

Shulin. The Nexan word for coupling. Relief washed through her, and her muscles relaxed. She'd tell him what he wanted to hear and—

"However, if you lie to me or evade my questions, then I will take you in every way that I know. All night."

She choked. "I…I won't answer questions that will…incriminate me."

He smiled slowly. "Fair enough." Gripping her robe, he backed up to the overstuffed chair in the corner and pulled her into his lap. She squirmed until he asked, "Would you rather talk on the bed?"

She froze, sitting rigidly upright on his knees. Wetting her lips, she said carefully, "No. Here is fine."

When amusement flashed in his eyes, she hated him a little. He had her as trapped as if she were in one of their restraint pens.

With firm hands, he leaned her back into the curve of his arm, increasing her feeling of vulnerability. And then he deliberately pushed her robe more open and set his hand on her breast. Even through the thin silk, his fingers felt warm on her chilled skin. "When did you make love for the first time?"

"The first time?" She'd expected questions about her marriage. Nathan. Or stealing. "Um. Five years ago, when I mar—" She bit the word back. "Five years ago." A fine and proper wedding with her parents so pleased and Nathan so attentive. She'd been excited, knowing she would soon discover the secrets her body had cried out for… She sighed at the dismal memory.

"That is not the sound of a woman remembering passion." He curled his arm around her, pulling her closer to his warmth, an almost comforting feeling. "When was the last time you made love?" he asked quietly. When she looked down, he murmured, "Keep your eyes on mine. How long ago?"

His eyes were such a dark gray, almost black. "I think…" Why would she remember that? It wasn't important. Nothing had been very important since her parents—

"Stop. Tell me that thought."

She stiffened. "That's personal."

"And you will have no personal secrets from me," he said softly. "Tell me what put the look of grief on your face."

Did he see everything? He waited, stroking down her neck, massaging the tight muscles in her shoulders. His body felt solid and strong beneath hers.

"My parents and sister died in a hovercar accident," she said finally.

"When?"

"About a year ago." A frozen year when nothing could break through the ice coating her emotions and heart. She didn't need warmth; she didn't *want* warmth.

"Ah." He ran his knuckles over her cheek, his eyes gentle. "I'm sorry, laria. That's a devastating loss. Did your mate—"

"No!"

DAIN TIGHTENED HIS arm around the stiff little body in his lap. She didn't want him to know she was married. Why? Another rigid Earther custom?

On Nexus, a contract for reproduction required fidelity only until confirmation of pregnancy and paternity. But Earth contracts might include more restrictions. "It is true that the law dissolves your marriage during your indenture. Afterward, will your spouse react badly when he finds you've served as an unshuline?"

He saw the lie form in her eyes and get rejected before she spoke. She was learning. Good.

"We're not married anymore."

Her emotions jangled until he couldn't get a clear reading.

"He doesn't even know where I am right now."

Truth.

Was she married or not? Dain frowned. And did Earthers care so little for their mates that they'd lose them among the planets? He realized she'd made no attempt to notify a spouse that she'd been sold. He felt a surge of pity for this fragile woman who had no one to run to for succor.

He'd known that she hadn't been intimate with anyone recently. Her sheath had taken too long to adjust to him.

Then there was her amazement at her climax. She should not have been so surprised, even if years had passed. In fact, he had to wonder if she'd ever reached release before at all.

He smiled. Nothing pleased him as much as a new mystery. But he had to solve the current question first: why she had withdrawn into herself so tightly? He cupped her breast, enjoying the heavy weight in his hand. Through the thin gown, her nipples were pale pink, far lighter than a Nexan's dusky brown. Yet even if her body was different and her culture strange, pain was universal. "Your grief took you from the world of the living."

Although she shrugged, her shoulders stiffened.

Mourning for loved ones was not unusual. But he saw that, though her grief remained, the pain of loss had eased. So why did she still hide within herself?

He pulled her braid forward and started undoing it with one hand. The cool strands glowed with the colors of fire, much like the little Earther. Cold on the outside, but last night, he'd found heat on the inside.

To him, her spirit seemed to waver, as if in a doorway, unsure whether to return to living or bury itself even further into coldness. Something had opened the door for her, for she'd been alive when he'd captured her outside his club. And their intimacy and her release last night should have reminded her of the joys of the body. Why did she not step completely out into the world?

A memory came to him from his early days as an enforcer. A friend whose partner had died in a port brawl had tried to follow him into death. Not just because of the loss, but also… Dain flattened his hand between her breasts, over her heart. "Do you feel guilty for being alive when they are dead?"

Her heart gave a heavy thud, and her whole body stiffened like a *relix* preparing to strike. Her voice came out hoarse. Harsh. "I am guilty." She turned her face away, trying to retreat from his hand and failing. "They were coming to hear—to visit me and died. If I hadn't wanted... If I had said not to come, they might—"

"They would have died anyway, laria." He laid a hand along her jawline, feeling the fragile, stubborn bones beneath her satin skin as he turned her face back to him. Her drenched eyes were green as a high mountain lake. He kissed her forehead. "Ekatae, the death goddess, claims us when she will."

She shook her head in disagreement, but he could feel the minute relaxation of her muscles. His words had penetrated and would be considered. In turn, he would reflect on what he had discovered. One insight he had gained: she had been left too long alone in her grief, and no one had insisted she return to the world. The more he learned about this planet Earth, the more disgusted he became.

He could feel tiny trembles running through her body, although her spine stayed straight, and her face composed. She was a strong woman, despite her vulnerable heart and small size. "Come, laria, let us rest. Tomorrow you may return to being an unshuline; for tonight, you will simply sleep in my arms."

Her gaze jerked back to his. Had she expected to spend the night alone? Foolish little Earther. He carried her to the bed. Ignoring the rigidity of her body, he turned her on her side and curled around her in a protective position, one heightened by the difference in their sizes—and her softness within his arms.

Slowly, as his body heat warmed her, she relaxed, stiffening only for a moment when he slid his hand around to lie in the soft valley between her breasts. "Sleep, little one," he whispered. Her wavy hair teased his face, silky soft with the fragrance of *ronves* and vanilla. Her round ass nestled against his groin.

It was odd how this woman from a distant planet could feel so right within his embrace.

SHE AWOKE FROM deep sleep, lying on her back. Hard hands moved over her body, stroking up from her waist to massage her breasts.

Opening her eyes, she tried to sit up, and he pushed her down with a firm hand on her chest.

Dain straddled her hips, his balls pressed against the junction of her legs. "Lie still, Mella, or I will restrain you."

The memory of her wrists in cuffs, of his enjoying free rein over her body, sent a wave of heat through her—one she ignored. She glared at him. "We had a deal. I answered your questions."

His grin was a flash of white in the dark face. Whiskers shadowed his jaw and chin, making him look even more dangerous. As dangerous as the hands on her body. "The night is over, little one, and a new day has begun." He teased her nipples gently until they pebbled into an aching tightness. Then he slowly pinched the peaks almost to the point of pain.

She gasped at the intensely erotic sensation and shoved at his hands, trying to push him away.

With a low chuckle, he grasped one wrist. He leaned forward and then his heavy weight came down on top of her so hard and fast that the air exploded out of her. By the time she could breathe, he had fastened both her wrists to the headboard chains. Pulling her leg out from under his hip, she tried to kick him. Evading her easily, he rolled off the bed. He caught her foot in his hard hand and, to her horror, tied her ankle to the footboard with soft silken ropes. Ignoring her frantic thrashing, he secured her other leg.

Spread-eagled, she lay helpless, tugging at the ropes. "Do Nexans have to tie their women down to have sex with them?" she hissed. "This is rape."

He joined her on the bed, lying beside her. Leaning on one elbow, he fondled her breasts, this time without her interference. "I fear that word does not apply to indentured slaves, Mella. Especially one who begged me to buy her." His look was piercing.

Guilt settled like a hard knot in her stomach. She *had* begged.

"If you don't count criminals convicted of injuring another, very, very few people are raped on Nexus." He licked a finger and circled her nipple, smiling as it tightened to a jutting peak. "You see, the penalty for rape on our planet is to have one's male parts cut off and then banishment to the mines for the remainder of a miserable life. There, any male without his *shultor* and *globes* is considered fair game for use by others."

She looked at him, her eyes wide. "That's horrible."

He nodded. "And effective."

"Then if you don't usually buy unshulines or take women against their will, why do you have these?" She tugged on the chain attached to her indenture bracelet.

"Because I like them." He chuckled, low and deep. "I read about your planet now and then, little Earther. Your people spend an excessive amount of time watching vids." He took her nipple between his lips. His mouth was hot. Wet. Exciting. After the roaring left her ears, she realized he'd leaned back to study her with that unsettling gaze. "Our technology is limited, and noninteractive entertainment is restricted. So for our entertainment, we sing. We dance. We play in bed."

Her other nipple received the same treatment, long and hard. When he finished, the nub was a dark red, and its throbbing wakened her private parts. "We like sex, and nothing is considered improper as long as the players agree." He grinned. "I believe on Earth, everything having to do with sex is considered sinful, yes?"

She managed to nod, although following the conversation was growing more difficult.

"Now, I enjoy the sight of a woman tied down for my use. Open and available." His gaze traveled over her slowly, his pleasure obvious, and she became acutely aware of the way her raised arms lifted her breasts and of the vulnerable area between her widespread legs.

"But that's rape," she whispered.

"Ah, it is not if the woman enjoys being restrained. If she wants someone to take his pleasure…"

She closed her eyes, tried to ignore the growing need of her body. A woman would do that…willingly? Surely not. Would everything she believed about right and wrong be twisted on its side?

When she opened her eyes, he hadn't moved, as if he was waiting for her to finish thinking. Now he straddled her, his buttocks resting on her thighs. His erection was immense, jutting out slightly from his body. He saw her staring and closed his fist around it. "This says I want you, yes."

"But I don't want you, no." She yanked at the restraints, saw a faint smile on his hard face.

"Perhaps. One thing I do know, Mella." He leaned down and touched her breast with one finger. "You aren't occupied with grieving at the moment."

The unexpected statement stabbed right into her heart. "Damn you."

"It's time to move on, Iaria. You are alive, and I can't imagine your family would begrudge you your survival. They would not want you to remain frozen." His serious eyes captured hers. "Am I wrong?"

Mama and Papa would have been very unhappy to see her mourning so long. And Kalie had loved life.

He waited for her reply.

She shook her head in answer, unable to say the words.

Slowly his lips curled into a dangerous smile. "So I now have a sweet Earther female, just waiting for me to take her." He studied her with a penetrating gaze. "She can't move, can't do anything to help herself."

His words sent disconcerting warmth flooding through her. Heat pooled low in her stomach as she tugged on the ropes in response to the heat. A flash of satisfaction showed in his eyes. He leaned down to her, his lips a breath away from hers. "Kiss me, Mella. As long as you're kissing me, I'm not doing...other things."

Without waiting for her answer, he took her mouth, his lips firm, experienced, teasing her lightly before he plunged within. His tongue stroked over hers, coaxed it into responding. Only his lips touched her, yet she could feel the dark heat of him pour into her.

She felt...awake. Roused. Hot. And when he drew back, her breath came hard.

"Very nice, Iaria," he murmured. He looked at her breasts and smiled. "So much to enjoy. These need more attention, I think." He leaned down to circle one nipple with his tongue, his hand cupping her breast and holding it for his lips. "You're so pale and pink." His mouth closed over her nipple, and he sucked, drawing strongly until each pull sent a current running to her…her clit.

As she arched from the bed, he sat back. His finger circled the peak, the sunlines beside his eyes crinkling. "Very nice."

He teased her other breast, switching from one to the other until they were swollen and aching and she was appallingly wet below. How could he do this to her? She shouldn't be get getting hot for—

He shifted to kneel between her legs, then stroked up her left thigh and slid his hand through her wet folds.

"Aaah!" She jerked on the chains. She'd forgotten how intimately he'd touched her yesterday. How could he do things like this? Nathan had only put his hands down there long enough to push his shaft into her. "*Women are messy,*" he'd said.

She wiggled uncontrollably as Dain's fingers, slick with her wetness, slid from the top of her mound almost to her anus. "What are you planning to do?"

"Just touch you, Mella." His voice was lazy and deep.

She realized his eyes had never left her face, even as he stroked her. Suddenly his finger glided up and over her clit, and she sucked in a breath as a wave of excitement shot through her. He set his free hand on one breast, gently fondling it, and then he pinched her sensitive nipple. The electric feeling sizzled straight to her clit. Before she could recover, he opened her folds and pressed a finger into her— right inside her—and she gasped at the riveting pleasure.

Her legs trembled with the strain of trying to pull away—and trying to get closer. She couldn't do either.

With a low growl, he nipped her on the thigh, and the sharp pain seared through her, making her gasp. He bit her higher, again and again, moving up her leg toward her pussy. Each stinging pain made her skin more sensitive and the sensation more erotic.

She could feel the trickle of moisture through her folds and couldn't find any embarrassment within her. Just need.

When his mouth closed over the tender skin at the crease of her thigh, she trembled, feeling his breath on her most intimate places.

He'd done this before, put his mouth…there, but that time she'd been wild with the drug. Now…now her lower parts ached for his touch, but she could control it. Could control herself.

"No," she whispered. "Please don't." A shaft being pushed inside her was uncomfortable, but bearable. Having his mouth on her was different. Too personal. Too intimate.

He didn't move, just looked at her private area, at a place always hidden. "Ah, Earthers and their prudery." He touched a finger right at her opening, pressed in a centimeter, and she quivered as new sensations awoke and bloomed outward. He rose to smile at her. "I remember reading that before the emigration to the planets, sex was considered a normal and pleasurable part of life on Earth. Anything was allowed, as long as the partners agreed. Much like we deal with shulin here on Nexus."

She couldn't look away from him, from his intense gaze. His finger remained just barely inside her; she could feel her tissues throbbing around it.

"Did your lovers never do this?" He lowered his head, and his warm tongue replaced his finger, delving between her folds. When it pushed inside her, the feeling was so overwhelming, she started to pant. Her legs wouldn't close. *I can't stop him.*

"No, you can't stop me," he murmured, and she realized she'd spoken aloud. His eyes crinkled at the corners. And then his tongue stroked right over her clit. Her body went rigid. Soaring, burning arousal ignited in her, as if everything that had come before was but a drop in the lake of her need.

He was watching her again, and amusement glimmered in his eyes. "Now you look almost like you did with the drug."

She felt his fingers on her, touching her folds, and the muscles in her legs tightened uncontrollably. Her hands pulled on the chains, to no avail.

His eyes went dark and satisfied as she struggled. His mouth lowered onto her. The hot, wet feel of his lips felt indescribable. His fingers opened her farther, and his tongue found her exposed clit. Sliding up one side. Rubbing. Over the top to the other side. Rubbing.

Her body tensed, coiling tighter and tighter as he continued. Her breathing turned to low moans, then to panting. A finger slid into her, sparking new nerve endings to life, sending her closer to the edge. She couldn't think, could only wait for the next slow slide of his tongue, the movement of his finger inside her. His tongue on her was more intensely pleasurable than anything she'd ever felt before. She never wanted it to end, and yet her hips strained upward, desperate for more, for release.

The slow, firm slide of his tongue alternated with the slow in-and-out movement of his finger. Faster—she needed faster as pressure built inside her. Her body hovered on the precipice, rigid, waiting for the next...the next...

"Oooh!" A star went nova inside her—searing pleasure bursting outward through her whole body. Her insides pulsed convulsively around his finger, each spasm sending glorious waves through her. Her hips tried to buck, and she realized his forearm pinned her to the bed, keeping her right where he wanted her, and the knowledge shot her into another spasm of pleasure.

He lifted his head, a faint smile on his lips. "I think I like your release more when no drugs are involved. What do you think?"

She could only stare at him, her heart pounding like it wanted to burst from her chest.

His finger ran through her folds again, and she gasped as her vagina clenched.

"You're nicely wet, Iaria. Let's put that to use." He came down on her, his body solid muscle. His left hand cupped her breast, thumbing the nipple and shooting small explosions through her. His right hand pressed his erection against her opening. "I didn't take you very hard the other night," he told her, holding her gaze. "I will now." And he pushed into her.

She was so wet, he slid in easily, moving deeper and deeper inside her. She whimpered as the feeling of fullness increased, as he stretched her to the point of pain until her vagina throbbed around him. He's done this before, she tried to tell herself, and it got better. She panted, trying to get air.

He stopped, and she could feel his balls touching her pussy. "Look at me, little one." His big hand cupped her cheek as his dark gray eyes focused on her.

When he shifted inside her, the sensation was…terrifying. The huge feeling moved through her swollen tissues, retreating, surging forward again. She closed her eyes.

"Look at me," he growled.

Chapter Six

WHEN SHE OBEYED, Dain was pleased to see the glazed look in her eyes. Not only an Earther, but a very innocent one. Her husband must have been as sexless as an agrustal in dry season. As Dain increased the pace and force of his thrusts, he felt her *inmaline* stretch to accommodate him, and the soft, wet feeling of her around him was finer than any other sensation. He could feel his globes tighten, demanding release. Each plunge of his shultor edged him closer, but he drew it out, balancing on the peak, enjoying the little thief's response. Her lips were swollen from his mouth. Her nipples peaked into hard points against his chest as she climbed back to arousal.

In the restraints, her hands had fisted, and her shallow pants heated his face. He smiled. From her reaction to his touch on her somaline, she hadn't been pleasured there before. More might be nice. He reached down and slid his fingers through her wetness, before firmly stroking the engorged nub.

As if zapped, her body arched to a rigid bow, and she fell into her release with the sharp scream of someone falling off a cliff. Her inmaline clenched around him, spasming so hard it ripped away his own control, and he shot into her, over and over.

She'd closed her eyes, he realized, at the height of her orgasm, but he'd seen the sheer shock in there, just as she'd come. By the four gods, he enjoyed taking her more than he had any woman in a long,

long time. He nuzzled her face. Her body had lost its tension, turning to softness around him and under him. He kissed her, coaxing her lips to respond.

"Well, little Mella, do Nexans make love differently than Earthers?"

When she didn't answer, he moved inside her, felt her inmaline tighten as she gave a soft gasp. "Mella?"

"Um." Her cheeks shaded to an appealing pink. "I-I suppose. But I've only been with one man, so…" Her frown indicated she was recovering rapidly. "Of course, he never had to buy me or tie me down to—"

"To have you reach climax? Make you whimper with pleasure?" He slid in and out and enjoyed the way her heart rate increased. By Cernun, if he stayed inside her and teased her much more, he'd end up taking her again. He sighed. He didn't have time to spend the day in bed.

And now that he wasn't occupied, he realized his knee ached like someone was poking knives into the bone. With regret, he pulled out of her, enjoying the flash of dismay in her eyes. Much as she wanted to deny it, she'd enjoyed herself as fully as he had.

Lying beside her, he propped up on one elbow. The scent of shulin filled the air, and he could smell himself on her. He liked that small sign of possession. Smiling, he ran one hand over her breasts. They were so beautifully lush, he couldn't keep his hands off.

"Let me loose," she demanded.

"Did you just give me an order?" he asked mildly.

When he pinched the velvety nipple under his fingers, her breath caught, and a telling shiver ran through her.

Ah, did she enjoy a touch of pain with her pleasure? To test the idea, he said, "I believe you might want to curtail your tongue, little thief. Indentured slaves may be beaten. Would you like my hand applied to your ass?"

"You wouldn't," she gasped.

With his palm on her breast, he felt her pulse increase. From the way her pupils dilated slightly, she found the idea of being beaten—by him—exciting.

"Oh, but I would," he murmured. Under his thumb, her nipple had contracted to a tight point.

And he hardened. By Cernun's spear, he needed to get out of this bed before he taught her all about pain and pleasure. "Get up and have some breakfast, my thief. A seamstress should be here by midmorning."

THAT EVENING, IN an emerald green gown of heavy satin, Mella accompanied Dain up a grassy path to an elegant stone mansion. Her fingernails dug into her palms as she tried to conceal her trembling.

Dain glanced at her. "You look lovely, laria. Stop fretting."

Sure, she *looked* fine, but being so visible terrified her. Would Nathan come to this planet? And what if the Nexan enforcers who'd tried to kill her were here? How had Nathan managed to hire the police to do his dirty work, anyway? If only there weren't cops involved, she could have turned to them for justice. If only she weren't on a foreign planet; on Earth, she'd have had people to call upon for help. A shiver went through her as she thought of all the things that might go wrong tonight.

Dain stopped and leaned on his cane. His warm fingers curled around her bare upper arm. "Now that I think about it, you aren't fidgeting with your hair or gown. Your appearance isn't what worries you." He held her in place as he studied her. "What are you afraid of?" he asked softly.

Could she tell him? Would he believe her and protect her? The thought of sharing her fears, her betrayal with someone was so compelling. "I—"

"Dain!" a woman's voice called from the entry. A willowy brunette in a glittering silver gown hurried down the path. She elbowed Mella to one side and wrapped her arms around Dain. "Where have you been for the past month?"

Dain set the woman from him and glanced at Mella. "I will require an answer to my question later," he warned before returning his attention to the woman. "Atrilla, you look lovely tonight. Let me escort you back to the house." Yet rather than offering his arm to the woman, he pulled Mella to his side, his arm like an iron band around her waist.

Atrilla raised thin eyebrows and looked down an equally thin nose at Mella. "Really, Dain. Did you have to bring your unshuline?"

"I enjoy her company." His tone was mild, but his voice had turned to ice.

Silenced, the brunette excused herself even before they reached the house. Mella understood completely. Dain had a talent for intimidation that was worthy of a divine interrogator. A rather odd talent for a businessman, but probably quite useful in long meetings.

At the door, a butler in red livery bowed low, then motioned them into a marble-floored entry. They walked through open double doors into a huge ballroom with a high-domed ceiling. When Mella looked closely at the arched windows, she could see heavy metal gridwork outside the glass. Flying predators… What a strange world.

People crowded the center of the room, weaving an intricate dance to music reminiscent of the Renaissance period. Around the edges, others mingled. Only a few lighter-skinned foreigners were sprinkled among the Nexans. The excessively tall Nexans, Mella thought, feeling like a fat dwarf. After another look, she realized the males outnumbered the females by almost three to one. "Don't Nexan women enjoy parties?" she asked. "There are hardly any here."

"On Nexus, male births have always outnumbered female. It's why many marriages have two or three men to one woman."

Mella blinked in surprise. "A marriage is one man and one woman."

He gave her an amused look. "Not on Nexus. Actually, kinlines known for dominant males tend to have one on one, except for the

Arewells. But in the less…ah…testosterone-laden families, multiple males in a marriage are common."

Heavens. No wonder the Prophet had only bad things to say about this planet.

Dain chuckled and ran a finger down her cheek before moving on.

As she and Dain made their slow way around the room, everyone greeted him. Mella received several interested glances before the men spotted her indenture bracelets, and then they stared at her like a stray mongrel in a fancy kitchen. Reproving looks directed at Dain bounced off him—or perhaps he didn't even notice. She'd never met a man so self-confident.

Even his mother's annoyance didn't budge his equilibrium. "Dain, I left word for you not to bring this—your slave," the older woman hissed.

"How are you, Mother?" Dain gave her a formal embrace. "You look lovely, as always."

"Dain, did you hear me?"

"I believe you've met Mella," he said, a hint of steel in his voice.

His mother tightened her lips before giving Mella a frozen nod. "Good evening."

Mella returned the nod. "Ma'am."

The woman frowned at her son and then sighed. "Please do not do anything else to embarrass the kinline."

Dain tilted his head in lieu of an answer. His mother walked away, spine rigidly straight. She nodded at two black-clad enforcers as she passed.

A tremor ran through Mella at the sight of the black uniforms and zappers. When Dain moved toward them, Mella dug in her heels. She couldn't stay here any longer. What if those two enforcers who'd killed Cap and her crew came to the party? "I can wait outside. In the carriage. Or on the—"

"No, laria." His attention turned to her like a powerful spotlight. "I prefer you with me."

Anger lit inside her like a tiny flame. "And do you always get what you want?"

"Not always, no." Wrapping his hand around the back of her neck, he dragged her closer. His warm breath tickled her ear as he whispered, "But with a little unshuline? Always."

The feel of his firm hand sent chills through her, as if he had her in his bed again, and when he pulled back, she could only stare helplessly into his dark gray eyes. Smiling, he rubbed his knuckles against her cheek. "Come, little thief. I have two or three more friends I wish to see. Then we can leave."

Over the next half an hour, as he talked with various people about planetary policies and new laws, Mella realized just how powerful a man he was. Great choice of victim to rob, she thought bitterly. Yet his arm around her seemed more for protection than humiliation. Despite the raised eyebrows, not one person offered her anything less than a polite greeting.

"Remember the ship that blew up at the port recently?"

The question caught Mella's attention, and she stiffened, looking for who had spoken. She finally spotted an elderly woman, her gown crusty with sequins, who confided in her friend, "I just found out on the infonet today—the ship belonged to Armelina Archer. Such a tragedy."

"Oh my. I didn't know. May Ekatae be gentle with her," the other woman said, putting a hand over her ample breasts. "Her 'Lament for a Lost Spring' is the most beautiful thing I've ever heard. I cry every time the clanae lets us play it."

My last song. She'd written it after her little sister's death and, hidden in the church alcove, had sung it for the first and only time at the funeral. Someone must have recorded it. As she thought about that day, she remembered the darkness inside the church with even the stained-glass windows appearing somber. As the coffin lid was lowered, she'd felt as if her heart were being buried in the metal box with her sister.

Now surrounded by music and light, Mella rubbed her chest, feeling the rhythmic pulse. Her heart was alive again, and somewhere along the way, her loss had become less devastating, the ache more distant.

She huffed a laugh. And now that she could consider living, the monster had targeted her for death. *Life is just full of surprises.*

Hard fingers raised her chin, tilting her face up for inspection. "Are you all right, laria?"

"I'm fine."

"Try again."

"You didn't buy my emotions along with my body." With a sarcastic bite, she added, "Sir."

To her surprise, he only laughed. "The title sounds pleasing coming from your lips." His finger traced her mouth, leaving tingles in its wake. "And I bought everything, my little thief, including your emotions."

When Dain turned his attention toward two men and a woman, Mella breathed a sigh of relief. She stood silently with his arm around her, her bought-and-paid-for emotions swirling through her like jangling harp strings.

The next person Dain greeted was a Nexan woman with a lighter complexion than most. "Triscana, I didn't realize you'd come to the city."

The woman's gaze dropped. "Kinae Dain."

After hooking his cane over his arm, Dain lifted Triscana's face until she looked up at him. He smiled. "I have fond memories of our time together."

The woman flushed and whispered, "As do I, sir." When someone hailed her from nearby, Triscana flitted away after giving Dain a very warm look. An...inviting look, Mella thought, unsettled at the annoyance curling within her.

"Dain, you old *wulkor*. How's the knee?" called a muscular man in black pants and a dark tunic with red embroidery. He strode through the crowd toward them, people parting before him as they did for Dain.

"Blackwell, I looked for you earlier." Dain grinned and clasped the man's forearm. "My leg is improving."

"Then why the cane?"

Mella felt shame sweep through her, abrading her self-respect. *I hurt a person for my own gain.* She waited miserably for Dain to tell his friend.

"I bumped it the other day. I hear you're negotiating a generation contract."

"Your news is outdated, wulkor. My very fainthearted proposed mate failed to win my approval." Blackwell's face tightened, and then he shrugged. "The thought of shulin with me frightened her; living in our clanhome made her quake. What kind of timid child would she have borne me? The clanae agreed."

"With the way your clanae checks genes, I'm surprised she wasn't weeded out long ago," Dain said.

"Perhaps she'd never had the opportunity for a good scare," Blackwell added drily, "until she met me." His gaze turned to Mella, and his icy blue eyes examined her as if she were a mannequin on display. "Interesting, Dain. You go from never buying an unshuline to bringing one to a party. But she appears a nicely soft choice."

"Thank you. I'm quite pleased."

The man's grin lightened his rough face. "Bring her with you to the LastDay festivities. She'd be a pleasure to share."

Share? Mella ventured a look up at her owner, met his eyes. He smiled slowly. "I'll consider it."

Chapter Seven

THE CHILL, LATE-NIGHT air carried the scent of the spice fields as the horses clopped down the dirt road. Dain held the reins with one hand and kept an arm around Mella's curvy body, pointing out various Nexan plants and animals. More relaxed since they'd left the party, she actually argued with him on which ones had been carried over from Earth with the first colonists. Finding out that horses—and people—were the only imports that had not been radically mutated rather shocked her.

Dain watched the Earther's reactions on the slow journey to the enclave. Apparently, on Earth, everyone traveled in enclosed hovercars. Although Nexans used solacars during 'stal migrations and when in a hurry, most preferred a horse and carriage. The world, like women, should be savored slowly.

Only two moons, Morrgan and Neman, rode high in the sky by the time Dain guided the animals through the gate and to the back of the enclave. The stableman took the reins from Dain and jerked his head toward the clanhome. "Think you might be needed in there, Kinae."

Even from the yard, Dain could hear the uproar. Taking Mella's hand, he limped inside.

"Kinae, thank Cernun you've returned." The clan butler hurried down the hall.

After divesting himself and Mella of their outer garments, Dain turned his attention back to the butler. "What's going on, Yorest?"

"Wardain cut his hand playing with his father's sword, and Felaina took the child to the hospital by solacar."

"All right. So what is the problem?"

"The problem is that Nanny Karesta left yesterday to visit her grandchildren, and the new girl is useless." Yorest sniffed contemptuously. The Hermest kinline had served the Zarain clan for centuries and made up the majority of the servants on the estate. But Dain's sister had wanted a younger nanny and had hired one from the unaffiliated Junant kinline instead. "Cannalaina is having hysterics, and Reblaini won't stop crying."

Dain scrubbed his face. He'd rather face a Port City riot than deal with his young nieces when they were upset. They had inherited all Felaina's stubbornness. "I'll see what I can do." He took a step forward, reached back, and grabbed Mella's hand. "Come, little Earther. I need reinforcements."

"But..."

Felaina's family rooms lay on the west side of the house, decorated in the green colors she loved. Standing in the tiny hallway to the bedrooms, Dain winced at the sound of screeching and courageously assigned himself Cannalaina's room. He deserved a medal for this. He pointed Mella toward the other room from which he could hear sobbing. "Reblaini is five, and she gets upset if her mother or Nanny Karesta aren't here."

"But..."

Trying not to smile at the horrified look on the little Earther's face, Dain stepped into Canna's room and shut the door behind him. He surveyed the situation and sighed. Maybe he should have stayed in the militia; it would have been safer.

Kneeling in the center of her bed, the slender seven-year-old pounded the mattress with her fists. In the corner, the thoroughly cowed young nanny wrung her hands. Dain gave the nanny credit for not having fled; the noise level was worse than a Port City bar during festival.

At least Canna didn't normally act like this. Neither her mother nor Nanny Karesta would have permitted it. But they weren't here, and she couldn't be allowed to think she could trample people with impunity. The Zarain kinline prided itself on self-control. Leaders didn't have tantrums—more's the pity.

So.

He plucked her mechanical clock off the wall and strolled over to the bed. Setting it in front of Canna, he tapped the unit. Her gaze dropped to the timepiece, although her screaming didn't abate. Personally, he thought a single swat on the bottom would be an appropriate punishment, but corporal discipline was left up to immediate family and the clanae, which, thank Cernun, Dain wouldn't be for many years.

"Cannalaina, I tire of the noise." He spoke loudly enough that she could hear his voice. "For each minute it continues, I will toss a toy out the window. In the morning, those toys will go to the hospital as gifts."

Only a second's pause indicated she'd heard.

After one minute, he threw a stuffed felin out the narrow arched window.

The screams grew louder.

Two minutes. A kaleidoscope hit the grass.

On the way past the shelves, he picked up a stuffed *canin* with round paws and floppy ears—one he knew was a favorite.

Silence.

She glared up at him, looking so much like her mother had as a child that he almost swept her up in a hug. But rewards and affection were for proper behavior, not tantrums. He put his hands behind his back. "You will offer suitable apologies to me, to your nanny, and tomorrow to Yorest for this disgraceful display. When your mother returns, you will explain to her what you have done and accompany her to the hospital to give your two toys away. Is that clear?"

"Yes, Unka Dain." Her eyes brimmed with tears. He rarely spoke harshly to her, and it seemed his anger bothered her more than the loss of the toys. She took a shuddering breath. "I am sorry for m-my—what I did."

He considered, decided the apology was sincere, and wrapped an arm around her. "Forgiven, Niece. Give the rest of your apologies. Then Nanny will help you prepare for bed."

"Yes, sir."

His lips curved as his memory brought back another voice saying *Sir*. He should check how Mella was doing. Undoubtedly not well, since no one could console Reblaini. But as he stepped out into the hall, he heard only silence. Fear hit him. Surely she wouldn't have hurt the child...

And then he heard Rebli's high, sweet voice. "Sing another one, Mella? It makes the hurty part go away."

A husky laugh. "Well, we can't have a hurty part. All right, then. This is a song my mama used to sing to me."

Amazing. Dain took a step in that direction, then froze as her voice lifted into an ancient Earth lullaby. *What a voice.* Clear yet resonant, filled with so much emotion that his chest tightened. He usually preferred instrumentals to vocals, but he could have listened to her all night. As could his niece, obviously.

He felt a presence beside him. Yorest, eyes half-lidded, mouth curving. The fussy butler had perhaps smiled twice in his entire lifetime. One of those times had been when Dain was appointed head of Planetary Security. Here was a third.

They simply stood and listened to the song as it drifted down the hall. When silence fell, Yorest nodded to Dain and disappeared.

Dain walked over to the door. Looking into Rebli's room, he saw the little girl had fallen asleep, snuggled in the Earther's arms as if she'd found warmth in a cold world.

SHE'D ACTUALLY BEEN singing. Mella stood in the center of her bedroom and shook her head. She'd tried to sing once or twice during the past year, but nothing had come out. It was as if her mourning had cut her throat and let all the music bleed away. But tonight she hadn't even thought twice about singing a lullaby to Rebli.

After stepping out of her fancy green slippers, she started on the tiny hooks running down the front of her new gown. Singing had felt…good. Like she'd stood only on one foot for a year and now had two. Had achieved a little balance.

But how totally stupid had it been to sing at all? Thank heavens Dain obviously hadn't recognized her voice. Far too many people would, she knew, even here on this benighted planet, where the five clans regulated recorded music and vids.

She felt him a second before he moved behind her, and she froze. The man walked much too quietly.

"You have a lovely voice." Dain kissed her nape and sent goose bumps down her arms.

"Thank you." Her fingers hesitated on the hooks. She'd thought she was alone. But now…

"Do you need help, laria?" Leaning against her back, he reached around and, with very skillful fingers, unhooked her gown until the sides flapped open, exposing her breast binder. No panties. He ran his hand over her bare stomach and down to cup her mound. She inhaled, feeling her traitorous body waken.

His other hand curved under her breast over the binder. When he nipped her earlobe, she jumped, even as excitement ran through her. And with his hand between her legs, he must feel how she dampened. His arm locked her against him as his fingers slid lower, separating her slick folds to stroke her clit.

Throbbing grew inside her to an urgent heat. Her legs began to quiver, and her breathing grew more rapid. Just that easily, he'd made her want him. Made her want to couple. Humiliation followed the thought yet didn't decrease the excitement growing inside her.

"The ice appears to be cracking," he murmured. His lips against her shoulder made her shudder with need. Ignoring her murmur of protest, he stripped off her gown, then pulled her binder off. When she reached for her nightgown, he caught her hand. "You won't need that."

Cupping her chin, he forced her to meet his gaze. His eyes were dark pools. "Get on the bed, laria. Wait for me on your hands and knees."

"But—"

His lips curved into a hard smile. "You do not have permission to speak. I want to hear nothing from you except whimpers."

Chapter Eight

THREE DAYS LATER, Dain took a solacar into Port City. The car hummed past fields greening with new plantings. Spring was a beautiful time on Nexus.

Mella hadn't wanted to come into the city. Odd that. Most women he knew preferred the bustle of the city to enclave life, at least now and then. But Mella had hidden places in her—unhappy ones she hadn't shared with him. Yet.

Much of the fear had disappeared from her eyes over the past few days. Not all, though. His mouth tightened as he remembered the terror that flashed across her face at times. No woman should be afraid, not even a thieving one. Although he had to admit, a woman stranded on an unfamiliar planet might have more reason to fear than most.

Out of the corner of his eye, he saw a relix freeze. The lizard darted forward almost too fast to follow and caught a *flutter* in its pointy mouth. As it scrabbled back into the underbrush, Dain tapped the steering wheel. Dangers filled the world. But what exactly was the Earther afraid of?

She appeared to be adapting to enclave life. Although she avoided his family and other clan members as if they might bite her—not unreasonable, considering the way his mother had acted—she spent time with the servants. The staff had taken to her. He grinned, remembering the floppy hat Quenoll had given her and how adorable she'd looked in it. Dirt smudged across one cheek, scratches on her arms from weeding the sun garden with the old gardener, new freckles on her pale skin, and happiness in her big green eyes.

Dain smiled. He had competition for her favors—an old man approaching the century mark. The sight of the little thief looking so content pleased him.

Her attitude toward shulin had eased, and she welcomed his attentions, even becoming more assertive about what she liked, as her experience grew.

She still shocked easily, though, didn't she?

Yesterday in the garden, she'd demanded a lower undergarment that she called *panties*. After motioning for the gardener and apprentice to leave, Dain had flipped up her skirt, bent her over the stone bench, and demonstrated why he permitted neither underwear nor trousers on his unshuline.

For the rest of the day, she'd blushed every time she looked at him. By Cernun, she was sweet.

Dain slowed the car to allow a herd of deerlets to flow across the road in graceful leaps. Two more curves and he'd reached the outskirts of Port City.

The small city enclaves gave way to the businesses that crowded the port, and a slight distance farther stood the Planetary Defense and Planetary Security buildings. The Council of Five had requested his time and oversight on the investigation of a ship that had been blown apart in the port. Once the identity of the ship's famous owner became known, pressure had increased to find the culprit responsible.

What a mess.

"YOU DON'T HAVE to work like that, you know."

Kneeling in a flower bed, Mella jumped at the sound of the soft voice, and the thorny bush scratched down her arm. She gritted her teeth at the stinging pain and turned.

Beside the tiny altar, a woman about Mella's age stood in the entrance to the blue garden. Gemstones woven into the woman's braided black hair sparkled in the sunlight. Mella grimaced. Another tall, slender Nexan woman—didn't they have any small, pudgy ones like her?

Miss Incredibly Gorgeous rushed forward. "You're bleeding. Oh, sweet Herina, I'm sorry. I didn't mean to startle you." From the fineness of the pale blue skirt and silky green tunic, the woman must be one of the Zarain family, not a servant.

"It's nothing," Mella said, flushing and uncomfortably aware of the indenture bracelets on her sunburned arms. Over the past week, she'd avoided Dain's family. Dain hadn't noticed. He stayed so busy, she never saw him outside of the evenings. Apparently her luck had run out.

The woman pulled the scarf from around her neck, wet it in the splashing fountain, and tied the fabric around Mella's forearm. "There, that will do until Ida can put some of her special salve on it. Considering how often Wardain manages to slice himself up, I've had a lot of experience using it."

Wardain. She'd heard that name before. Heavens, the boy who'd cut himself on his daddy's sword. Dain's nephew. She'd seen him running around the gardens with the two little girls trailing after him, or indulging in mock fights with some of the other clan children. Then this must be Dain's sister.

"Thank you," Mella said. "If you'll excuse me, I'll go to the house and take care of my arm." Mella forced a smile onto her face, hoping to escape before the bracelets registered. She doubted that this finely dressed woman would behave any nicer to an unshuline than her mother.

"I'm Felaina. And you are Mella?"

Mella glanced at the bright bracelets and sighed. Like any other unshuline lived here? "That's right." Mella pushed to her feet and nodded her farewell. "Good day."

"Wait." The woman's frown looked just like Dain's, and a funny feeling tickled Mella's throat. "Did I do something to offend you?"

"I'm an unshuline."

"Well, yes, I know that." Felaina settled onto the stone bench and smoothed her skirt. "You helped Rebli when I took Wardain to the hospital."

Eyeing her warily, Mella nodded.

"I wanted to thank you."

"It was nothing. I was pleased to help," Mella said stiffly.

"You seem to like to help a lot. Ida says you assist in the kitchen; Quenoll says you're out in the gardens every day." Felaina tilted her head. "Did anyone tell you an unshuline isn't expected to do servant work?"

Did that mean she couldn't work anymore? As Mella thought of the long, useless days, her hands fisted at her sides. "I'm sorry if I bothered—"

"By Mardun's sword, you're taking everything I say wrong." Felaina scowled. "Ida and Quenoll love having you help, and you're allowed to do anything you…" She stopped and burst into laughter. "You should see your face. Like I was a parogan that pecked your nose."

"Well…" What kind of a conversation was this? "Then you don't mind if I help out?"

"Of course not. As long as you realize it's not required." Dain's sister grinned. "Dain said you're from Earth and don't know our customs. Sometimes he's so terse… I just wanted to make sure someone had told you."

The expression on Felaina's face seemed as far from contemptuous as could be. Mella knelt back down in the soft grass. "I'm sorry. I guess I'm oversensitive."

"Not surprising." Felaina's voice softened. "I daresay Earthers wouldn't approve of unshulines at all."

"Well, no." Whips and stones would be the least of what came her way. "Ida told me I didn't need to work, but I want to." Mella looked around. In the blue garden, purple grass as fine as fur covered the paths. Water lilies of pale purple and white filled the pond, and crescendos of lavender blossoms spilled from vines that arched over a pergola. The garden seemed a refuge of coolness no matter how hot the day. "I never knew how satisfying gardening could be."

"Good enough." Felaina rose to her feet. "Let's go and have Ida put some ointment on that scratch…and maybe you can tell me about Earth?"

The warmth settling around Mella's heart felt oddly like contentment. "I'd love to."

Chapter Nine

TWO DAYS LATER, Mella stood at the kitchen counter, her hands buried in warm bread dough. The lovely scent of yeast rose around her as she kneaded and watched the vid in the corner. The newscaster had just introduced the Council of Five.

In another fifteen minutes, the tiny screen would click off—Nexus only allowed broadcasting from six to eight each morning and evening. Dain hadn't lied when he'd mentioned the planet's abhorrence for artificial entertainment.

She folded the dough in on itself and pressed again, enjoying how the texture grew elastic. Ida glanced over, silently checked her progress, and nodded in approval. Mella smiled. She'd learned more here than just about coupling. By the time she left, she'd possess some decent cooking skills.

Each morning, she arrived a little earlier to enjoy the homelike atmosphere in the big kitchen.

She could also keep track of the news.

On the vid, the five clanae finished discussing the increase in taxes, and the view changed to the lead newsman's report on Port City crime. One rare murder in the Old Quarters. A brawl in the plaza between off-worlders. Two robberies inside the port. The display switched to the port gates and a flower-filled altar set up there for Armelina Archer. The newsman reported about the stalker who had followed the singer from Earth and then bombed her ship.

Her lips quirked. So now stalkers engaged in interplanetary travel?

The scene changed to a plaza hotel and then… Nathan appeared on the vid. Evil incarnate. He walked out of the hotel and stood on the top step, facing a horde of reporters.

Iron bands closed around Mella's ribs, and her heart slammed into her rib cage as if trying to break out. *He's here. In Port City.* After a strangling gasp, she forced herself to breathe slowly and knead the bread. *Turn, press, fold over.* The tightness in her chest eased.

Nathan's on the planet.

Well, she'd always known he might come. Wouldn't it look suspicious if the husband of a famous singer didn't collect her body and help investigate her murder? He'd never foolishly ignore the proprieties.

But seeing him… Her stomach knotted. The picture on the screen blurred into his face on the holocard, the one the murderers had given her. He'd been her husband for over five years, and she'd almost not recognized his picture on the card that night. His eyes had looked flat, almost lifeless, and his smooth voice nonchalant, as if he spoke of an evening's entertainment, not her murder. *"You're going to die now, Armelina. Sorry."*

Just the memory… She clamped her jaws together at the surging fear. *Don't panic.* He couldn't know she'd escaped the bombing. He'd undoubtedly arrived to ensure suspicion fell on the stalker.

"All right be you, Mella? You be white as winter fur on a *greiet*." Ida poured a glass of fruit juice and set it on the counter. "Sit yourself down and drink."

Prepared to refuse, Mella nodded instead. Her legs wobbled as she walked to the table. She sat and watched the vid.

When a reporter asked why Armelina Archer had left Earth, Nathan answered, "I urged her to get away. I thought it would be safer for her because of the stalker. But he must have followed her off-planet." He choked and turned away.

The glass halted halfway to Mella's mouth. She'd received letters and calls from that stalker, hadn't she? Had he even existed? Knowing her deepest fear, had Nathan invented him to scare her to the frontier planets, where he could have her murdered more easily? *"I don't want anything to happen to you, darling. While you're on vacation, I'll make sure the police catch this man."*

Oh Prophet, how blind she'd been. She took a sip of juice and choked at the sound of Dain's voice.

"I have to go to Port City, Ida." He strolled into the kitchen and stopped beside Mella. "Do you ladies need me to pick up anything while I'm there?"

With a hand on Mella's shoulder, he leaned her against his hip. He touched her constantly, from hugs to playing with her hair to full embraces. Nexans were so different. No one kissed or hugged on Earth, not casually.

She'd miss his comforting touch. When she looked up at him, his eyes darkened. "What has upset you, laria?"

She swallowed her initial words and tried for a half-truth instead. "The news was ugly today."

"Mmmph. It's ugly far too often." He traced her lips with one finger before glancing at the vid, where the reporter spoke of women calling the Planetary Security building, claiming to be Armelina Archer.

"How in the world can the enforcers know if someone's lying without a truth-reader?" Blani asked. "No one knows what Armelina Archer looks like."

Dain chuckled. "The enforcers hired two of Archer's fans to screen the callers by listening to them sing. Apparently, Archer's voice is unique."

"As you'd know, if you ever took time to listen," Ida said with a sniff as she handed him a glass of juice. "She has an extraordinary voice."

"So her fans say." He drank, then added, "I'll return after lastmeal, Ida. No need to save me anything." He studied Mella's face again, gave her a hard kiss, and left.

Rather than returning to her room, Mella escaped to the inner courtyard. Near the walls, tiny streams of water curved through purple grass and brightly colored flower beds, then flowed under small wooden bridges until reaching the clear blue pond in the center. Bright little parogans lined up on the stones, preening in the fine spray from the arching center fountain. The flowering, dwarf fruit trees added a tropical scent to the moist, green fragrance. So quiet and serene.

Mella sank down on a cushioned chair near the tiny altar by the water. This altar held a hand-sized statue of a woman with her arms lifted in victory.

At a flash of color, Mella looked up to see a little bird flit through the heavy screening overhead. The large size of the openings in the barrier implied that the flying predators must be bigger than three feet. *What a horrible thought.*

But safety existed nowhere in the galaxy. She'd learned that.

Still… The enclave had come to feel like a sanctuary. When she first arrived, she'd considered running. The gardener's apprentice had told her of a Port City man who removed indenture bracelets. *For a price.* Her stomach twisted at the thought of paying that price.

Eventually, she'd realized the foolishness of trying to flee. She was well hidden here. Safe.

Maybe. His face—Seeing his face brought everything back.

A tiny wind whipped around the courtyard and spray from the fountain misted over her, cold against her heated skin. She heard Dain's solacar starting up, and it sounded far too like a zapper's fire. A shudder shook her as she remembered how Captain Anderson had fallen. The heavy *thud* as his body hit the deck.

Guilt tasted bitter in her mouth. She should have saved them or avenged them…somehow. But everything she'd done since her ship blew up proved how weak she was. Mella's hands shook as she laced her fingers together. Could she have done something different?

She and Cap and the engineer, Johnnie, had been in the galley, eating a greiet stew. Johnnie'd pushed the vegetables on his plate away from the meat; he liked everything separated out. And then the copilot, Pard, had walked in with two enforcers. Having met the cops when the ship cleared customs, Mella had smiled at them. That memory made her feel sick now. Why hadn't she felt the evil coming from them? Something, before…

As Johnnie turned to greet them, the dark enforcer shot Cap with his zapper. That horrible whining noise... Cap's body went rigid, his gentle hazel eyes wide, and then he toppled from the chair.

Mella screamed. Before Johnnie could move, the dark enforcer whipped around and buried a knife in his throat. Blood sprayed. Red everywhere.

Mella shoved back from the table and charged the blond enforcer even as he stabbed Pard. He blocked Mella's first punch, and the dark one threw her into a bulkhead. She slammed hard and dropped, hitting her head on the rigid deck. Stunned. When she opened her eyes, she stared at Johnnie, into his lifeless blue eyes. An hour earlier, he'd shown her the picture of his petite girlfriend on Delgato. He'd asked Mella to help him pick out a pretty gift.

"I wish these benighted zappers would hold more than one charge," one enforcer said.

"You should carry two, like I do. Is she alive?"

Something dripped on her face, and she struggled to look up. The blond stood over her, his knife bloody. "Yeah, she's moving."

"Don't kill her. She's got to read that letter before the ship blows. With our luck, her husband is a truth-reader."

The ship blows? Husband? Pain stabbed through her skull when she tried to move. *What did he mean?* She couldn't look away from Johnnie's face. They'd killed him; he was only twenty-two, and they'd knifed him. They'd only zapped Cap, though; surely he'd be alive... She pushed up on an elbow. Her breath hitched as she saw the blood pooling around the captain's body. They'd stabbed him too, that sweet old man so full of stories of his early adventures.

"By Mardun's sword." Still standing over Mella, the blond turned to glare at his companion. "You're as timid as a greiet. Let's just get those explos—"

She'd kill him. Kill him dead like Cap and Pard... Head splitting with pain, Mella kicked hard and connected with the blond enforcer's leg. He fell back.

A high whine... Her body spasmed as streams of agony seared down every nerve. Paralyzed. She couldn't even moan. Every breath hurt, and drool ran from her mouth.

The dark enforcer glared at the blond. "Cretin. Get her out of here so I can finish. We don't have time to screw around. I still don't like this."

"Yeah, but we'll be set for life. Lie low for a while. Then go off-planet and never return." Taking a handful of her clothing, the blond dragged her to her cabin. "Here, Earther, your husband sent you a message." He stuffed a holocard into her tight top, groping her in the process. "There, now we can honestly say you got the card." He stepped out. Her cabin door slid shut, and something thudded on the other side.

After a minute, she rolled over. Her muscles spasmed and burned. Two tries to stand; two falls. Stomach heaving, she lurched to the door. It didn't open.

Dear Prophet, he'd destroyed the controls. Legs buckling, she fell against the door.

She could hear them moving through the ship, discussing where to put each bomb. *Bombs.* They were going to blow up her ship?

Terror filled her, drowning her beneath its weight. Screaming, she slammed herself against the cabin door again and again, clawed the controls.

Laughter.

The sound sliced through her hysteria like a knife. Panting, heart hammering, sweat cold on her body, she stared around the cabin. What would open the door? Nothing. Cabin doors were recessed, airtight in case of hull breach. Nothing would... Her gaze fell on the tiny refresher.

She fell once on the way, and then she stood in the coffin-sized shower stall. Hands shaking, she pushed on the plas-tiles like Cap had shown her. "*Four down, two across, one up.*" With the seventh tile, something clicked. She set her shoulder against the wall, shoved, and a three-foot section opened like a door.

Behind the wall was only blackness. A chill shuddered through her. *No flashlight.* Could she open the hatch at the far end by touch, or would she die there in the dark?

She sucked in a breath. Hesitated. Silence. The men had gone. *No time left.* After scrambling into the access tube, she crawled until her head thudded into the outside hatch. Where were the manual levers?

She fumbled blindly, remembering the day Cap had shown her his secret. Six locks to ensure an airtight seal. Five of them flipped under her fingers. *Where is the last one?* Her hands felt numb, icy as she started from the top again. Halfway down, she found the one that she'd missed before. *Please, Prophet...* She shoved the lever and jammed her shoulder against the door, pushing with all her might.

It opened soundlessly. The old smuggler had even mentioned that. "*After all, little miss, you don't want anything squeaking when you're illegally off-loading.*"

Docking cribs usually lit only a ship's side hatches and front. The stern lay in a pool of darkness. She dropped the ten feet or so to the asphalt. Her legs buckled, and she fell hard, scraping her hands, bruising her knees. She clamped her lips tightly over her whimpers of pain and fear. Pushing to her feet, she staggered through the shadows toward the far end. She made it past an empty dock, another ship—

With a series of ear-deafening blasts, her ship exploded. She went face-first into the concrete.

Bleeding, aching, and crying soundlessly, she hid. People arrived, running. Yelling. Medics and port staff. And *enforcers*.

In the midst of the chaos, she walked right out of the port.

Two miles later, in a small park, she remembered the holocard the blond had stuffed into her shirt. She pulled it out.

Nathan's face appeared above the card, bobbling since her hands wouldn't stop shaking. "*You're going to die now, Armelina. Sorry. You shouldn't have taken an interest in your accounts.*" He smoothed his hair and smiled. "*I'd hoped you'd kill yourself, but nooo. So I'll help.*" When he smiled, she'd taken a step back. "*You always like the cards I give you for special occasions. I thought you'd enjoy one for your death.*"

She stared at the card, stomach twisting. *No...no!* Although silent now, the hologram of his face still hovered above the card. His eyes gleamed. Amused. She remembered how two dogs had fought to the death in their street. Rather than pulling them apart, Nathan had watched, the same look in his eyes.

Mella's fingers clenched convulsively, closing the card, making the hologram disappear. Just as Nathan had made her whole life disappear.

A SPARKLE OF song broke into Mella's thoughts, and she shook herself and blinked. The enclave. The courtyard filled with bright flowers and birds. The high melody had come from a tiny golden bird on the rocks. It finished its song and sidled closer to its mate. Mella choked on a bitter laugh. Her mate hadn't been so loving. She wrapped her arms around herself.

What she couldn't get past was that Cap and Johnnie and Pard had died because of her. She hadn't killed them, but if she hadn't been on the ship, they'd still be alive.

Tears seared her cheeks, and her breath hitched. She'd never told them how much she cherished their friendship. Their laughter in her gray life. How Cap had teased Pard about adding hot sauce to everything. Johnnie's addiction to magnetic jigsaw puzzles that always had a piece missing. The card games and how they'd taught her to bet. The fact she was quiet and solemn hadn't annoyed them like it had Nathan. They'd treated her so gently. Sometimes Cap would wrap an arm around her and squeeze her, as if to let her know she wasn't alone.

And he was dead now. *I miss them, miss them so much.*

Mella hauled in a shaky breath and wiped her face. Nothing had changed, even if Nathan had arrived on the planet. Her plan to wait out her servitude, take her earnings, and return home would still work. Her fingerprints and retinal patterns were on file on Earth, and once she'd proven her identity, things would change. She had a few friends—very few—who would help her obtain a lawyer, police, whatever she'd need. Even on paternalistic Earth, money still talked loudly.

She looked down at her hands and watched them close into fists. And then she'd make sure Nathan paid for what he'd done to Cap and Johnnie and Pard.

Chapter Ten

"A DANCE?" MELLA pressed her hand over her chest, trying to settle her pounding heart. "Now? Tonight?"

Dain turned away from his bedroom armoire to look at her. "An evening meal and then dancing, yes. At the Felin's Rest Hotel. The Council of Five begins a new session, and they like to mingle in the evenings. As one of the council, Grandsir will be there, so it's expected that I will attend."

She didn't move, and he frowned. "Go to your room and get dressed, Mella. Attire is festive, but not formal. We'll leave in about an hour."

Nathan might be there. The monster loved parties, and as the widow of a galaxy-famous star, he'd surely receive an invitation to any prominent events. "I won't go," she said. She gripped her hands in front of her. "I don't feel well."

Dain's eyes narrowed. "Mella, have I mentioned how I dislike being lied to?"

"Fine. But I won't go. You don't want to drag a kicking, screaming slave to a party, do you?"

Crossing his arms over his wide chest, he leaned against the wall and studied her. "Why now? You've accompanied me before."

She couldn't answer that question. "I-I just hate being stared at...or looked down on like I'm dirt. It makes me sick."

"Bothers you, perhaps, but makes you sick is another lie," he said softly. His face hardened. "Be dressed within the hour, or you will go naked. If you need to scream, so be it. The Felin's Rest has a restraint pen for obstreperous slaves."

Damn the man. "I'll be ready." She walked out of his room on shaky legs.

AFTER SHOWERING, DAIN stepped out of the bathroom, thinking about the unusual reaction of his little thief. Although she had a sensitive nature, Mella hadn't appeared quite so unnerved since she'd arrived at his home. Why now?

Frowning, he turned away from the formalwear and pulled on a pair of casual pants and a loose tunic. Arriving late didn't bother him; Mella's attitude did. Before they left, she'd explain exactly why a party—this party—caused such concern.

On the way out the door, he heard a soft chime. After returning to the bedroom, he pressed the house comunit button on the wall. "Speak."

"Sir, we have an alarm at the back gate," reported the guard on evening shift.

The little fool. As he moved up the ladder to his current position, the enclave's security had increased until it now rivaled that of the Council Building. No one could enter—or leave—the grounds without the security staff's knowledge. "Put a level-five charge through the gate, Garwell. I'll handle the rest."

"Sir, don't you want some guards to—"

"No need."

By the time he reached the back gate, the little Earther had recovered enough to move. Somewhat. She tried to stand and made it to her knees. From there, she stared up at him, eyes huge in the light of the three moons. Almost unconsciously, she put her hand to her mouth, undoubtedly to soothe the burn on her palm from the charged gate. Dirt streaked her face and her clothing.

Thank Cernun that she hadn't made it past the gate, or he'd have been forced to cane her.

"Not a well-thought-out escape, was it?" he asked. His anger faded slightly at her pitiful appearance.

She shook her head.

"Come." He didn't wait for compliance but grasped her wrist and hauled her to her feet.

The walk back to the house and then to his rooms was accomplished in silence, his disappointment rising as his anger diminished. In his bedroom, he halted by the chair in the corner and secured both her wrists in one hand. It was past time for her to experience the consequences of dishonesty. "Mella, did I tell you not to lie to me?"

She stood silent, not meeting his gaze. Would there come a time she would look him in the eyes without masking?

"On Nexus, our children are spanked for lying. You obviously did not get those lessons in your youth. You will now."

SPANKED? HORROR FILLING her, Mella tried to yank her wrists away, but his grip didn't yield.

"You can submit to your punishment and receive seven swats." His voice was low and even. The muscles in his face were hard, his eyes level. "The longer you fight, the more blows you will receive." He paused. "Mella, you cannot escape this discipline."

She tried anyway. She couldn't pull her hands free, so she kicked at him. He didn't react at all to the impact of her soft shoes.

"Eight."

She rammed her shoulder into him, hoping to loosen his grip. It felt like hitting a rock wall.

"Nine."

Finally she stood, rigid, straining away. He'd never get her to bend.

He sighed and shook his head. "Ten." And faster than she could believe, he dropped into the chair and yanked her, stomach down, over his knees. With his left hand, he pressed on her shoulders, then swung his right leg over her ankles.

She squirmed against his restraint, but his ruthless strength pinned her in place.

"This will hurt more if your muscles are tight," he remarked easily, not even out of breath.

As he lifted her house gown, cool air touched her bare thighs and bottom. "No. You can't do this to me."

"Actually, Mella, I can." His hand came down on her buttocks with a resounding *smack*.

She screamed, more from outrage than pain. *He hit me.* "Let me go!"

Slam. Slam. Slam.

Pain burned across her bottom like a fiery brand.

He slapped one side, then the other—*slam, slam*—and stopped.

Tears slid from her eyes, dropping to the wooden floor. "You barbarian," she gritted out. "You stupid Nexan. I hate your guts."

"I know, little thief. I know," he said, gently. *Slam.* "Before you leave my estate, I will find you a better means of survival than stealing." *Slam.* "And you will no longer lie to me or try to escape." And delivered two more very hard slaps to her bottom.

She went limp, tears scalding her face, the pain and humiliation overwhelming. When he turned her, she hit at his hands, trying to get away from him, but he handled her easily, sitting her on his lap. Fury burned within her so hot, she felt as if she'd smother with it.

And yet his strength pulled her. The urge to confide in him and let him take care of her crept into her, sneaking around the rage.

But she didn't dare tell him. People would do anything for money. Look how easily Nathan was able to hire enforcers to do murder.

Dain seems honest. And that meant nothing. She'd thought Nathan had loved her.

And I have no one at all.

"Let me go," she gritted out, her breath hitching. His arms only tightened like steel bands, caging her. An ugly sound escaped her as she tried to choke back her grief.

"I'm not going to let you go," he murmured. His big hand pressed her face against his chest. "Cry, laria. Cry."

She held herself rigid. His lips brushed her hair, a kiss like her father used to give her when she'd skinned her knee. Like a hulled ship spilling everything into vacuum, she felt the pain ripping out of her.

Sagging into Dain's arms, she cried. Horrible, wrenching sobs that shook her body. She couldn't bear it anymore. Betrayed, trapped here, humiliated. Her friends lost. Left alone—*left alone.*

Her crying slowed to shuddering breaths. She blinked swollen eyes; her cheeks felt raw from the tears.

He hadn't spoken, hadn't pulled away, just enclosed her in warmth. His hand stroked up and down her back. As she slumped against him, she felt the strength of his arms, the hard chest she rested her cheek upon. His heart beat slowly and evenly; punishing her hadn't even raised his pulse.

Her bottom burned like fire. No one had ever hit her or spanked her. And since she'd been a child, no one had held her when she cried. But Dain had cared enough to deal out punishment—and even comfort—despite his anger. Something tightened inside her. This felt right—too right.

She sighed and pushed herself upright.

Dain grasped her chin and wiped her wet cheeks. After a long minute's study, he kissed her softly. "Tomorrow we will discuss your feelings about going out." He rose and set her on her feet. "And we'll both skip the party tonight." A glint of humor filled his eyes. "Especially since sitting down at a dinner table might present a problem for you." He slid his hand over her tender bottom.

The stinging pain made her jerk, and she pushed him away. "Don't."

His mouth firmed. "Little thief, I can touch you however and whenever I desire. Not only does the law state I have this right, but you gave me the right. Or have you forgotten?" He waited for her answer.

"*Please,*" she'd begged him from the auction stand. "I remember."

"For twenty-nine more days, Mella, your only rights are water, enough food to prevent starvation, and protection from permanent damage. A lot can happen to a person before lasting damage is incurred." He gave her a thin smile. "Perhaps the Indenture Hall didn't explain, but I can also sell or give your contract away. Are you starting to understand?"

She took a step back in disbelief. He could actually sell her? To anyone? "I understand." And her emotions swung right over from gratitude to hating him with everything inside her.

"Clean yourself and then return here in your robe and night-gown." His hard look said he intended to couple with her this night.

WHEN SHE RETURNED, he waited in his chair, although he'd changed into his black robe. He set the reader on the side table and snapped off the light, leaving only the glow of candlelight. The open door to the courtyard let in the scent of moisture and the gentle splashing sounds from the fountains.

He leaned back and considered her for a long moment. Her nipples tightened beneath the silky nightgown. How could she feel so angry and still want him? The shepherds were right—women *were* weak.

He had noticed her response, of course. Crinkles appeared around his eyes.

She flushed and took a step back toward the door.

He shook his head. "Mella, I am too tired to play Chase the Thief Around the Bedroom tonight. I'm more interested in another game— an adult version of one that Nexan children play."

A game? From the uncompromising look in his face, she'd probably not like this sport. Her gaze dropped.

"Come here." He motioned to a spot directly in front of his knees.

She had to force her feet to move across the room. Prophet, she didn't want to be with him. Not tonight. Her emotions felt like a shaken carbonated drink, bubbling through her painfully. She stopped in front of him.

Leaning forward, he ran a finger around her jutting nipples. "Your body is interested in playing."

She shivered at the teasing touch. Her eyes met his.

"I am very, very good at reading what a woman's body says," he said softly. His gaze never left hers as he rolled her nipple gently between his fingers. Heat shot through her so fast, her knees almost gave way. "So," he continued. "This is how the evening will go. I tell you to do something, and you obey. Quickly, eagerly, and without speaking."

Her lips tightened. This really didn't sound like a game she wanted to play.

His eyes darkened. "Now we can keep our activities in the bedroom, or we can go to my club and you can show my friends how well you follow instructions. It's your choice, little one."

"That's not much of a choice," she muttered.

"Did I give you permission to speak?"

Her mouth opened, but she reconsidered and shook her head. Her bottom still burned from his hand.

"Very good." He leaned back. "Take your robe off."

She shrugged it off her shoulders and let it drop into a heap to the wooden floor.

His eyes warmed. "The nightgown is lovely on you, Mella," he said, and his deep voice roughened. "Sit on my lap."

Obeying him seemed wrong, as if she willingly surrendered, yet she wasn't afraid. Not really. His eyes didn't hold cruelty, just enjoyment. And determination. She smothered a moan when her sore bottom scraped over his rock-hard legs, then sat, keeping herself stiffly upright.

He chuckled. "Lean against me and put your head on my shoulder, little thief."

His chest felt hard, his silky robe rubbed her cheek. She inhaled the clean scent of soap and man. Why did he have to smell so good?

His arm curved around her back, and his hand gripped her hip, holding her in place. "Are you comfortable?" he asked.

As if he cared. "Yes, I guess."

"Ah. The correct answer is either 'yes, sir' or 'no, sir.' Nothing else. Now try again."

"Yes, sir," she whispered.

"Very nice," he said, his voice warming. "That sounded just right." His free hand caressed her breasts through her gown. She tried to flinch away, but the arm behind her was unyielding. He cupped each breast in turn, as if savoring their weight, and his thumb traced circles around her increasingly hard nipples. In her private areas, a throbbing started, then grew in urgency as he rolled the tips between his fingers.

"Put one leg on each side of mine and your back against my chest," he murmured.

Now *that*, she didn't want to do. Straddle him? Without waiting for her compliance, he shifted her into the position he'd ordered.

Now her back was against him, and he curved an arm around her. Putting his hand under the gown's bodice, he fondled her breast. When he kissed her neck and she jumped at the feel of his warm mouth on her skin, his arm tightened, easily holding her for his touch. "Your skin could make a saint into a sinner," he said, nuzzling where her neck met her shoulder and sending goose bumps up her arms.

He had one hand on her breast. Her head spun as she tried to think, as sensations rippled through her. Where was his other hand? Then he slid her gown up her thighs, exposing the V between her legs. With her legs dangling on each side of his, her attempt to draw her thighs closed got nowhere.

"Uh-uh," he chided in her ear. "You will not move. I intend to enjoy touching you—everywhere."

Embarrassment heated her cheeks when his hand settled over her pussy, when his fingers slid into her folds. "You're wet for me, little thief. Your mind might not agree, but your body enjoys my touch." His fingers never stopped moving. When two fingers slid into her, she gasped at the intense rush of pleasure. Her hands clamped down on the arm around her waist, and he chuckled.

His thumb settled over her clit, right on top, barely brushing the increasingly sensitive spot. She froze. He was playing her body as easily as she played the harp, and her emotions wouldn't stay separate her body's responses. Part of her wanted to shove him away, to escape to her room, the other part clamored for his touch. She shook her head in confusion.

"You're thinking too hard, little Earther," he said and bit her shoulder. The sharp pain sent a streak of erotic pleasure through her, and her vagina tightened around his fingers. He moved his knees apart, spreading her farther open to his touch. She shivered.

Hot. Wanting. *Vulnerable.*

His thumb traced circles around her clit, and she clenched her hands as her body started to burn. He rolled a nipple between his fingers, this time the pinch just short of pain, and fire singed downward to meet the increasing need surging upward.

Her hips tilted, trying to increase the pressure on her clit. He chuckled and removed his hand, leaving her lower half throbbing. "Stand up."

"But—"

"Mella." He waited.

She struggled to her feet, closing her thighs over her wet, swollen private area. He pulled her to stand directly in front of him.

"Remove your gown."

After the gown dropped to the floor, she stood naked, raising her hands to cover her breasts and mound. She'd been unclothed with him before. Just…not standing in front of him like this. She realized that the light was more than sufficient to display her size and shape. "*Short and fat.*" That's what his mother had said. Maybe she should cover her stomach instead of her breasts. Or her hips… She averted her gaze as a wave of humiliation ran through her.

"Lower your hands. I like to look at you, laria." The chair squeaked. "Keep your eyes on mine."

She turned back, meeting his dark gaze, and a frown appeared on his forehead. "More than modesty," he muttered. "Come here." He pulled her so she stood between his open legs. "Why do you not like being in front of me? And don't tell me it's wrong, little Earther. What else?"

Her cheeks heated. "I—You are all so tall. So thin and hard—even your women. Why—I don't see why you bought me. I'm fat. Ugly.

Can't you understand that?" she finally snapped out and tried to retreat.

His legs closed, trapping her between his thighs. His lips curved into a faint smile. "Laria, if you were any more beautiful, men would fall down, frothing at the mouth. Perhaps Earther standards are different. Then again, each man has his own ideal of beauty. You happen to be mine." He ran his hands up the backs of her thighs and squeezed gently. "I am hard, you're right, so why would I want a wiry woman in my bed?"

His hands moved to rest on her wide hips, and he dug his fingers in. "This is the perfect cradle for me. And you are so little that I can hold you easily and move you as I will."

She flushed, remembering how he'd done just that last time.

He leaned forward to nip at her rounded stomach. "Softness and curves everywhere I touch." He licked over a nipple, making her jerk. "And these…" His eyes were half-lidded as his hands curved under her breasts. "I don't believe I could ever tire of touching these. You please me very much, little thief, and I have trouble keeping my hands off you. During the day, I think about everything I want to touch and kiss at night." His lips quirked. "And the enclave's business suffers because I find you so lovely."

Dain never tried to disguise his words in easy lies; the man took directness to new levels. And he thought she was lovely. A glow started in her stomach, and for a moment she could see herself as he did, lush and soft. Her spine straightened, pushing her breasts even farther into his hands.

His grin flashed. "Now I want you on your back on the bed."

When she hesitated, he slapped her bottom lightly, and the sting combined with the lingering soreness shot through her and straight to her clit.

His eyes crinkled, and he gently pinched her nipples, which had suddenly peaked. "Get on the bed before you persuade me that you'd enjoy another spanking."

Oh Prophet. She almost tripped in her rush to back away, yet she'd become even wetter between the legs. That spanking had hurt. Why hadn't his slap on her bottom this time hurt as much? She sat on the bed, frowning.

"Mella." He silently gestured for her to lie back. Another flush heated her face as she complied. As he stood looking down at her. This just felt so different from before, so—

"Lift your knees."

"W-what?" She stared up at him. Her legs dangled off the foot of the bed, and he'd moved to stand between them.

He set something down on the bed, then grasped and bent her legs until her knees rested on her chest. The pose tilted her hips and left her exposed. He clasped her arms around her knees, then gave her a stern look. "You stay in this position, little Earther, or I will tie you here."

"But—"

"You do not have permission to speak."

She swallowed once, then again when he pulled his chair forward and sat right...right where he could see everything in the candlelight. She started to bring her legs down and received a sharp slap on her exposed thigh. Gritting her teeth, she laced her hands over her bent knees.

He touched her.

Just the slow glide of his finger over her burning folds sent heat through her. Her body quivered uncontrollably.

"You're very wet, Iaria," he murmured. "I think you must like this game." His finger slid up beside her clit, moving and teasing.

Chapter Eleven

WITH A SLICK fingertip, Dain teased the tiny hood covering her somaline until the nub pushed out. Glistening and engorged and delightfully pink. Her breathing turned ragged, and he could see her fingers digging into her knees. Curving his hands under her round ass, he secured her, then used his thumbs to open her farther. The gasp of worry and anticipation she gave pleased him.

Bending forward, he licked through her folds, stroking his tongue on the sides of her somaline in long, heavy laps until her muscles tightened under his hands. And he backed off.

"Do not come yet, Earther," he murmured, lifting his head to watch the color rise in her cheeks as she bit back her protest.

As her tension relaxed, he slid a finger into her. Her cry of surprise hardened him further, if possible, considering his shultor already ached from being erect so long.

Her sheath felt snug around his finger. Hot. Welcoming. He thrust in and out, then bent and duplicated the movements with his tongue. Never too close to her nub. Her hips tilted, trying to get more. He brought her to the edge again. He heard her panting, felt her vagina tighten around his finger.

And backed off.

She moaned, long and low, as her head thrashed back and forth on the mattress.

He slid a rubber cover over his finger and oiled it well. Her eyes were closed, so he bit the inside of her thigh and watched a tremor run through her body. Her eyes opened, slightly glazed with unsatisfied need. When he had her attention, he smiled. "Do not move your legs, little one. Do you understand?"

"Yes, sir," she whispered.

He lowered his head, using his tongue and the fingers of his left hand to bring her to delightful need. And then he brought forward the other hand.

DEAR PROPHET, SHE was so close. Her arms shook with the effort of holding her legs up. Her legs trembled uncontrollably as Dain licked her down there, each stroke showing he knew exactly how to tease her. And his finger acted like a man's shaft, pushing in and out of her until her whole pussy felt on fire, so tight... If he'd only touch her there. Just move his mouth up a little. She whimpered when he lifted his head, one finger still deep inside her.

"Don't move, Mella," he said again. Then she felt something push against the rim of her back hole. Her mouth dropped open in alarm. "No. You—"

"Silence, little thief." The finger in her vagina pressed deeper, and he slid a finger into her other hole. Her whole body tensed as more nerves sparked to life, as she felt horribly, intimately taken yet unbearably excited. He started to thrust his fingers in and out, a compelling rhythm that pulled her higher and higher until each stroke left her quivering on the precipice, excruciatingly poised—

Sweat broke out on her skin as he kept her there. Whimpering. She couldn't...couldn't—

His tongue stroked over her clit, hot and hard, and his fingers hammered into her. The candlelit room turned a brilliant white as pleasure exploded inside her. The searing ecstasy shattered her control, sending heat outward until her fingertips throbbed.

Her body quivered with aftershocks, over and over. Finally his fingers stopped moving.

"Very nice," he murmured, withdrawing his fingers from her anus and vagina, leaving emptiness behind. "You almost made it all the way through."

What? And she realized her legs lay sprawled open, no longer held against her chest. When had she let go?

He stripped something off one finger, then removed his clothes and lay beside her, one hand idly stroking her breasts. His lips were firm as he took her mouth, plunging inside as thoroughly as he'd taken her below.

She could taste herself on him. "How can you do those things?" she asked when he pulled back.

"Do what?" He plucked at her nipple, sending little erratic jolts of arousal through her, like the sputtering of a damp candle.

"Use your mouth. There. Doesn't it—"

"You taste like an aroused woman, Iaria, and nothing in the world is as delightful." He licked his lips, and a grin flashed over his dark face. "Using my mouth and hands means I can concentrate on your pleasure. To bring a woman to fulfillment is satisfying." His steel gray eyes were knowing as he added slowly, "I also enjoy making a woman whimper, quiver, and not come until I permit."

He must have seen her eyes widen, for a crease appeared in his cheek. "And you enjoy being that woman, Iaria."

"Oh."

"I've neglected your education, if you have to ask a question about taste." He rolled onto his back and patted the mattress beside him. "Kneel here."

Giving him a quizzical look, she complied.

He took one of her hands and placed it on his hard shaft. "Use your hands on me, Iaria, and then put those soft lips around me."

Her mouth dropped open.

He chuckled, tracing her lips with one finger. "Yes, exactly there."

She couldn't move, could only stare at him. After a minute, he released her fingers to put his hand behind his head and waited, studying her with a smile. He looked as if he'd wait all night for her to begin. Her gaze swept over his body. So...so male. Hard muscles covered his broad chest, and his biceps bulged where his arm flexed under his head. His abdomen was flat, with horizontal, muscular ridges. Her gaze skirted the next part to run down his thighs, which were dusted with black hair. Even his feet looked strong.

She glanced at Dain. Amusement danced in his eyes, but he didn't move. All right, then. She looked at her hand lying on his shaft and pressing it against his stomach. It was so big; she still couldn't believe that it fit inside her. And so hard, only... The skin covering it felt softer than her own. The head bulged out like a mushroom cap, but slightly darker and smoother than the rest of his shaft. Like velvet. She ran her fingertip around the head, and his shaft twitched. She snatched her hand back. "I'm sorry," she whispered. Had she hurt him?

His deep, infectious laugh pulled a smile from her. "Little thief, when I lick over your somaline, do you jump because I hurt you?"

The heat in her cheeks told her she was blushing. Again. But relief outweighed her embarrassment. She hadn't caused him pain. In fact, he had basically said he liked that.

As if he'd read her mind, he added, "I like your hands on me. Do to me whatever you enjoy having me do to you, laria."

She bit her lip. Wasn't it strange how touching him made her center all melty? Curving her hand around his thickness, she stroked up and down and felt him tighten. Increasingly interested, she played with him, tracing the curling veins, discovering the heavy balls buried in thick hair. Soft and crinkly. But she returned to the shaft. He'd licked her...

Bending, she ran her tongue up it and heard him take a quick breath. A hint of a salty taste. His masculine scent was stronger, but almost heady, like when the orchestra starts to build and the parts come together. Curling her hand around him, she swirled her tongue on the tip and then took him into her mouth.

He groaned, and not from pain. She hesitated. He was too big to lick like he had done to her. How did—

His hand tangled in her hair, tugging her head down until his shaft went deeper in her mouth, then back up.

Ah. She widened her knees for balance, gripped him more firmly at the base, and slid the top in and out of her mouth. She found that using her tongue made him fist his hand in her hair. Moving her hands up and down in the same way as her mouth made the muscles of his stomach tighten. Sucking netted her another groan.

And made her wetter. Why did doing this for him excite her?

He'd said licking her did the same to him.

She could feel him getting harder. He pulled her away and flattened her on her back beneath him. Her head spun.

He kissed her, long and hard and deep, before murmuring, "I haven't had my control tested like that in years, little Earther."

After nudging her legs open, he knelt between them. Then, his grip ruthlessly strong, he set her feet on his shoulders, making her hips tilt up and exposing her below. "Stay right there," he ordered.

Her heart seemed to stutter at the dark look he gave her, and then he pressed himself against her and slid in, so hard and fast, she cried out. He went so deep, much deeper in this position, and she couldn't find her breath. Yet the feeling of him inside her, taking her over, filling her impossibly full sent a shudder of need through her. Her insides burned for more.

His hard mouth curved into a dark smile. "Look at me, Iaria." He held her gaze as he moved within her, in, out, plunging harder and deeper as her body relaxed to his invasion. Then, he hammered into her, and the driving need lifted her hips to match his thrusts. She began to tighten inside and tried to arch her back. *More, more.*

Resting his weight on one arm, he set his other hand on her breast. His fingers circled her nipple once and then squeezed the peak.

The tiny pain was like the falling leaf that sets off an avalanche. "Oh, oh, ohhh." Not an explosion, but a wave of exquisite sensation starting from where they joined, and it didn't stop. The incredible pleasure rippled outward, expanding until even her fingers tingled.

She barely saw his grin before his face went taut, the cords in his neck standing out. His short, hard strokes made her shudder, and then he groaned, and his shaft jerked inside her, making her vagina spasm again.

With a sigh, he dropped onto the bed beside her, and for one second she felt abandoned and lonely. Unwanted.

He pulled her up against his side and pushed her head into the hollow of his shoulder. He curved an arm around her back to stroke her, and contentment blew through her like a warm wind.

"You know, Mella, I thought you said you had been married."

Her fingers ruffled the crisp hairs on his chest. His nipples were flat, almost hidden. "Um. What?"

"Married?"

She stiffened. "I was." But I'm not now. *The judge said so; I say so.* She didn't want to think about Nathan, not now.

"Do Earth men not have the same equipment as Nexans: a shultor and globes?"

"Of course they do." Lethargy dragged at her limbs, and her brain felt like an underpowered ship trying to escape gravity. "What kind of question is that?"

"Obviously you've never touched a man before—or even seen a man's shultor. How can that happen?"

Her finger circled one flat nipple. Such soft satin skin on this hard man. How strange.

He squeezed her shoulder. "Mella, answer me."

"On Earth, we don't believe in—You're not supposed to look at…or touch…things…when you couple. It's a sin." She made a noise of complaint when he rolled her over and stared down at her.

"You did not caress your husband, and he did not fondle you." The disbelief in his voice gave way to disgust. "What kind of a culture…? Shulin is a gift from the gods to humans. Given to us for joy."

And that was exactly what he'd given her, she realized. The tiny pain of a pinch and even her embarrassment had only led to increased arousal and deeper ecstasy. She reached up to brush her fingers over his solid jaw and high cheekbones. His firm lips had the same satin texture as the nipple she'd just stroked.

To touch another truly is a kind of joy.

His lips curved. How could gray eyes appear so warm? "You've never touched me on your own before, laria." He pressed a kiss into her palm as she moved her fingers over his face. "Perhaps we should let you explore further."

UNABLE TO FACE Dain the next morning, Mella sneaked out to the sun garden at dawn. Pulling her robe close against the chill air, she settled onto a stone bench. The purple grasses wet her toes with cool dew. Fiery red birds darted between the two tall fountains, snatching small insects out of the air. Considering the exhaustion weighing down her limbs, the birds' enthusiasm seemed excessive.

Thinking of enthusiasm led her back to why she'd come out here. Somehow she needed to understand her behavior. Last night had been… She'd never felt like that with Nathan. Not only reaching climax after climax, but being so aroused, so willing to do anything. What she'd let him do… A rush of heat ran through her like fire.

He had ordered her, told her exactly what to do. She'd not only followed his commands, but his control of her had excited her. Just the memory of his hard hands holding her immobile made her dampen. On Earth, she'd stayed as independent as society allowed, running her home, her career, and caring for Nathan and her family. But she sure hadn't acted independent last night. Had being a slave done this to her?

"What has you concerned, Mella?"

Mella jumped and turned.

Dain walked down the path toward her. He wore loose black pants and an embroidered white tunic that displayed his bronzed muscular arms. His scent wrapped around her, strongly masculine with a slight forest tang, and she realized her skin still bore traces of it, as if he'd marked her with himself.

Watching her face, he straddled the bench, facing her. In the morning light, his eyes were a smoky gray. "Mella?"

"I'm not concer—" When his black brows drew together, her lie stuck in her throat. Pulling her gaze from him, she stared down at the funny-colored grass, so soft under her bare feet. "Last night," she managed finally.

"Ah."

She looked and saw amusement in his eyes as he said, "You wonder about your response to me—no, not to me exactly, but to my control over you."

Her cheeks heated.

He smiled slowly. Still straddling the bench, he slid her closer, until her legs bumped against his. Until her hip nestled against his groin and she could feel his hard shaft. He pulled her to his chest, his warmth comforting in the chill of the morning—comforting, until he slid his left hand inside her robe and captured a breast.

"Hey." When she struggled and tried to push his hand away, he tightened his arm, keeping her immobile, and her efforts failed dismally.

To her horror, her nipple bunched to a peak under his touch, and she grew wetter. Why was this happening to her?

"You prudish Earthers have so many limits and rules." His thumb circled her nipple, and the slight roughness of his skin against her sensitive tissue was incredibly exciting. "Until last night, I had no idea how limited your experience was."

She could feel her heart rate increasing as he fondled her breast.

"Shulin—sex—can have more variations than birds in the sky." He glanced at the nearest tree, where a flock of multicolored avians bickered over nesting grounds. "A man and woman sharing equally is only one option."

He held her immobile as he nuzzled just below her jaw. "Other choices can include various positions as well as participants of either sex. And there are differences in the power each brings to the relationship." He bit the muscle in the curve of her neck, and heat shot straight through her body.

"Dain—"

"Don't move. Don't speak," he growled, and she froze without thinking. "I am a male of the Zarain kinline, which means in my relationships, Mella, I dominate, and my partner submits—to anything I ask of her. I find the sight of a woman surrendering—everything—incredibly arousing."

She swallowed. His words alone made hunger roll through her, and the heat of his hand on her breast grew unbearably exciting.

When he rolled her nipple between his fingers, she couldn't contain the moan. His lips curved. "To be fully aroused, you, little thief, have a need to submit. A need to give up control."

The thought appalled her, releasing her from the spell. She shook her head, starting to—

"Don't move," he snapped, and her body stilled. "On Nexus, we accept that mutual pleasure comes in various ways."

"I don't like being controlled," she said, trying to ignore her body's response.

He chuckled and tipped her backward. As she grabbed his shoulders, she felt his hand between her legs, sliding in the telltale wetness there. To her shock, he pushed one finger deep inside her, and she inhaled sharply at the overwhelming sensation. Keeping her trapped and helpless, he tapped his thumb against her clit, raised an eyebrow at her betraying quiver, and gave her a level look. "Now tell me that being controlled is not exciting to you."

"It…it—"

"Do not lie to me, Iaria. Not unless you need another lesson over my knees."

The memory of his hand slapping her bare bottom made her vagina clench around him. "It's exciting," she whispered. It was the truth; she couldn't hide from it.

His cheek creased as he smiled. "Yes, I dominate, and you submit because that is what inflames you. We suit rather well, don't you think?" His eyes crinkled as he slowly removed his hand and held up his fingers, which glistened with her arousal in the early-morning light.

Chapter Twelve

AS SHE WALKED out of the kitchen two days later, Mella heard Cannalaina arguing with someone in the family room. The child sounded close to tears. "I can't play it. I'm too dumb, and my fingers don't move right." The unhappy *twang* of a plucked harp string echoed in the hallway.

Mella's feet took her in that direction before she realized she'd moved. The clan's family room was huge. Soft carpets covered the floor, and rich tapestries of historical events hung on the golden walls. A stone fireplace with glowing coals dispelled the morning chill. Each corner held a group of overstuffed chairs, couches, and floor cushions: one area for talking, one for watching vid, and one with a table for card playing. Another table boasted a massive puzzle. The wall farthest from the heat was the music space, where Cannalaina and her mother glared at each other.

"Everyone in our kinline masters a musical instrument, Canna. And you chose this one." Felaina's voice had the level tones of someone trying not to yell.

"Nobody can play this stupid thing." Cannalaina scowled, looking like she wanted to kick the freestanding harp. "Not even you."

Mella smothered a smile as she crossed the room. In their occasional meetings, Dain's sister had always acted friendly. Maybe Mella could return the favor. "I can play it."

Canna's mouth dropped open, and then her little brows drew together in suspicion. "Can you really?"

"Really." After seating herself in front of the harp, Mella plucked the strings. The resonant sound ran through her in a joyful hum. "This is one of the pieces I learned when I was your age." And she played Beethoven's lovely *Moonlight Sonata*. Out here on this frontier planet, after their long isolation, would the Earth classics have survived?

Her thoughts slowly disappeared as the music pulled her into its embrace, which was both comforting and exhilarating.

Canna edged a few inches closer, her gaze fixed on Mella's fingers as the piece reached its perfect conclusion.

"This is one I …learned…as an adult." With a soft breath, Mella threw herself into the song, losing herself in the joy of the music she'd composed during a week she and her family spent at a storm-torn Pacific beach. Now the intricate harmonies splashed like breakers into her soul, washing away the traces of grief. As the song came to an end, she lingered on the last few notes before settling her hands in her her lap. Her fingertips burned, and she frowned at the reddened skin. "I haven't played in a very long time."

"That was 'Poseidon's Rapture.'" Felaina rested a hand on Mella's shoulder. "I fell in love with the music the first time I heard it, and it's one of the few songs from off-planet that Grandsir allows. The song is one of Archer's best, I thought, and yet you play it even better than she did."

"Added depth, maybe?" Dain stepped into the family room. "I daresay Mella has experienced more sorrow than some rich and famous vocalist."

The music still sang in Mella's body, ever joyful. And yet Dain's observation contained truth; her grief had added something, let her find the deeper elements in the song.

He lifted her hand and kissed her fingers. "Thank you, laria."

She smiled at him, unable to say how much his open pleasure in her playing meant to her. So she turned to Canna instead.

The lure of the harp had drawn the child forward until she leaned against Mella's knees. "Can I can learn to play like that?" she whispered, eyes shining.

Mella could almost see melody of the girl's spirit, and she touched the child's cheek. "Yes. If you want it badly enough, you can."

"Will you show me?"

"I will."

THAT EVENING, DAIN found Mella in the blue garden making notes on a piece of paper. Engrossed, she didn't hear him approach, and he paused a moment to enjoy the sight of her. The dark red color of her loose hair rivaled the sunset behind her. Her white teeth bit into her pink bottom lip as she scribbled on the paper. She hummed a few notes, then wrote again. He stepped closer to see the paper.

Music. She was composing music.

He shook his head. He didn't know her last name, her clan, how she had gotten stranded on his planet, or apparently very much of what she liked at all. He'd had women over the years, but none as reticent as this one. "I haven't known many Earthers," he said.

She startled, dropping her pencil and paper.

Bending, Dain ran a finger down her cheek. Softer than silk. "Do they all keep secrets as thoroughly as you do?"

She looked at him blankly, obviously still absorbed in the music she'd been writing. Then her big green eyes focused. "Well. Probably some do and some don't."

"I see." He'd made a good start at learning the secrets of her body, but each day he discovered new facets to her personality. More mysteries in her past. Did she realize how intriguing riddles were to someone in law enforcement? Just to watch her mentally sidestep, he asked, "Did you leave anyone behind on Earth?"

A lie hovered in her mind, and then she paused and frowned. He could see her shift, the pain from her spanking recent enough to bring discretion. "Um. No one important to me is there now," she said carefully.

Clever little Earther. He chuckled, hauled her up, and took her mouth. He had only planned to taste, but her lips were soft, her mouth warm and welcoming, and the slight hitch in her breathing had him wanting to bend her over the bench and take more. Give more.

With a sigh, he stepped back, running his hands up and down her bare arms. "My grandfather, Clanae Solain, thinks we've hidden out long enough. We are to join the family for the lastmeal."

In a supremely feminine gesture, she touched her hair, then frowned at her simple house gown. "Now?"

"Yes, laria." He set her composition into her hand and gave her a push toward the arched opening in the hedge. "If you run, you can put your music away and find some shoes."

She looked down at her bare feet in horror, then darted away. Before she disappeared through the archway, he had time to note how enticingly her bottom bounced with her running. Already hard enough for discomfort, he growled and headed for the dining room. Duty called, although he'd far rather strip her bare and sink his teeth into a curvy buttock.

"GRANDSIR, THIS IS Mella from Earth. Mella, this is Solain, the clanae of Clan Zarain," Dain said.

Seated at the end of the crowded dining-room table, Solain rose to his feet.

Mella looked up at the older version of Dain. Solain had the same straight, broad shoulders and lean, hard face, although his eyes were black rather than dark, dark gray. The clanae's hair was mostly silver, the darkly tanned face deeply lined, but Mella could see that his grandson would only grow more attractive as he aged.

When she glanced at Dain, she saw the silver strands sprinkled through his hair, and a heavy feeling settled in her stomach. Someday, he would grow old. And no matter how well he aged, eventually he would die.

Why did the thought make her want to cry? Ignoring the way Dain's brows had drawn together and his hand had tightened on her arm, she returned her attention to the old warrior in front of her. Forcing her lips into a smile, she said, "I'm pleased to meet you, sir."

With a finger, the clanae turned her face from side to side. "Few Earthers come to Nexus. In the last few years, I've seen a dark-skinned, tall Earther female and a slender blonde with golden skin. And now you—a redhead with translucent skin and lovely curves. Is this diversity normal on your planet, or do only the odd ones leave?"

Had that old man just called her odd? Glaring, Mella pulled away from his touch and stepped back, not caring if he thought her rude. Lifting her chin, she let her voice take on an instructional tone, as if he were a grade-school boy. "Earth has the most diversity of the known worlds. Emigrants to the frontier planets were more homogenous since they tended to be from one country or even one clan. I can recommend a book for you to read, if you'd care to increase your knowledge."

"Feisty little slave." The clanae's grin looked so much like Dain's that it made her heart thump. He gave Dain an amused look. "A shame Earthers are so small, or we might consider breeding a few to add variety to the kinline." A ripple of laughter ran down the table.

"An interesting suggestion, Grandsir."

Mella turned her glare toward Dain and saw his lips quirk. After bowing to his grandfather, he pulled out a chair for her, then sat beside her on the clanae's right. Across from them, Dain's mother sat to Solain's left, followed by Felaina, her spouse who had just returned from the militia, and her children. A variety of kinlines oathbound to the Zarain clan filled the rest of the long table, and she noticed the higher proportion of males to females held true here also.

After glancing around, she dropped her gaze and flinched at her impossible-to-overlook indenture bracelets. Dain's family must look at her and see a criminal bought for sex. Biting her lip, she tried to tell herself this was just another formal dinner in a long line of formal dinners. *Really*. Her parents had loved to entertain. And Nathan—his ambitions had dictated they attend any event to advance his position.

She frowned, remembering him strutting through a room full of guests, his bearing pompous. An elder in the church, he wielded an exorbitant amount of power, and he enjoyed using it. He'd hated when he couldn't boast about being Armelina Archer's husband. That was the only thing she'd ever denied him, her anonymity more important than his pleasure. She had never performed in public. Ever. So no one had discovered that Nathan's wife, Mella, was the famous singer Armelina Archer. Not until now.

She bit her lip, feeling it quiver. *Nathan never wanted me, did he? Not even in the beginning.*

A warm hand curled around hers. Dain kissed her chilled fingers. "You look very unhappy, little one." He tilted his head, silently requesting an answer.

She shook her head and tried to ignore the disappointment in his eyes.

Then his lips curved. "My life has lacked challenge recently. Perhaps it's time to work on your secrets. You're trapped here long enough for me to discover everything about you." He nipped her thumb sharply and made her jump.

Unease shivered through her at his threat, and she looked away, only to see the people down the table watching them. *Dear heavens*. She frowned at him. "Behave," she whispered.

"Make me, laria." With his other hand, he tangled his fingers in her hair and pulled enough to tilt her head back. "Or should I make you behave instead?" he murmured. He tightened his hand in her hair, forcing her to meet his penetrating gaze. Slowly, the table of noisy people disappeared, until there was only Dain and the rapid thudding of her heart in her ears.

"Dain, stop that." His mother's sharp voice breached the fog.

Releasing Mella, he turned to speak with his mother. Mella sagged back in her chair, experiencing the same feeling as when he released her restraints in bed—relief and a strange sense of loss.

Pull yourself together. Giving herself a mental shake, she straightened and caught the scent of grilled meat. Somehow in the last minute, a servant had placed a filled plate in front of her. She started to pick up her fork and realized Dain still held her hand as he talked with his mother. With a scowl, she tugged, only to have his grip tighten.

She huffed in exasperation, then saw his grandfather's frown. The old man's gaze went from their joined hands to his grandson's face to hers. She felt herself flush and pulled harder on her hand.

Dain glanced down at her, and his eyes crinkled. "Sorry, laria. I enjoy touching you."

He'd said the same thing the night before, even as he'd held her thighs apart and... She swallowed hard.

His eyebrow went up, and then his fingers slid down to her wrist, resting on her fast pulse. His gaze intensified, as he took in her heated cheeks. When his eyes focused lower, she realized her breasts felt tight and swollen.

"Well." Lifting her hand to his lips, he murmured, for her ears only, "Perhaps we should take a nap after lastmeal."

Releasing her, he returned to his conversation with his mother and Felaina. Mella clasped her hands and fumed. Her whole body felt hot. Needy. And yet he hadn't done anything except pull on her hair and hold her hand.

He laughed at something Felaina said, the sound so deep and resonant, it sent chills through her. No musical instrument could achieve the controlled power of his voice. She gazed at his strong profile, his square jaw, and firm lips. His lips had touched—She jerked her eyes away. *Prophet have mercy.* What was wrong with her? She needed to remember that he owned her. She was his toy—his sex slave, nothing more. When her indenture period ended, he'd hardly notice her absence. He might even buy a new unshuline in the market to take her place.

The thought of him with another woman jabbed her in the chest, so hard it took her breath.

As she stared down at her hands in her lap, she concentrated on settling herself using the techniques she'd mastered as a child for performance anxiety. Her breathing slowed; her mind cleared. After a minute, she picked up her fork and looked around.

Her eyes met the clanae's. He was watching her, his face as unreadable as Dain's.

Chapter Thirteen

TWO DAYS LATER, tired of her dismal thoughts, Mella left her rooms and headed down the hallway. *Blast that man.*

Last night and again that evening, Dain had gone into Port City, leaving her at home. In fact, he hadn't asked her to accompany him once since her attempted escape. The relief of being safe and hidden in the enclave mingled with an unsettling jealousy.

Was he dancing and flirting with city women like the one who'd thrown herself at him outside the party? Or like that Triscana, who had lowered her eyes until Dain made her look at him. Mella recognized the woman's behavior now. Triscana was submissive, and Dain had coupled with her. And enjoyed it.

The thought hurt.

Dumb, dumb, dumb. She'd coupled with a man and, in spite of knowing better, had let her emotions get tangled. Dain certainly didn't feel any involvement. She was his unshuline and nothing more. In twenty-some days, she wouldn't even be that.

Yet the thought of losing him—not seeing the molten silver of desire in his eyes, feeling his hard hands on her body, or hearing the laughter in his deep voice—made her chest feel hollow, as if it would echo with emptiness when she left.

But she would leave; she must leave. Every morning, she watched the news in the kitchen. The investigation of her death had stalled, in spite of the public's outcry against the stalker. Mella laughed cynically.

Considering the bombers were the same men investigating the crime, the so-called stalker would never get caught. Very clever of Nathan.

If only they would simply close the case. Then Nathan would leave. And Mella might talk Dain into taking her to Port City again.

She shook her head. *Pitiful.* She was acting more like a wife than a slave he'd bought. With a sigh, she walked into the family room and paused for a moment. Rebli and Canna sat on each side of Felaina as she read them a story. A wistful ache settled in Mella's chest. She'd never been around young children and never had a baby. Nathan had said she must be infertile. She had missed more than she'd known.

"Mella!" Rebli ran across the room, her shoulder-length braids bouncing madly. "Are you going to play for us like yesterday? Can I help?" As Mella knelt, the little girl jumped straight into her arms, hugging her neck, and it felt as if she trailed happiness in her wake.

Were all Nexan children so exuberant? On Earth, the shepherds would consider Rebli far too loud. Too forward. The young were to remain silent and in the nursery. Mella frowned, remembering when she'd been a child and darted out of their apartment, screaming in joy because her daddy had returned from a trip. He'd laughed and tossed her into the air.

The dour shepherd next door had reported them. After that, Mella had attended the sector nursery like other children rather than staying home with Mama. Her parents had become quieter, and happiness more elusive.

All for laughing too loud. *Earth was wrong. The Divine Prophet was wrong.*

Mella hugged Rebli hard and received a delightful stream of giggles and a kiss. When Mella rose, Rebli grabbed her hand and dragged her to the *pianete*, close kin to an Earth piano. "This one, Mella. I want to play this one with you."

"Well…" Mella glanced around.

On a couch by the music area, Canna snuggled against Felaina, both of them smiling. "Reblaini, Mella may not want to play right now," Felaina said.

Biting her lip, Rebli looked up pleadingly, her dark eyes like Dain's in miniature.

This is how his daughters would look, Mella knew. And his son would look like Wardain with mischief dancing in his eyes. Raised here in the clanhome, this is how they would be—cheerful and cherished. Her heart tugged, as she wished for impossible things. "Of course we can play together." She pulled the child down beside her on the bench and placed her tiny fingers on the keyboard. "This is a C chord. When I nod my head, you do your chord."

The simple tunes Mella played were made splendid by the joy in the child's face.

Canna demanded a turn on the pianete and then had her harp lesson. After that, Felaina requested quiet music so the children might unwind before bedtime. Mella ignored Rebli's begging her to sing and played lullabies on the harp. No more singing, although it became harder and harder to suppress the melodies bubbling up inside her. Mama had always said that she'd sung before she learned to speak.

A short time later, the children hugged Mella, and Felaina herded them off to bed. Now the room seemed too silent. Pushing away from the harp, Mella stretched and rose to her feet. And froze.

Both Dain and the clanae sat at a card table across the room, watching her. When had they come in? Dain wore dark formalwear with silver embroidery flashing on the neckline and sleeves. His expression unreadable, he leaned back in his chair, his long legs extended before him.

The clanae frowned at her.

An uneasy feeling slid into Mella's stomach. Had she done something wrong? Perhaps unshulines were not to associate with the precious children of the clan. Maybe Felaina didn't realize that. After all, Dain said he hadn't bought a sex slave before. The thought of losing the children's company filled her with unhappiness. How had they become so important to her so quickly?

As she approached the two men, Dain's brows drew together. "When you looked at us, the happiness left you. Tell me why, laria."

She glanced at the clanae, but his expression didn't change. "I... Um, are there rules about un"—the word was hard to say, harder to apply to herself—"unshulines being around children? Am I supposed to stay away from them?"

"Ah." Smiling, Dain took her hand and pulled her into his lap so easily, she had no time to resist.

"Dain, stop," she hissed. Horrified, she glanced at the stern old grandfather. His hand was in front of his mouth, rubbing his lips.

Dain ignored her, settling her in his arms to his satisfaction. "To answer your question, there are no rules about you associating with the children. In fact, Felaina is delighted you've taken an interest in them. Music isn't one of the talents bred into the Zarain line."

Bred? The clanae and Blackwell had used that word also. Surely she misunderstood. "You...breed...for certain things?"

The clanae leaned forward, resting his forearms on the table. "The Zarain kinline breeds for leaders and warriors. For courage, strength, intelligence, and the ability to command. We select our mates according to those criteria. Only under moonless nights during Starlight Rites are our requirements relaxed."

Well, she fell short in every category. Good thing she had no interest in staying on this planet. *At all. Really.* Her stomach felt funny, though, like the old man had hit her with his fist rather than his cold words.

Dain made a growling noise. "Grandsir, that's enough."

The old man raised an eyebrow but sat back in his chair. "We plan to play cards, Earther. It's a shame you don't know how."

"Oh, but I do," she said coolly, bursting his bubble with pleasure. Not that his assumption about Earth wasn't correct. Card games were forbidden. However, Cap and his crew had played constantly and insisted on her joining them, especially for... "Do you know how to play poker?"

They didn't.

She soon had a nice pile of royals in front of her. Cap had coached her on hiding her "tells," and apparently whatever devious method

Dain used for catching her lies didn't work with bluffing. At least, not at first.

But with this hand, she raised and saw skepticism in his eyes. *Better quit while I'm ahead.*

"Well, gentlemen, it's been fun." With a smile, she repaid Dain's loan and tucked her winnings into her dress pockets. The heavy royals clinked as she moved, a sweetly satisfying sound. She'd won half the price of a ticket to Earth in just one night. Rather than thieving, she should have set up a gambling table in the plaza.

Rising, Dain grinned and ran his hand down her arm. "*Little thief* is a good name for you. I haven't lost like that since my first year in the militia. How about you, Grandsir?"

The old man's black eyebrows drew together as he looked her up and down. "You're smarter than you look, Earther."

THE HIGH-PITCHED SCREAMS had turned to grunts of agony by the time Armelina reached the stage. Her hands slid in the blood on the floor as she crawled to her friend and froze in horror. Slashes everywhere, blood streaming from them all.

"Wake up now, Mella." The authority in the deep voice pulled her out of her dream and into reality. Iron-hard arms cradled her against a broad chest, and she breathed in the scent of safety.

"Dain?"

"Be at ease, laria. I'm here; you're safe." He rolled far enough to turn on the bedside light, then sat up against the headboard with her in his lap. "A nightmare, little one?" He pushed sweat-dampened hair from her face.

She trembled, still caught in the aftermath. "Yes."

"Tell me about it, so it will go away."

Her cheek against his chest, she shook her head no.

"I have them too, you know," he murmured, stroking her hair.

"You?" He seemed so powerful, like nothing would ever bother him.

He huffed a laugh. "I'm only human, and I've lived with violence all my life."

He said he'd been in the militia. "It bothers you?"

"I wake up and think I'm covered in blood," he said. "Hearing screams. Seeing people die. Killing."

She wrapped her arms around him and hugged him hard.

"I haven't had one since you came to share my bed, little thief." He pressed a kiss to her hair. "You lighten my world."

"I'm glad," she whispered.

"Now tell me about your dream."

She hesitated, and her resistance broke under the weight of his concern. "I was twelve, and I'd stayed late at school to finish an assignment. I heard screams coming from the auditorium on the third floor." She swallowed. Running down the hallway at the School of Music, hearing the teachers stampeding up from the first floor, where they'd gathered for a meeting. She had hit the double doors so hard, they slammed against the walls as she burst into the auditorium. "My friend—I saw her lying on the stage. Bleeding."

She'd dropped down beside Cecily, seeing nothing but her. The blood flowing from…everywhere.

A scraping noise and she'd looked up. Redness glinted on the knife as the gaunt man stepped out from behind the stage curtains. His voice whined eerily like an overburdened engine. "*You all sing bad songs. Wrong. The Prophet doesn't want you to sing.*" His eyes insane, his face distorted. She had scrambled back and slipped in the blood pooled on the floor.

"He tried to get me, but a teacher tackled him."

Sticky, warm blood all over her—Cecily's blood. The teachers had surrounded Cecily, but Mella had frantically pushed between them. Her face had been the one Cecily focused on as she shuddered, as her feet drummed staccato on the wooden stage. And although her eyes remained open, she was gone.

There is no music in death, and no angels sing.

A growl rumbled through Dain's chest. "They should have protected you better."

Cecily had been famous, a child prodigy with a high, clear voice. Fame attracted the insane. The violent... "No one can keep everyone safe all the time." And Mella had decided then and there that she would never, ever perform in public. No one would know her face. No violence would find her.

Her breath stuck in between a bitter laugh and a sob.

"They should have tried harder." Dain's arms tightened. "Rest assured, laria, while you are here, in my care, I will keep you safe."

With the deep certainty in his voice, the slow *thud* of his heartbeat under her ear, and his hard arms holding her against him, she drifted off to dream of gardens and tinkling fountains and music spilling through the air.

As Dain drove the carriage into the enclave, the fragrance of blooming ronves drifted through the cool evening air. With a sigh of relief, he handed the reins over to the stableman and eased out. Carefully. His knee burned like someone had poured hot pepper sauce into the joint. Perhaps visiting the farm enclave hadn't been the wisest decision, but with the council in session, Grandsir didn't have time to check on the proposed changes to the planting schedule. Unfortunately, Dain hadn't realized he'd need to visit each field on foot.

Limping, he went in the back door, wanting only a hot shower and a comfortable chair. And a sweet little Earther to hold. He wanted to tell her about his day and hear about her adventures in gardening and cooking. To enjoy her comparisons of Nexan and Earther culture and creatures. To listen to her soft laughter, which soothed something deep inside him. He increased his pace.

As he walked past the family room, he heard her voice and turned in.

The children and Mella were listening to Felaina read a story. Dain smiled at how comfortable the little Earther looked in the middle of his family. Rebli must have undone Mella's usual braid, for the child fingered the long strands, seeming fascinated by the different colors glinting in the firelight. Wardain sat at his mother's side, watching with a smile.

Canna spotted him first. "Unka Dain, you missed supper."

"Unka Dain! Did you buy me something?" Rebli asked. "Tomorrow is Artema's FirstDay."

"Was I supposed to buy you something?" Dain asked, smothering a laugh. "No one told me."

"Unka Dain, everyone gets presents the first day of festival. You know that." Rebli scowled at him, crossing her tiny arms.

Dain crouched in front of his niece and tugged on a black braid. "I do know, little one," he said. "And I do have gifts for you, Wardain, and Canna. But it is not polite to ask if someone bought you a present. Can you remember that next time?"

"Oh." Rebli leaned back, and Mella wrapped her arms around the child, unconsciously protective.

With a smile, Dain said, "And what about you, little Earther. Are you wondering if you will get a gift?"

Mella blinked and then shook her head. "You've already spent more than you should, considering I'll be gone soon. I don't need anything."

Rebli's mouth dropped open.

Wardain protested, "But, Mella..."

Canna gasped. "No present?" She tugged at her mother's sleeve. "She doesn't want a present, Mama."

Felaina tilted her head. "Well, that's different." She looked pleased, obviously remembering Dain's last few women and how they had maneuvered for gifts and attention.

Over the past few years, Dain had realized he was caught in the same quandary as many men in the Arewell and Zarain kinlines. In the early days of isolation, the two families had bred intensely for strength and leadership and had inadvertently introduced a trait for dominance. Like his cousins, Dain wanted—needed—a submissive woman in his bed. But, by Cernun's spear, he really disliked timid women. His kinline valued bravery.

On Nexus, only a weak woman would ever give up control. So he was caught in a dilemma. Where did one find someone who was submissive in bed and strong outside of it?

And what if one found such a person, and she turned out to be a liar and a thief?

Chapter Fourteen

MELLA SPENT THE next day running back and forth from the gardens to the house. As Quenoll cut flowers—mostly blue, with some white for variety—he handed them over, instructing her to fill the vases on the tiny altars scattered everywhere, inside and out.

"Why not yellow or red?" she asked him on her fifth trip.

He gave her an appalled look. "You can't use Cernun's or Mardun's colors during Artema's Days."

"Oh. Of course," Mella said politely, taking the basket of blooms. If Artema was the name of the god here, then who were Cernun and Mardo or Marda or whatever?

Later, she kneaded dough for a special herb bread while Ida concocted a delicacy called *festival cake* filled with fruit and nuts. Ida had another recipe for ThreeMoon cake with chocolate icing that she stated they'd prepare on LastDay. Apparently, there were five days to cook for.

"Five days of partying?" Mella asked. Worse than Christmas on Earth.

"Different kinds of parties on each day," Blani said. "FirstDay is a family day, and on LastDay, each clan hosts a Starlight Rite." She giggled and rolled her eyes at Ida. "This year I'm going with my cousins to the Pegoson Enclave in Port City. Mama wouldn't let me go last festival on Cernun's LastDay. She said I was too young for the things they do. Honestly, though, they're not nearly as wild as some, like the Arewells." She flushed. "Of course, the Pegosons are more...energetic than the Vulacans. Anyway, I'm looking forward to it."

Cernun's LastDay? "Isn't this called *Artema's* LastDay?" Mella asked.

"Yes, but there's four festivals in a year." Blani handed Mella a Nexan spice that smelled like cinnamon and oranges combined. "One for each season and god. The spring festival belongs to Artema, one of the twins."

"You have more than one god?" Mella asked carefully. Surely that was blasphemy.

"Actually there be five, but only four have festivals. Cernun, the father, be god of winter and law. Herina, the mother, goddess of summer and fertility." Ida scooped a spoon into the cake batter, tasted, then nodded approval. "Mardun be Artema's twin, god of harvest and war."

How did they keep them all straight? "What about the fifth one? Why doesn't he have a party?"

Ida laughed and patted Mella's shoulder. "There be no season for death. All souls pass through Ekatae's realm and walk her sands on the way to their own god."

Sands? "Why the detour? Why not just go directly to...whatever god?"

"Her desert scours your soul clean," Blani said, her voice muffled as she dug through the tater bin.

"Be a way to break ties to the mortal world," Ida added. "Loves and longings must cast off be before returning to the god."

"If you're bad, you walk the scorching sands for long and long, and you suffer until all your bad thoughts and memories are burned away." Blani's shudder wasn't assumed. The girl believed what she said.

Well, something new to think about. Every time she thought she understood these people, they twisted on her. Breeding? Several gods? Dear heavens. But it was an interesting idea: to walk through a desert until all sins seared away.

Ida glanced at the timepiece on the wall. "Finish there quickly, Blani. Leave soon, we must."

"Where are you going?"

"FirstDay is for close kin," Blani said, popping a red *cherly* fruit in her mouth. "We'll spend the rest of the day in the Hermest Kinhome in Port City."

"All the servants get today off to spend with their families, and tomorrow to be with their clan. Even the indentured slaves. So you can…" Blani stopped, her face puckered with distress. "But you don't have family or anyone—"

"I may not have family here," Mella said lightly, "but I have friends. That makes me happy." And it did, actually. After she'd married, she lost her childhood friends. Nathan's doing. He hadn't wanted her to have anyone of her own, she realized suddenly, and over the years, her friends had disappeared.

"Yes, friends you have, child." Ida kissed her forehead.

Blani sprang next, a whirling tornado, hugging Mella. "You can come with us to—"

"Be not a silly *podnat*," Ida said. "Himself won't leave her to loneliness. As unshuline, she be part of the Zarain kinline unless other family be there for her."

"Of course, you're right." Blani's troubled face cleared, and she beamed at Mella. "The kinae won't let you be lonely."

"Very true." The deep voice rumbled through the kitchen, shivering across Mella's skin like a bass drum.

Dain crossed the room, his bearing straight and his gait more even than she'd seen it in a while. He was using the cane less and less. "She will be welcomed in our kinline this FirstDay," he told Blani before kissing Mella's cheek. His masculine scent sent a thrill through her and weakened her legs. She clutched at his arm.

Firm hands around her waist steadied her, at least until he leaned forward and whispered, "I enjoy having you on your knees before me, little Earther, but this is not the place."

The memory of kneeling between his legs, holding his…his shaft in her hands and licking… The kitchen suddenly felt very warm. And the wicked expression in his eyes only made it worse. She glared at him. His growling laugh made her insides quiver.

He rubbed his knuckles gently across her cheek. "The family will gather for lastmeal early tonight, around five. We'll all help cook"—he grinned at Ida—"whatever is left to prepare, and then eat together in the shade garden."

The talk of relatives and festivities had made her feel very lonely, Mella realized. But Dain hadn't forgotten her. He'd come to find her, and she had someone with whom to share a holiday. Looking down, she blinked hard against the burning in her eyes. Who would have thought something like that could mean so much?

ON THE LAST day of festival, Dain came into Port City in response to a request. Two of his enforcers, Hanwell and Nilard, wanted him to check over their reports of Armelina Archer's death and determine if they could call the case closed. Since Dain hadn't officially returned to work, he had instructed them to meet him at a local restaurant for breakfast.

To Dain's disgust, the singer's husband had arrived with the enforcers. Nathan Hamilton had grown increasingly demanding. Since Earth couldn't process the woman's inheritance until Port City filed the final report, his impatience was understandable—and very annoying.

Even more annoying, some vid reporters had trailed the husband into the quiet restaurant. They'd eventually caused enough of a disturbance that the staff forced them to leave.

Peace. Finally.

Taking an occasional bite of his biscuits and baked greiet, Dain glanced through the investigators' reports while his men and Hamilton conversed quietly.

He flipped to the screen of data where the security vids displayed the alleged bomber. Medium height and weight, his face concealed by a hooded cape. Dain glanced over the bomb reports. The perpetrator had expertly placed the demolitions to destroy the ship and everything inside. The debris report showed nothing of concern. The... He frowned and scanned the list again. "Where is the biological report?"

"Hasn't come in yet," Hanwell said, tapping his thick fingers on the table. "The lab's backlogged. But there's probably no real need for—"

"No," Dain cut him off, not wanting to dress down his man in front of others. "I require every report before I sign off on this."

"Of course, sir." Hanwell's mouth thinned at the unspoken rebuke.

Dain leaned back in his chair as his instincts tickled up his spine like the feelers on a *sandroach*. Something was off. He glanced at the others.

Although Archer's husband appeared at ease, the muscles around his lips and eyes were tight, and he kept rubbing his fingers together. Definitely tense.

Dain glanced at his enforcers. "You've had no success in finding the bomber?"

Nilard, the more intellectual of the two partners, scowled. "We think he must have lifted off-planet in one of the holiday spaceliners."

Hanwell growled, "It's the only explanation. The cowardly *mounut* isn't here in Port City. We've checked everywhere."

Dain nodded and turned to Armelina Archer's husband, trying to get a good read on him. "Nathan Hamilton, do you have anything to add? The notes you brought from the stalker on Earth certainly point toward him being the murderer."

The man's face twisted in a grief-stricken pattern. "You've heard everything I know. If—"

Water suddenly flooded across the table, and everyone shoved back to avoid the deluge.

"By Ekatae's jackals," Hanwell cursed. "The glass slipped right out of my hand. I'm a clumsy regstal."

The accident had broken Dain's concentration. He wanted to leave anyway, before Nathan Hamilton started pushing. Again. As the waitress hurried over with cloths, Dain rose and told his men,

"Continue searching for the bomber. And have a copy of the biological report sent to my office when it comes in. At that point, I can close the case."

His men nodded their agreement. Dain tilted his head to Hamilton. "Good day, sir."

"LOOK, THERE'S HIMSELF." Hands occupied with peeling a tater, Ida jerked her chin toward the tiny vid in the corner of the kitchen.

Sitting beside Blanesta, Mella glanced over, and her heart jumped. Dain sat at a table in a restaurant. Wasn't that funny how he wasn't nearly as handsome as some men, but it didn't seem to matter? And even on the tiny viewer, he looked powerful.

She propped her chin in her hand. Part of it was his bearing: soldier straight, broad shoulders held back, every move controlled. And part of it was his face. His features were strong and hard. Even his lips were... She remembered how those firm lips felt against her skin, her breasts, her...

Her body awoke as if someone had snapped their fingers, humming with increased sensitivity. With need.

Honestly, how ridiculous. She picked the knife up and resumed chopping carrots. *Carrots.* All the frontier planets had unique fruits and vegetables, but all had remnants of Earth stock too. On cool, moist Maliden, they still had broccoli. Here on Nexus, potatoes and carrots survived. The carrots were slightly purple in color, but recognizable nonetheless.

"Aw, he looks heartbroken." Blanesta tore greens into small pieces, her gaze fixed on the display.

"Heartbroken?" *Dain heartbroken?* Mella frowned at the vid, and her breath clogged in her throat.

Nathan. The monster sat at Dain's table, laughing at something Dain had said. On each side of Dain were the two enforcers who had killed Cap and Johnnie and Pard—who had tried to kill her.

Oh Prophet.

"Mella! You're bleeding." Blanesta dropped the greens and jumped to her feet.

Mella looked down. She'd gashed her palm open with the knife. Blood splattered the table. She hadn't even felt it.

"Goodness, child." Ida bustled over and pressed a clean napkin to the cut. "Blanesta, fetch you the injury kit."

A few minutes later, with the slice across her hand glued shut and bandaged, Mella tried to choke down the tea Ida insisted on giving her. *What should I do?* She shivered, earning herself a worried look from Ida. "Mella, maybe—"

"I'm fine." Mella forced a smile. While Ida had tended her cut, the news had moved on to other matters. The latest in the Port City scandals, the increase in feral animals. "Why was Dain on television?" *Why was he with Nathan?*

"I bet he's investigating that poor singer's death." Blanesta bounced in her chair. "Sometimes he'll tell us about the stuff he's working on. Remember, Ida, when he directed the hunt for those terrorists?"

Coldness grew in Mella's stomach, chilling all the way up into her chest. "Directed the hunt? I thought he worked here, taking care of the estate business."

"Oh, he be here because the doctor won't let him return to work." Ida scooped the greens into the pot. "He be head of Planetary Security. That be why the enclave is well protected."

Blanesta smiled proudly. "He's in charge of every enforcer on Nexus. He knows everything."

Chapter Fifteen

S HE'D APPARENTLY TURNED so white that Ida had insisted she go
lie down. Mella hadn't resisted. Now she paced back and forth in
her room.

How could I be so blind? Again. She'd felt so safe with Dain, ignoring
the fact that he owned her, ignoring that he'd coupled with her. Or
maybe because of those things. He understood her better than anyone
had since her family had died. She'd started to trust him.

But he was a cop—an *enforcer* like the murderers. Horror twisted
her stomach until nausea rolled through her in waves. What were the
chances he hadn't known about Nathan's plan?

But...maybe he'd just gone to the restaurant to do his job. Checking on law stuff or something?

She shook her head, anguish settling like a stone in her chest, as
she remembered how he and Nathan had laughed together and how
comfortable the enforcers had seemed with him. And they'd met in a
restaurant—a social place—not at work. *Face the facts.* Dain and the
men who'd murdered Cap and Pard and Johnnie were friends.

Dain might even have set up the bombing. She swallowed hard.
She'd coupled with him. *Oh, please, no.*

Wrapping her arms around herself, she tried not to cry. Even
knowing what he might have done, she still wanted him. She craved
his presence like a plant needed water to survive. But she mustn't need

him or want him. *He is dead to me.* Grief blossomed within her until her body ached with it.

She squeezed her bandaged hand, the pain ripping through her grief. She didn't have time for sadness, not if Dain and Nathan knew each other. Sooner or later, either he'd mention his slave named Mella or Nathan would give him a picture of her or—anything could happen.

And then she'd die.

Would Dain kill her with his own hands? Those hands that had stroked her body so tenderly. Would regret show in his dark eyes? Her legs crumpled, and she dropped to her knees, hunching over to hold her chest. Her heart felt torn, savaged into pieces.

What was wrong with her that no one could—Dear Prophet, why couldn't anyone love her? Why was she fighting so hard to stay alive, anyway? *What in heaven's name am I living for?*

The sob broke through her control, burning its way past her throat. She shook as more and more sobs came, and tears scalded her cheeks. *Why, Prophet, why?*

The sound of footsteps pattering down the hall brought Mella back to herself. A tap on the door. She pressed her lips together, smothering…everything.

Silence. As the footsteps tapped away, Canna's high voice said, "She's not here, Rebli."

With a moan, Mella pushed to her feet. Her body ached like she'd suffered a beating, and her eyes felt puffy. But she was alive, and she would stay that way. She could do no less—Cap and Pard and Johnnie were owed justice.

And what of the others? What of the women in Nathan's future who might possess something he wanted? And the people the enforcers should protect but harmed instead?

She couldn't walk away, but that meant she had to escape. Lifting her arm, she eyed the indenture bracelet. No tool around here would get it off, but there remained one option. The person deep in the heart of Port City who would remove a bracelet for a price. Her stomach heaved, and she pressed her hands over her mouth. She knew the price the man would demand.

She'd pay it.

Nothing could come with her. Her mouth tightened. The holocard where Nathan told her he'd deliberately planned her murder was locked up with her clothing in the Indenture Hall. She'd not be able to use that for evidence. But it didn't matter; she had no choice now.

After walking across the room, she looked out the door into the enclosed courtyard. Like a prison within a prison. She couldn't escape from the Zarain Enclave. Dain worked as head of Planetary Security. She huffed a bitter laugh. No wonder they'd caught her so easily when she'd tried to run.

She'd have to leave from somewhere else. Anywhere else.

THAT EVENING, THE house emptied except for the children and the very elderly nanny who had arrived to sit with them. Everyone else had gone off to the LastDay festivities. And everyone seemed very...excited. They all had sex at those LastDay parties; Mella had figured that much out.

Lifting her chin for courage, she tapped on Dain's door.

"Come."

She stepped into the room. He'd already showered and donned black trousers and a black tunic embroidered with moons and stars in metallic silver thread. Unlike other clothing he wore, this tunic had no fastenings in front and displayed his darkly bronzed, muscular chest.

"You're leaving too?" she asked.

"Yes, Iaria." He walked over to her. "Our gods demand the attendance of every fertile person at the Starlight Rites."

"But...not me?" She forced herself to not retreat.

He stroked her hair. "No. You're not Nexan."

"No religious festival on Earth gets every person to attend."

"From what I understand, Earth's deity doesn't involve himself with his followers. Our gods are not so distant." Dain's mouth quirked. "In my childhood, I knew a man who didn't join the rite. His prize horse would foal that night, and he didn't want to leave."

"Sounds reasonable."

Dain shook his head. "Others could have attended the animal. If a child is seriously ill, for a deathwatch, or if the person is too ill to walk—those are about the only exceptions."

"What happened to the man? Did the church fine him?"

"Church?" Dain's brows drew together. "Ah, a religious organization. No, we have no church here. Cernun—it was his LastDay—removed the man's ability to procreate for an entire year. Until Cernun's LastDay arrived again."

"Ability to procreate?"

"If a man's shultor doesn't not become erect..." Dain shrugged and then grinned. "I've also heard of a woman who lost the capacity to enjoy shulin."

"Well." He actually believed his god had taken such a direct intervention? Probably guilt-induced psychosis. "I was looking forward to going to a party."

"I fear this is a Nexan custom you would not enjoy, little Earther. This is the gods' answer to our limited population—a way of ensuring that genes are mingled."

To mingle genes would require...mingling. "You couple with—"

"With everyone at the rite. Yes. From the time the last moon exits the sky until the first rises. Moonless nights occur only four times a year, and the festivals are set around those days."

Dear heavens. That sounded horrible. "Oh well. Maybe I'd better wait for a different party," she said lightly.

"After tonight, we take a break from parties." He rubbed his chin. "The next one is in two weeks, to celebrate the founding of Port City."

Two weeks? She couldn't risk that long. And how could she handle coupling with Dain during that time, knowing he'd probably been involved in killing her friends? Even now, her heart flip-flopped inside her chest with her wanting him and hating him.

"Oh." She pouted. "I'm getting housebound, I guess."

He sat down on the bed and pulled her onto his lap. "I understand, but there's not much I can do. An unshuline cannot leave the premises except with her owner. In fact, starting tomorrow, you probably won't get out much at all, since the doctor has cleared me to return to work. I have too many problems piling up to stay absent longer. Like the singer's death. There are still some issues—"

"You're going back to work," Mella interrupted. If Dain did that, he'd see those two enforcers all the time. And if he was in charge of her so-called death, he'd meet with Nathan, increasing the chances that the monster would discover she'd survived. A shiver ran through her.

"Mella." Dain ran a finger along her jaw, warm against her chilled skin. "Tell me what the problem is."

"No problem." She leaned her head on his shoulder, hating that she found his arms around her comforting. "I want to go with you tonight. To participate in your ceremonies."

His embrace tightened. "Laria, this night is about shulin. You have just accepted my possession. How will you feel when other men take you?"

The thought made her cringe inside. "I think it's time for me to expand my horizons, don't you? I really want to go with you tonight."

"I see. Well, the goddess will not refuse another set of genes." But his brows drew together as he studied her.

AN OCEAN BREEZE brought swirls of fog with it as Dain led Mella down a winding path through the Arewell Enclave toward a building designed just for Starlight Rites. All five of the clans hosted the rites, although the Zarain clan had moved their festival to Port City when Dain's career became a security nightmare. Oddly enough, the new location in the gardens behind a spice warehouse and store had proven a popular choice with the city residents.

One of the first enclaves created on Nexus, the Arewell Enclave, lay on the edge of crime-ridden Old Quarters. Statuary gleamed in the moonlight, and the briny scent of the sea mingled with the sweet fragrance from the formal ronve garden. The Starlight building hid within high hedges in the back corner. As they neared, Dain heard the unmistakable wail of a woman achieving release.

Mella stopped as if she'd hit a wall. "That—"

"There will be more of that tonight, if you stay. Are you sure, laria?" Dain asked. He couldn't believe she'd requested to join him this evening. He'd considered refusing her. But shulin on LastDay was sacred, and to turn away a willing female would anger the goddess.

If she were still willing. He tilted Mella's face up gently, seeing the stunned look in her eyes. "Sex happens here. And the shulin will not be...refined. The Arewell kinline is as dominant as the Zarain, Mella. This evening will shock your little Earther soul."

Her lips firmed, and she stepped away from him. "My soul is getting stronger by the day."

And her soul had moved away from his. Dain narrowed his eyes. Testing, he ran his hand down her arm and felt the involuntary withdrawal before she stilled. "Mella."

She looked at him, her face holding the same blank look as when she'd played poker with him and Grandsir. "Yes?"

"What has happened?" Had he violated some odd Earther custom?

She shrugged.

When she didn't speak, he stepped closer, letting her feel the heat and power in his body. "Answer me, laria."

But before he could pursue the matter further, a shout echoed across the enclave. "Dain!" Clad in Arewell colors of black and red, Blackwell strode through the open door, a grin on his lean face.

"Blackwell," Dain said, clasping forearms with his friend.

"I didn't know if you'd come here or go to your clan's location, but I'm pleased. I see you brought your unshuline." Blackwell motioned them into the building, which consisted of one huge center room, several secluded nooks, and a kitchen near the back.

Dain paused just inside the doorway, so Mella could get her bearings. A slapping sound drew their attention to a naked woman bent over a bench. A hefty-sized man serviced her from the rear.

Mella's mouth dropped open, and the little thief's eyes widened as she took in the rest of the room. A woman manacled to one wall, being driven into a sexual frenzy. Three men and two women having shulin on a wide padded platform. An Arewell woman ordering a man to kneel and lick her. Two brothers tag-teaming a woman on a bench.

"Oh Prophet," she whispered.

"No, the term is 'oh goddess,'" Blackwell corrected. "This is Artema's night."

"But they're coupling in public," she said. "That... I didn't think..." She stopped, too distressed to continue.

Blackwell laughed, obviously taken with her. After a glance at Dain for permission, he stroked Mella's cheek and lingered, like Dain, mesmerized by the silkiness. "Because of the solar storms, our people have frequent genetic mutations and decreased fertility. When kinlines began to practice selective breeding, the gods frowned on the increased inbreeding and demanded the Starlight Rites to increase the odds of conception and to keep the genes intermingled."

A clear explanation. Dain forgot sometimes that this ultimate in warrior breeding had also taught history.

Mella moved away from Blackwell's touch as she had Dain's.

She stayed silent as he walked her across the room to the buffet table. Neither of them had eaten lastmeal yet, but she didn't appear interested. Her gaze flickered to the kitchen, where servants came and went, bearing trays of appetizers.

Setting her small hand on his arm—the first time she'd willingly touched him all evening—she looked up. "Could I... I'd like a chance to regain my composure. Maybe I can sit in a corner of the kitchen for a while...so I don't disgrace you by behaving badly?"

His heart twisted. "I shouldn't have brought you here, laria. I'm sorry." He wrapped his hand around her nape, noting her chilled skin and the speed of her breathing. She was terrified and trying to hide it. "I'll take you home."

"No." She pulled in a deep breath. "I want to stay, but... Just give me some time to remind myself that these people aren't all horrible sinners." Her lips turned up in a smile that didn't reach her eyes. "It's something I've had to do often since coming to Nexus, you know."

"I know." Stubborn little Earther. "Take your break. I'll talk with Blackwell for a half hour or so, then return to get you." He tugged on her braid. "Stay in the kitchen until I come. If anyone asks or bothers you, tell them you're Dain's unshuline and off-limits."

Her eyes widened. "Someone might try to…touch me?"

"Indeed. Your bracelets are green. Gold bracelets restrict what an indentured slave can be required to do, but green means you can be used for anything—including shulin. And tonight everyone has shulin with everyone, remember?"

"I see." A shudder ran through her. "Well then, I'll stay put." Back straight as a graywood tree, she walked past the table, into the kitchen, and exchanged greetings with the staff there.

Too brave for her own good. Dain glanced around the room, looking for Blackwell. He'd give her some time to think. Not too much, because the doors to the building would be locked when the red moon, Neman, set and the goddess's avatar was chosen.

ALMOST AN HOUR later, Dain stood in the doorway of the kitchen. Servants bustled around, but he didn't see Mella anywhere.

He checked the refresher, then the main room. Not there.

Back to the kitchen. When questioned, the kitchen helpers said she'd wanted air and had stepped outside. She hadn't returned.

Blackwell called out servants to check the surrounding gardens and then the enclave itself. Anger sparked to life in Dain's gut when Blackwell reported back. No unshuline. The pity in his friend's gaze didn't help Dain's temper.

And neither did the realization that she'd conned him into coming to this party just so she could escape. His mouth tasted bitter as he used the comunit to call the Indenture Hall.

"Kinae Dain, how can I be of service?"

"Get tracking for me."

A minute later, he heard the gruff voice of the duty officer at the hall. "Kinae Dain, is there a problem?"

"I seem to have misplaced my unshuline. Name of Mella. Can you locate and make the data available on the city infounits?"

The tracking devices were located only in the city and could only sense the tiny bracelet pulse within a one-block radius. The Arewell Enclave sat on the edge of Port City. Hopefully she'd gone toward the city; if she had gone out the back gate into farmland, they couldn't track her.

The officer murmured, then raised his voice. "She is moving into Old Quarters. The city units will be kept updated until you notify me otherwise."

"Thank you." Dain slapped the Off button.

Chapter Sixteen

As THE MOON hung above the western skyline, Mella hurried farther into Old Quarters. She jogged past crumbling buildings, and her uneasiness grew. She was being watched.

When she'd lived on the streets in Port City, she'd kept to the respectable outskirts, forgoing the possibility of easier targets in favor of safety. There would be no safety in Old Quarters. Although she held a butcher knife from the kitchen hidden in the folds of her skirt, it wouldn't prove much use against more than one man, or even an experienced fighter.

She should have taken self-defense classes when Kalie had. Nathan had felt it unseemly. *Damn him to the hell he always spoke of.*

A stick figure in ragged clothing edged out from a doorway and regarded her with the sunken eyes of an alcoholic. According to Dain, fermented beverages were the one drug the Nexans hadn't managed to curtail, since liquor could be made anywhere.

A shiver ran through Mella. That man would slit her throat just to get a few royals to buy another bottle. She increased her speed. One more block to her destination. As stabbing pain cramped her muscles, she pressed her left hand against her side. The life of an unshuline hadn't prepared her for running so far.

She passed two derelict houses. Only another couple—

Three men appeared, emerging from hiding places as silently as ghosts. One had the swarthy-skinned Nexan coloring. The remaining two were lighter skinned and brown haired. Scum from the other worlds who had become trapped here in this Nexan slum.

Her legs felt like blocks of stone as she spun around. *Go back.*

Another man walked into the center of the street to block her. Blond hair streaked with mud, ripped clothing. He slapped a piece of wood against his palm.

Oh Prophet. Mella halted. Trapped. So she'd exchanged the clean death Dain might have dispensed for rape and murder in the filth of the street. Mouth dry, she waited, bracing herself. She wouldn't run, wouldn't flee to be caught and killed like an animal.

A knife glinted in the Nexan's hand as the other three men sidled closer.

Icy horror blurred Mella's vision. *A knife. Blood, so red and hot.* Her friend's small body on the stage and... She shook her head furiously.

All those years she'd jumped through hoops to prevent being identified as Armelina Archer. She'd done everything to avoid Cecily's fate, and everything she'd done had brought her here. All her ventures had doomed her to what she'd feared the most. The irony sang in her ears with the slow, creeping footsteps of the vileness that approached.

She kept the knife in the folds of her skirt. With surprise, she might get one at least.

At an unseen signal, they charged her. The first man to touch her, one of the brown-haired ones, got her knife in his upper stomach, but his twisting fall wrenched it from her hand. Weaponless, she jerked to face the next, and—

A solacar rammed into the man standing the farthest away. His scream of agony stopped abruptly when his head cracked on the pavement.

The door of the car slid open, and Dain emerged, leaning on his cane. Fear for him rushed through her, and her vision blurred. *Oh, Dain, no!* There were too many. Even now, two more slum dwellers stepped out of an alley. They'd take him down like a pack of dogs preying on a deer.

Her two remaining assailants abandoned her in favor of the sol-acar and obviously rich man. They separated, one on each side of Dain, moving in slowly.

No one watched Mella. She could run now. *Get away. Quick.*

I can't. With a scream of frustrated anger, Mella charged. She rammed into the back of the closest one and knocked him off balance. As she fell to her knees, she heard a *whishing* sound, a broken-off gasp. The man collapsed, blood pouring from his throat.

Dain whirled. The end of his cane gleamed wetly, and the blade slid into the oncoming man. The ragged Nexan dropped silently. Dain glanced around and spotted the two others hovering uncertainly. He smiled in icy amusement. Then he growled, "Leave." The power in his voice was almost palpable in the evening air.

The ghosts disappeared without a sound, edging back into the darkness to wait for their next victim.

Mella sucked in a breath. He'd saved her, kept her from being carved up like Cecily. The street had emptied except for them. A slight wind skittered past, rolling a can down the pavement. Grit stung her palms as she stared up at him—and realized she was alone with the man she'd tried to escape. *Oh Prophet.* She shoved upright, springing away from him.

And agony seared through her. Fire burned from her head to her feet. She hit the ground hard, her body convulsing uncontrollably.

When the pain stopped, she could only lie there in the filth as tears streamed from her eyes. Her muscles didn't work; her fingers couldn't move.

"Isn't it nice that I had a zapper in my solacar? I saved the charge just for you."

Filthy, cowardly Nexan weapon. She heard his footsteps, punctuated by the *click* of his cane, and then he walked into her field of vision. His face was cold. Harsh. Would he kill her now? Would she die here in this horrible place?

He looked down at her, and his mouth twisted in a bitter smile. "Well, little thief, you've stolen more from me than I thought to lose." He tucked his cane into a loop on his belt, picked her up, and slung her over one shoulder as easily as if she were a knapsack. She couldn't even scream at the pain of being moved. Her mind blurred.

An interminable time later, the solacar pulled to a stop, and Dain got out.

Mella's agony had eased, leaving her muscles aching and her thoughts racketing around her head. Feeling far too vulnerable, she pushed into a more upright position in the seat.

When he slid open the door to her side, she looked at his impassive face.

He studied her silently. "Do you want to tell me why you ran?" he asked finally.

She shook her head.

His lips thinned into a narrow line, sharp as a blade. "All right, then. Answer me this. What did the Indenture Hall require of an owner if a slave attempted escape?"

The staff had required that "*an indentured slave who flees be punished with ten strikes of the cane with enough force to create welts.*" Her throat hurt as she forced the words out. "Caning. Ten."

"Precisely." Leaning against the door frame, he said, "You requested that I buy you, Mella."

Guilt swept through her. She had. But then the memory of seeing him laugh with Nathan and the two cops who had tried to murder her returned like an icy dagger. If he realized her identity, she'd die.

"Have I treated you so badly that you felt you had to escape?" His jaw tightened. "I believe your life with me has been as gentle as any indentured servant might want."

"I-I... You..." She had no answer to give, not without revealing far too much. She stared at him helplessly.

"After your first escape attempt, I could have caned you until my arm wouldn't rise. I could have whipped you all night, as long as I didn't break the skin." He was furious. He was so controlled that she hadn't realized the depths of his anger, but when her gaze met his, she saw the flames in his dark gray eyes. "I had thought that you... Obviously you play your part very well, little thief. Since you find the idea of being my unshuline so abhorrent—"

"Kinae Dain, can I assist?" interrupted a servant, appearing at Dain's elbow. The servant's black tunic had red piping.

"I would appreciate your assistance, yes. Have her stripped and washed. If Blackwell has a suitable drape, she may wear that. Then return her to me, please." Without even looking at her, Dain walked away.

The servant picked her up easily. She shuddered as her oversensitive nerves spasmed. He carried her down a garden path that Mella suddenly recognized. Not a Zarain Enclave path, but an Arewell path—and this was an Arewell servant.

Dain had brought her back to Blackwell's party.

NOT MUCH TIME had passed—not nearly enough time—when the servant returned her to Dain. Mella's indenture bracelets had been clipped together at her back, pushing her breasts forward. The servants had dressed her in a nightgown. The bodice dipped almost to her nipples, and although the gown reached her ankles, the material could hardly be sheerer.

The servant bowed to Dain and Blackwell, then left. Released from his hard grip, Mella shook her loosened hair forward, trying to cover some of the bare skin.

Dain gave a short laugh and tossed her hair back over her shoulder.

Mella didn't move. She'd seen him mad before, but his anger this time seemed different. Colder.

Blackwell stood beside him, his gaze frozen. "I'll beat her for you."

Fear streaked down her spine. Dain wasn't the only angry one. Why was Blackwell furious?

"Mella," Dain said softly. "Do you want to talk to me now?"

She closed her eyes and shook her head.

"May I use your whipping post, Blackwell?"

"By Ekatae's sands." Blackwell scowled. "You don't like dealing out that much pain. Give me the form, and I'll sign it."

Dain shook his head. "No. The responsibility is the owner's. I gave my word to the Indenture Hall. Mella will survive a caning, and I will survive a few nightmares."

"You're too law-abiding for your own good." Blackwell growled something foul sounding under his breath. "I'll set up the whipping post."

Mella trembled. Dain would beat her. With an effort, she controlled her breathing. It was just pain. She could take pain, especially only ten hits. Welts didn't sound good, but it wasn't like being sliced open with a whip. *Was it?*

She looked up to see Dain's face an inch from hers. Deep lines bracketed his mouth, more between his eyes. He appeared as unhappy as he'd sounded.

"Mella." He cupped her cheek in one hand. "You will receive ten strikes with a cane."

She could only stare at him. Her mouth felt dry, and she swallowed painfully. At least he didn't look like he'd enjoy it any more than she would. She turned her head to watch him cross the room to Blackwell, his shoulders straight, posture proud.

THE LITTLE THIEF raised her chin when Dain returned, and he felt a surge of pride in her. Many women would have been in tears by now. Pleading. Not a Zarain or Arewell woman, of course, but the other kinlines didn't breed for bravery.

Grasping her by the arm, he guided her out the back door and across a wide lawn to the small discipline area, where Blackwell waited. As moonlight glimmered on the metal post, nausea swirled uneasily in his stomach. But he couldn't postpone this. Dain glanced up at the quarter moon. Neman had almost set.

At the post, Dain unclipped Mella's cuffs.

She yanked away, spinning around. Her punch grazed his chin before he grabbed her fist and secured her wrists in front.

Blackwell snorted a laugh. "Feisty little thing, isn't she?" He handed Dain the chain running through a ring at the top of the eight-foot post. Dain clipped her indenture bracelets to it and turned her to face the pole. Blackwell yanked the other end of the chain, raising Mella's arms until she stood on tiptoe, then secured the chain to a clip on the pole. "Ready for you, Cousin."

Dain rolled her nightgown up and tied it into a knot at her waist, baring her buttocks. Stepping back, he caught the long, slender stick Blackwell threw him. He swished it in the air a couple of times to get a feel for it.

The muscles in Mella's legs tightened as she identified the sound. Dain closed his eyes for a second, remembering being in the same position, how he had anticipated the searing pain to come. *Don't prolong the wait. Get it over with.* He met Blackwell's worried eyes and shrugged. His responsibility.

"Stubborn wulkor." Blackwell stepped closer to Mella and growled, "Worthless unshuline, you count for him. Out loud."

Gritting his teeth, Dain slapped the cane against her ass.

She jerked. "One," she spat out. Her fair, tender skin reddened immediately.

Another hard strike. "Two."

The sound of wood on naked flesh twisted Dain's stomach, and he swallowed. To be forced to cane a helpless person was the ultimate irony. Three more, quick but strong. He had to make welts; the hall would check.

Mella's voice began to tremble.

Two more.

"Seven." She sobbed then.

His gut tightened until he wanted to vomit. Forcing it down, he gave her the final three. *Thwack, thwack, thwack.*

"Ten."

With his jaw tight, he undid her nightgown, to cover her, and then released her from the post.

Her legs wobbled, despite her attempt to stand on her own. She turned her head away from him.

"Scorch it all." He lifted her up. And with his arms wrapped around her and her softness against his body, his nausea disappeared. The world felt right.

And yet he could feel her choking back tears, and his heart wrenched inside his chest. But reality was what it was, and a man couldn't demand that a woman return his affections.

She didn't, and he needed to remember that.

Nonetheless, he'd hold her until her tears stopped.

Chapter Seventeen

"WARRIORS, WE ARE locking the doors," someone called. Still in Dain's arms, Mella frowned as Dain moved faster toward the building, followed by his cousin. As they walked through the back door, one of the Arewell retainers snicked the lock. Why would they lock people in?

Once inside, Dain set Mella on her feet, keeping one hand on her arm. At the loss of his body's warmth against hers, she wanted to cling and ask him to hold her more. Why, oh why, couldn't he have been the man she'd thought he was?

What if she was wrong?

But every time she considered that, the memory of the restaurant and seeing Nathan laughing with him returned. *I'm not wrong.*

"How well is your Earther female going to handle the Starlight Rites?" Blackwell asked, staring down at her.

Dain frowned. "When she asked me to bring her, I was pleased. I thought… But she planned to escape, not to participate." He sighed. "I don't know, Blackwell. I don't particularly care."

"I'm no truth-reader, but even I can tell that's a lie." Blackwell scowled at Mella before turning his glare to Dain. "You do care. And you're worrying about her stupid Earther sensibilities, aren't you? Tenderhearted as a mother *pyr.*"

"Inbred greiet," Dain responded, but without any pleasure in the insult. "But yes, having every man here take her might be too much for her. You owe me a favor, Cousin. I call it in tonight. Give her the choice of goddess or guest."

"You would waste an Arewell debt on...this?" The scorn in Blackwell's voice sent a wave of humiliation through Mella. Despite what she'd done, Dain still wanted to protect her. "So be it, Cousin. I accept the call of the debt." Blackwell bowed, then turned to Mella.

"Stupid Earther, you got yourself into this," Blackwell snapped. "You have two choices. You can be the avatar of Artema tonight— touched by everyone, but taken by only one. Or you can be a guest and join the regular rites, and every man here will touch and take you. Choose."

Mella's stomach sank. The smell of sex filled the air, and her upbringing screamed for her to run. But they'd locked the door; she couldn't escape. "Neither of your choices appeals to me," she said, trying for dignity.

"And dishonest unshulines don't appeal to me. We both have things we must tolerate. Pick one, or I will choose for you."

Dain had called in a debt to let her be whatever this goddess thing was. "Goddess."

"Good choice," Dain said in a dry voice that grated along Mella's nerves. He glanced at Blackwell. "Do you have an extra play patch?"

Blackwell's dark brows rose. "Seriously?"

"Yes."

Blackwell held up a hand, and a servant appeared almost instantly, bearing a tray of drinks as well as a small metal box.

Dain removed something from the box, ripped the paper open, and stuck the patch to her arm just above her indenture bracelet.

"What is that?" Mella asked.

Dain gripped her chin. "From this point forward, you will stay silent." His eyes were cold. Indifferent.

She pressed her lips together to hide their quivering. Dropping her gaze, she blinked against the burn of tears. He was doing no more than what would have happened already if someone else had bought her. *Damn them all.* No person had a right to do this to her.

He stepped away from her, leaning hard on his cane, and she knew he'd have fully recovered by now if she hadn't damaged his knee. Because of her, he still limped.

Emotions swirled through her, a piercing symphony of guilt and hatred and fear. She looked up to see the men studying her, waiting for something, and suspicion thickened in her chest. *What did he put on me?* She opened her mouth to ask, caught Dain's dark stare, and shut her mouth before making a sound.

Suddenly a tremor ran through her, followed by a wave of heat.

Blackwell chuckled. "It's kicking in. Permission to touch?"

"Yes. But even with the patch, she won't appreciate it." Dain stepped behind her, and his hard hands curled around her cuffed wrists.

Blackwell laid his fingers lightly on her breast, fondling her through the gown. She gasped and tried to jerk back, but was halted by Dain's unyielding grip. Fire burst through her as Blackwell ran his hand over her, circling her nipple with his thumb.

Her body flamed, the V between her legs turning wet.

Blackwell chuckled. "The patch is definitely in effect. Do you want to do the honors of binding her?"

Binding? She remembered the equipment with people fastened to it. What kind of place was this? She shuddered, wrenching around to stare up at Dain. "Please," she whispered. "Don't."

Dain's eyes still held the coldness of interstellar space. "You begged me for something once before and played me for a fool. It will not happen again." Dain stepped away and glanced at Blackwell. "I'd appreciate it if you'd secure her."

Her throat closed when he turned his back on her, and her vision blurred with tears, despite the growing heat in her body.

With a merciless grip on her arm, Blackwell pulled her toward a stage at one end of the room. Her attempts to struggle had about the same effect on him as a buzzing fly would have; in fact, she doubted he even noticed. "Please don't do this." She gave up any chance at dignity and begged.

"You'll get no sympathy from me. Srinda told me the story, how you almost ruined his leg trying to steal from him. Then he not only buys you but treats you more like a guest than an unshuline. You've hurt him badly, Earther. Is this the way off-planet women act toward someone who is kind to them?"

"I-I…" She shook her head, unable to even swallow against the pain in her heart. She tried to look over her shoulder, to find Dain, but Blackwell gave her a shove, and she staggered up the steps.

On the stage, he stopped in front of a metal post, backed her up to it.

She gasped when the welts on her bottom brushed the cold metal, and then she heard a *click* as something fastened to her wrist cuffs. Pulling her emotions under control, she looked up to meet hard blue eyes. "What will happen now?" She tried to move, but he'd locked her cuffs to the post.

"Ah, more lessons for the Earther. Dain thought you might not like being taken over and over by strangers from moonset to moonrise, so you are designated to represent the goddess." He knelt and buckled a cuff onto her ankle.

"What does that mean?"

"A man who can bring a goddess's avatar to joy with his hands alone has good luck during the year." He cuffed her other ankle. "Later tonight, rather than having shulin with all, the avatar of Artema gets to choose her mate." He smiled at her coldly. "You will be taken tonight, but by only one, and you get to select whomever you wish."

She lifted her chin. "And if I don't?"

"Then as the host, I'll use you myself." His gaze ran across her body. "I'd not find it a hardship to bend you over and release into you, Earther. Dain has been my friend since I was seven, and I've never seen him look like this."

There was nothing she could say.

"Spread your legs open," he directed. "And keep them open."

She shook her head. "I will not."

His grin didn't reach his eyes. "I love feisty slaves." Walking over to a nearby pole, he grabbed a chain and returned to attach it to one ankle cuff. He did the same on the other side, ignoring how she'd clamped her legs together. After standing, he motioned to a burly man. "Take the right, Darwell. She refuses to place her feet for me, so I intend to spread her wide."

Darwell barked a laugh and walked over to the other pole. A second later, the chains tightened, inexorably dragging her legs apart, despite her efforts to keep them closed. Open...then more open...until her legs wouldn't separate farther. Only her cuffs clamped to the post kept her balanced.

A hand grasped her chin, tilting her head up to meet blue eyes with the warmth of a glacier. "A valuable lesson for you, unshuline. Anytime I am refused, there will be no further request, and I will take what I want without compassion. Do you understand me?"

She nodded, shivering with fear and embarrassment.

"I like seeing you tremble, little slave." He pulled a knife from a boot sheath, and she cringed. Rucking her gown together, he sliced it up the center in one stroke, then let the pieces fall down her arms. He stared, his lips curving. "No wonder Dain kept you to himself." Callused fingers caressed her breasts, making her body go rigid. Burning heat sizzled through her as his thumbs rubbed over her nipples.

"Don't touch me, dammit." She tried to jerk away but only succeeded in making her breasts shimmy within his grasp. He rolled one nipple between his fingers, and electricity shot straight to her clit. She bit back a moan and hissed instead, "You bastard, get your hands away from me."

Even knowing he might hit her couldn't keep the words back. Blackwell glanced at something over her shoulder. She started to look, but he pinched her nipple—hard. When she gasped, a rolled-up cloth was shoved between her lips. She felt someone tie the gag behind her head.

She let out a scream and heard only a muffled sound...and Blackwell's laughter.

"There's a pretty pink color," he said, stroking her cheek. "I'm going to touch you some more, and then I'll leave you for the others, although I wouldn't mind staying for a bit." His thumb and fingers grasped her chin as he forced her to look at him. She felt his other hand stroking her intimately, probing at the lips of her pussy.

Her eyes widened in shock. Heat flared inside her, and she dampened.

Blackwell chuckled, watching her intently as he spread the wetness in increasingly wide circles over her labia and up over her clitoris.

She jerked, struggled as his finger rubbed the nub in a demanding rhythm. She could feel her clit swell and harden, and a throbbing need grew inside her.

"You're a responsive one, all right," he murmured. "Dain didn't give you a strong dose, but he knows you well, doesn't he?" With a low laugh, he released her face and stepped back. Raising his voice, he announced, "This soft Earther is the avatar of Artema tonight. Pleasure her as you will." Without another look, he walked away.

No no no. She struggled against the bindings as two men approached. Typical Nexans, tall and dark haired, one had disconcertingly pale green eyes, the other had a white scar running down his face, with more white lines tracing across his hands and forearms and stomach. Clad in the usual loose black Nexan pants, they wore nothing to cover their heavily muscled chests.

The scarred one caught her chin, turning her face from side to side. "She's had a dose of aphrodica."

"There's a patch above her cuff. She still doesn't look too happy about this," the other said. He eyed her. "But she's a pretty little goddess."

"Well, Brother, let us do our duty to the goddess, then." The scarred one licked his finger and circled her left nipple with a wet touch, sending fire through her body. When the other man did the same on her right breast, she arched uncontrollably. They laughed, and their rough hands fondled her breasts without hurting her. The pinches on her nipples stopped just short of pain; the scratching from callused fingers only increased her sensitivity. When they finally moved back, her breasts were swollen and tight, with red, distended peaks. Her body burned with need.

"Good start," the scarred one said. "We'll continue. I'm not finished playing with these toys yet, so you may have the bottom."

Green eyes crinkled. "My pleasure...but not hers. Not yet."

As abrasive fingers closed on her nipples, she saw the green-eyed one kneel, and she shook her head and moaned.

Firm fingers stroked through her folds. "I like how open she is," he murmured. "Blackwell doesn't usually chain them this tight."

Scarred One chuckled. "Maybe she annoyed him. He gagged her too." His fingers pinched her nipple as he studied her face. "You must have quite a mouth on you, girl."

"Ah, but she has the softest maline, Brother." A hand cupped her, brushing through her folds a few more times. Then his thick finger opened her, sliding into her. She made a sound, strained, trying to get away from him even as arousal shot through her. "By Mardun, I'd like to taste her."

"Rules be rules, Brother." Scarred One gave a hard laugh. "Get up here and let me play for a moment."

They traded places, and then rougher hands pressed open her labia even farther. A finger traced over and around her clit, slick and hot and slightly scratchy, making her quiver. Her clit swelled under the firm strokes.

She lost track of place and time as one man fondled her breasts and the other teased her below. Her legs strained against the chains, quivering uncontrollably. Her insides coiled tighter, each touch filling her world until she poised, awaiting the next. Her hands closed into fists as she panted.

"Now," the man standing at her side said.

Suddenly fingers pushed into her, thick and rough, even as he pressed down hard on her clit. Every nerve between her legs exploded in pleasure. Fingers squeezed her nipples, the pressure unrelenting, and she screamed through the gag as the maelstrom of intensity burst within her. Her hips bucked against the hammering intrusion as the unceasing waves of sensation rolled through her, over and over.

Heart slamming in her chest, she would have fallen if the cuffs behind her hadn't held her in place. She blinked and felt a trickle of sweat roll down her cheek.

The scarred one rose to his feet, sucking on his fingers. He gave her a quick grin. "You taste like sweet sin, girl."

The green-eyed one pressed his hand against her pussy, making her shudder and her vagina spasm again. "By Mardun's sword, that was fun. A shame we can't take her now." He stroked through her slick folds, and then licked his palm as he looked around the room. "Let's double-team the big female from the Vulacan kinline. I like the way she shrieks as she reaches release."

As the two men sauntered away, Mella closed her eyes, trying not to cry. She'd come, but she felt…used. When Dain took her, she felt cherished. Wanted.

Not now.

The next man had softer hands, but a slower stroke, and she seemed to writhe forever under his touch before she came. Another one pushed her, hard and fast. And the next… She lost track of the times she'd come. She sagged against the pole, her inner thighs wet almost to her knees.

SITTING AT THE drink table, Dain watched the little thief be roused and then satisfied, again and again. With the lighting focused on the stage, he could see her every expression. Satisfaction, yes, but humiliation and anger also. His heart ached for her.

He scrubbed his face with his hands, feeling as if he'd kicked a baby canin. She wasn't prepared for this or for what would come next, damn the sands. Earthers didn't understand Nexan customs, and the government made no attempt to change that. Four times a year, during the night of the Starlight Rites, off-worlders were restricted to the plaza hotels for everyone's safety. *A planetary orgy* one off-planet magazine had called the LastDay celebrations.

They weren't too far wrong. But the customs of Nexus had kept the people strong for generation upon generation after the abandonment. Other colonies had failed or weakened. On Dan's Folly, the colonists had become so inbred that their children required surgery to walk and often died before reaching five years. The population of Artonia had halved over the centuries.

Yet Nexans had flourished, despite their genetic mutations, despite the unexpected predator migrations that had almost destroyed the first settlement. With their colony in shreds, the original settlers had become brutally practical, and survival had taken precedence over monogamy.

Now, centuries later, women fought for the chance to serve the goddess during Starlight Rites. But that didn't mean much to the little Earther suffering onstage. He shook his head.

"Neman and Morrgan are down; Bab is setting," Blackwell called, stepping up beside Mella on the platform. "Let us see if Artema accepts her avatar, and then the avatar will choose her mate for tonight." Pulling off the play patch, he released Mella from the restraints, holding her up when her legs sagged.

She scowled and pushed him away. "I won't pick anyone."

People around the stage gasped, but Blackwell only laughed and fisted his hand in her hair, running the other over her breast. He whispered something in her ear, and Mella's mouth tightened. Although Blackwell probably enjoyed threatening her—his protectiveness of his friends was legendary—it wasn't necessary. If Artema took Mella, she would need and want to mate.

Dain didn't fully understand why, no human could, but Nexan gods were more...involved than on other planets. The most accepted doctrine said they'd enjoyed the arrival of humans so much that they intervened to ensure the colonists' survival.

The door was unlocked. Stripping off any remaining clothing, people streamed into the enclosed festival garden. Under Dain's bare feet, the grass was soft, the evening air warm and moist. Only an edge of the moon glinted on the distant mountains. Forming a circle around the edges of the space, the women sang to Artema, asking for healthy children, that Nexans might live. The men chanted the beat, one word, over and over: *choose, choose, choose.*

Gripping Mella's upper arm, Blackwell guided her around the inside of the circle, pausing in front of each man. At a hard look from Blackwell, Dain joined the line, taking a place at the end. No man could refuse the avatar on this night.

Mella chose no one. Finally she reached the end, and Dain. A shimmer of power danced on the surface of her pale skin, and her pupils had widened until only a tiny emerald circlet rimmed the black. Dain sighed and bowed his head for a moment in recognition. The goddess had indeed accepted the little Earther.

She studied him for a minute, then spoke, her voice resonant with unworldly power, but still Mella. "You hurt me; I accept that. You gave me to those men…and now…" She frowned at her glowing arms. "I understand a little." Her eyes met his. "I don't trust you. I can't. But it's you I want tonight."

Dain held his hands out, palms up. He could no more refuse Artema's wishes than Mella could. When their fingers touched, fire seared Dain's skin and swept through his body, followed by uncontrollable lust, although he'd already been hard all evening from watching Mella being pleasured. He'd wanted her then; he still wanted her. Darkness rippled inside him at the memory of her running, that his desire and care hadn't been enough for her, and then he set the unhappiness aside.

This was the Starlight Rite, and the last moon was setting.

As the circle waited, Dain pulled the goddess's avatar into his arms, the feel of her lush body making him harden to the point of pain. Gripping her waist, he lifted her high in the air, so the very last of the moonlight glimmered on her pale skin. For a moment, he held her over his head, and then he lowered her slowly, impaling her on his rigid cock. The hot, wet feel of her pulled a groan from deep inside him.

Her legs wrapped around his waist, and she clenched his shoulders. Holding her ass in his palms, Dain raised her up and down. He thrust into her with a fury he didn't recognize. Mating frenzy. His strokes grew harder, faster, and he felt her inmaline tighten. Her body stiffened, straining, and as her back arched, she screamed her release to the heavens. The hard convulsing around his cock forced his own climax, and he jetted into her in body-jolting spasms.

A second later, the last glow of the moon disappeared, and the clearing darkened. Only the stars overhead shimmered, not enough light to distinguish person from person. As Mella slumped against him, her cheek resting on his shoulder, Dain heard the rustling of grass as people moved toward the center of the circle. When a man touched a woman, he took her. Then searched for the next, for during the Starlight Rite, a man's stamina was akin to a god's.

The babies conceived this night would carry genes that ensured genetic diversity. And the people would flourish.

Dain turned his attention to the woman in his arms. Mella's skin no longer burned where he touched her; her eyes were green again.

She swallowed. "I... Did I just...?" She stiffened at the unmistakable sounds of shulin, of women moaning, men's grunting exertions. A woman's voice rose in staggered cries as she came.

Dain felt the clench of Mella's vagina around his shultor and smiled. Artema enjoyed her visits on the planet. Holding Mella in his arms, he knelt and laid her down on the grass.

"Dain... I—"

"Shhh. Words do not belong in this time of the gods," he whispered as he feasted on her breasts. The moan of her response was an aphrodisiac. Her nipples jutted hard, almost as hard as he'd grown once again.

HE'D TAKEN HER over and over—so many times. And now, Mella watched a pale glow dance on the city skyline, portending the rising of a moon. Her body had returned to her control, although a whisper of the goddess remained, and she saw the energy of each person as a swirling vortex of color. Above her, Dain's outline shimmered a deep red with a rich blue center. More beautiful than anything she'd ever seen.

When his hot mouth closed on her breast again, when his teeth touched her nipple, every thought fled under the onslaught of returning need. She tangled her fingers in his hair and heard his low laugh. And then, with unyielding strength, he turned her over, putting her on hands and knees.

She shivered, uncertain if she could endure coming again, especially without Artema's desire burning within her. She tried to move away. He pinned her in place with rough hands on her hips, pushing her legs farther apart and placing himself between them. His cock nudged at her center, and then, with one hard thrust, he entered her. The feeling of his large shaft in this position shocked through her, taking her breath away.

He cupped her breast in one hand, holding himself up with the other, and set his chin on her shoulder. She felt engulfed by his body, surrounded and restrained and filled completely on the inside. Keeping her immobile, he began to move, his thickness sending shock waves of pleasure running through her.

She thought at first she could just enjoy the ride…until his hand left her breast and his fingers slid into the wetness between her legs. With every thrust, his fingers stroked her clit, one side, then the other. The oversensitive nub engorged under his fingers until each touch turned to an exquisite sensation. His strokes sent need rioting down her nerves. Her fingers curled, clawing the grass. She braced herself, trying to push against his thrusts, trying to urge him to greater speed. The night seemed too hot, and sweat ran down her back as she panted.

She'd come so many times that her body wouldn't come again. It couldn't. She needed more, something more…

Each nerve inside and out thrilled as his thrusts deepened. His fingers stayed on the boundary of her clit, never on top. *Damn him.*

She poised on the edge, whimpering, her thighs trembling, her body rigid. Waiting…waiting…

Then he cupped his hand over her clit, directly over it, pushing firmly as he groaned, shooting hot inside her, and the sensation sent her over. His hand hard against her, his cock hard inside, her bundle of nerves trapped between the two. Convulsions shot brutal pleasure through her whole body. Mewling, she bucked against his palm in little jerks, each motion increasing the pressure and sending her into more spasms.

Screams echoed in the small glade from people everywhere doing the same. The slap of flesh against flesh, moaning, incoherent begging.

Dain's arm came around her like steel bands as he sat on his heels, pulling her back with him, still firmly embedded within her. Her bottom rested on his thighs; the pain of the welts from the caning made her wiggle. His arm tightened, holding her against his chest. His hand stroked her breasts; his lips nuzzled her shoulders.

Her body felt limp, hugely satisfied, and yet tears burned her eyes. She needed to curl up and cry somewhere alone. She'd always wanted to be held like this, not just the orgasm, but the loving afterward, feeling protected and cherished.

But what would he do if he knew who she really was. Keep her? Or kill her?

She stiffened in his arms and heard him sigh.

Chapter Eighteen

PEOPLE RETURNED TO the building to dress then left quietly, exhaustion obvious in every step. Dain waited, leaning against the door frame of the building until one of Blackwell's servants brought Mella out, showered and dressed. Her mouth was swollen from his kisses, her face beard burned. She'd been well used and looked it.

And his heart felt like a boulder within his chest. He grasped her arm and nodded to the servant. "Please give us a minute."

With a bow, the man moved to a discreet distance.

Mella looked up.

"I didn't want to leave without saying good-bye." Dain ran a finger down a strand of her red-gold hair and watched it shimmer in the morning sunlight.

Her fine red-brown brows pulled together. "Good-bye?"

"Yes. You made it clear that my ownership doesn't please you. I'm returning you to the Indenture Hall. Perhaps your new master will prove more to your liking." He might as well have taken a knife and shoved it into his own gut. The thought of her living with another man, being taken… His hand pressed against his stomach as if he could cover a wound. Not this wound.

She didn't speak. Had not spoken to him since he'd ordered her to be silent. Her big green eyes filled with tears, but she gave him nothing else, nothing to pin hopes or dreams upon. Nothing to change his decision.

His chest tightened with disappointment. He motioned for the servant. Giving his little thief a nod of farewell, Dain turned and left her behind.

And felt his guts being pulled out of him, inch by inch.

MELLA WATCHED HIM walk away from her. She forced herself to keep from running after him. From begging him to let her stay. Breathing into the pain, she raised her chin. He was a murderer, if not directly, then one who'd had a hand in it. Just because he could make her body respond didn't mean she should abandon common sense. Cap and the others deserved better.

After a minute, she realized someone stood beside her, also watching, and she looked up. Blackwell's face appeared as hard as the mountains on the western horizon.

When Dain disappeared, Blackwell grasped Mella's arm. "Let's go, Earther."

The solacar was too silent, Mella thought, as Blackwell drove past Old Quarters and toward the center of Port City. She glanced at him from the corner of her eye and saw a muscle pulsing in his tight jaw. "What?" she asked.

Each word clipped and cold, he said, "When I was a skinny seven-year-old, two addicts in Old Quarters attacked me. They had me belly up on the ground. Then Dain charged in. He won, but by the sword, he almost died of it. The scars on his face and arms are souvenirs. He was only ten."

Blackwell's fingers tapped the steering wheel. "A couple of months later, a pack of regstal attacked his parents. Ripped apart his father and put his mother in the hospital for months."

"By what?"

He gave her an impatient look. "Regstal. Reptiles with big teeth. Everyone thought the season's migration finished, but this pack came through late. Perhaps delayed by a closed mountain pass. Dain's folks were in a carriage when the regstal scented them."

Mella shuddered. Ripped apart? Her heart tugged. What could be more horrible than to lose a parent like that?

"Dain went to a Zarain clan relative who liked to cow children into obedience. As you might have noticed—if you weren't a totally blind Earther—Dain doesn't cow easily. So the beast beat him. Daily. Usually with a cane, sometimes a whip."

"Dear Prophet," Mella whispered. "How could someone do that to a little boy?"

"The old man was sick in the head. Dain lived there until his grandsir visited and saw his bloody tunic."

"I hope the clanae beat that man up."

Blackwell barked a laugh. "He did, actually. And brought Dain home." His face hardened again. "Seeing, hearing someone being beaten makes Dain sick. Having to wield a cane himself..."

That's why he'd looked so unhappy, why he'd held her so tight. *Poor Dain.*

"I don't like you, Earther. You have hurt him in ways he's never been hurt before." Blackwell brought the solacar to a stop in the tiny alley behind the Indenture Hall. After sliding back the door on her side, he pulled her out. His unyielding grip on her upper arm quashed the impulse she'd had to flee. The door opened to a small reception area, a duplicate of the larger one on the plaza side. Behind the desk, an older man rose and bowed. "Colonel Blackwell. How can I serve you?"

"I am returning this unshuline, named Mella, for reassignment."

The manager blanched, and he quickly poked the keys on his infounit. "Can you tell me the problem? If she did not give good service, perhaps she should go to the mines."

Blackwell's mouth tightened. "Appealing as the thought is, General Dain requests that she merely be given a new owner."

"General Dain? The kinae of Zarain?" The manager appeared to have trouble breathing. "He was... She..." He tapped more keys. "Black sands, an escape attempt. She will be severely—"

Blackwell interrupted, "The general handled her punishment already." In illustration, he patted Mella's bottom.

She hissed in pain and jerked away, glaring at him.

"I enjoyed that," he said softly enough that only she heard.

The manager nodded. "I'll note she's received her discipline." He tapped a few keys. "Does the general desire a refund or a replacement?"

"No."

"Very good. In that case, I'll simply put this unshuline up for tomorrow's auction."

"Thank you." Blackwell gave her a cold look and walked away.

Mella clasped her hands together and tightened her lips. He hated her. Dain hated her.

I'm alone. Again.

The manager pressed a button on the desk, and Handler appeared. His brows drew into a line when he saw her. "Your indenture be not finished yet."

"She tried to escape yesterday," the manager said. "General Dain has returned her. She'll return to the auction stand tomorrow."

Handler nodded.

"Please verify that she has received suitable punishment, and then put her into a cell until tomorrow morning."

"Yes, sir." Handler pushed her through the door to the inner building. The overwhelming smell of cleanser couldn't eradicate the scent of fear, and Mella's stomach clenched.

Abelosh came down the hallway. "Manager sent me to help. She's back, eh?"

Handler nodded, then asked Mella, "Be you caned? And where?"

"My bottom." She felt her face flush.

"Bend over." When she'd complied, Handler set a hard hand on the back of her neck, keeping her there. "Check the beating," he ordered Abelosh.

Mella felt her skirt being raised, exposing her bottom. A painful touch on a welt made her jerk and caused Handler's grip to tighten.

"One. Two," Abelosh said, pressing hard on each stripe as he counted. "Nine and ten. Exactly ten, no more, no less."

"Good. Escort the unshuline to an empty cell and notify the kitchen she be added to the rolls." After letting her stand straight,

Handler frowned at her. "Be you sure that your next master will know you attempted escape. Not again will it happen."

FEELING AS IF he'd left part of himself back at Arewell Enclave, Dain arrived at the Planetary Security Building. At least his return to work would divert his mind from the little thief. His office smelled stale, and paper piles cluttered the desk's surface. One corner of his desk had a stack of comunit messages with a framed photo lying on top to prevent them from toppling.

Dain picked up the picture of Rebli and Mella that he'd brought in last week. His niece knelt beside the little thief in the shade garden while Mella wiggled a long string in front of a felin. The memory of her infectious laughter when the felin had pounced stabbed into Dain's chest, leaving an ache behind.

Jaw tight, he set the photo on his desk and picked up the stack of messages. With a sigh, he dropped into his chair and started reading them.

After a minute, he turned the photo to face away. *Scorch it all, anyway.* He put in a call to Blackwell and then forced his mind away from curves and softness and comfort.

He had work to do, starting with the notifications and reports clogging his infounit's in-basket. A LastDay party had grown too raucous. Fighting. Not unusual for the Trytron Enclave; seamen liked to brawl. His enforcers had handled the infractions well. He punched Delete.

Someone had robbed two great houses, but the detective on the case had a good lead. Delete.

Wulkor attacks had increased in the backcountry. He tagged a note to ask Planetary Defense to send a militia squad to help eliminate the predators.

The final report on the singer's ship explosion waited for him, along with the form to release the death certificate. Dain started to hit his Signature button, then remembered he'd asked for the biological report from the lab. He brought it up and glanced at it.

Then stopped and read it again.

When the singer's ship had docked, it carried the captain, two crew, and one passenger—Armelina Archer. But the report noted only three bodies in the debris. Now, with an explosion and a fire, the lab's estimate could be wrong, but... He frowned at the signature on the bottom. The head of the lab, Old Argulinin, was known as Anal Argulinin because he never missed a detail and never made a mistake.

So unless Ekatae's blazing sands had frozen over, someone from that ship had survived.

He was deep into reviewing the reports when his secretary signaled. "General, Nathan Hamilton has arrived for his appointment. Colonel Blackwell is here also."

Dain went to the door and saw the singer's husband sitting in a chair in the reception area.

And Blackwell... Dain gave an exasperated sigh. Blackwell was leaning over Esosha, one hand on her desk, the other on her chair, fencing the secretary in. Esosha's face was flushed, her voice sounded husky. Thrilled and intimidated.

By Cernun's spear. Best deal with Blackwell first, before Esosha got too flustered to do any work at all. Dain nodded at Nathan and held up a finger. "Give me one more minute, and then we can talk." He turned to his cousin. "Blackwell, leave my secretary alone."

Blackwell grinned and ran a finger down Esosha's pink cheek before strolling over to Dain. "I heard you wanted to speak with me. Since I stopped next door to check on the new soldiers assigned to my battalion, I figured I'd convince you to have lunch."

Dain glanced at the clock. Almost noon. He'd been busy all right. And still was. "I'm too behind for a break. I wanted to ask you for a favor. Another one." His jaw tightened. "You left Mella at the Indenture Hall?"

"I did."

Conscious of the fact that his secretary and Hamilton were present, Dain lowered his voice. "Buy her. She deserves better than being a *doshuline* in a brothel, even if we didn't suit."

Blackwell's eyes narrowed. "She caused you pain, Cousin. You sure you want her in my hands?"

He hadn't thought about Blackwell's overprotective loyalty and how he'd probably take his anger out on Mella. "Just for the moment. Buy her, and I'll find her somewhere else to go."

"You're as softhearted as a pyr sleeping with new lambs." Blackwell scowled. "Fine. I'll get over there sometime today. But you'd best remove her quickly, or I'll show her how that beating should have been done."

"Thank you, *panthat*." Dain squeezed his shoulder and then turned to the Earther. "Nathan Hamilton, please join me."

Hamilton entered the office smiling. "It's good to see you again, General Dain. And please, call me Nathan."

Ignoring the request, Dain politely shook the man's hand Earther fashion and motioned for him to have a seat.

Smoothing his blue silk suit, Hamilton took a chair. "I want to leave the planet today. Is the certificate for the Earth officials ready? You told me it wouldn't take more than a couple of days."

"I believe I said that just yesterday." Dain kept the irritation off his face and didn't add that the finalization grew more distant by the moment.

An hour ago, he'd pulled a young enforcer off patrol to review the dockside security vids from the evening of the bombing. If a body was missing, then that body must have left sometime before or after the explosion.

He'd ordered another tech to examine the vids of the stalker more closely. Perhaps Hanwell and Nilard missed a clue. His gut told him something was off. Very off. He tilted his head at the annoying Earther. "I have a few details yet to tie up. I hope the wait hasn't proven too onerous for you."

Hamilton's smile thinned. "Nexus is an entertaining planet, but I have business to return to. I need you to get this fini—" He choked, his eyes widening.

Did the man have heart problems? Dain rose to his feet. "Are you ill?"

Hamilton gave a weak laugh and leaned back in his chair. "No. I just got something stuck in my throat."

Lie.

Dain had long ago abandoned trying to truth-say constantly. It was a truism that everyone lied, and people constantly used white lies in everyday conversation: *You look fantastic. I feel fine. My husband has asked after you.* But a perceived heart attack had shot Dain's adrenaline level up, and stress strengthened the truth-reader talent.

Hamilton hadn't choked. "For a minute, I thought you were having heart problems."

"Nah. My health is fine."

Truth. Then what had disturbed the man? Something on the desk?

Before Dain could pursue the matter, Hamilton stood, pulling his cuffs down. "Well, if I can't collect the death certificate, I'll get going. Hopefully I can postpone my business a bit longer. If not, I assume you can send a courier with the papers to Earth."

Still standing, Dain nodded. "Certainly."

As the man hurried out of the office, Dain shook his head. Earthers were strange. After taking the chair where Hamilton had sat, Dain eyed his desk. All the reports lay too far away for Hamilton to have read them. The only thing that the Earther could have reacted to was the picture of Mella and Rebli in the enclave garden.

He tapped his fingers on the arm of the chair and frowned at the photo. Mella came from Earth. Did Nathan Hamilton know her? If so, why hadn't he mentioned it?

A crawling sensation crept up his spine, like when he'd hunted wulkors with a spear, knowing their pack lurked nearby. *Danger.* Hamilton was hiding something. But what?

He raised his voice. "Esosha, please summon Hanwell and Nilard to meet me in half an hour."

"Yes, General."

Dain punched a number into his comunit. "Have you discovered anything interesting?"

"I have, General." The tech's voice was filled with excitement. "But something entirely different from what you wanted. I'm uploading the data to your infounit now. Let me explain…"

MELLA PACED HER cell, rubbing her arms. Fear of tomorrow's auction prickled her nerves like dissonant music. Uncomfortable, but nothing close to the pain of losing Dain. That reverberated through her body like a heavy bass drum. Blinking back tears, she remembered how his eyes had looked so unhappy, his face so strained.

And then her mind presented her with the happier times. How he'd smile, his cheek creasing, the sun lines around his eyes deepening. How strong his arms were when he held her and how safe and wanted he made her feel. His lips would tease hers, and his fingers would play her body as surely as she played the harp.

Stop thinking of him as a lover. She dropped onto the cot and winced when her tender bottom hit the hard mattress. *Think about seeing him with the murderers and Nathan and how friendly they all appeared.*

Safety didn't lie in his arms; safety required distance from him. He was evil. *Think about the way he'd hurt her, caning her so hard she couldn't sit comfortably.* He was an abusive bastard who liked to… She sighed. No, he hadn't enjoyed it. She'd seen the pain in his face, and Blackwell had confirmed it. Dain hadn't wanted to hurt her, but he'd given his word to the Indenture Hall, and he wouldn't lie, even about something so small.

But that didn't make any sense. He wouldn't lie…because he was law-abiding. Honorable. She curled her hands around her knees, trying to think rationally, despite the hope rising in her chest.

Last night, Blackwell hadn't appeared surprised that Dain didn't evade his responsibility. He'd disliked seeing Dain suffer, but he'd known Dain would see her punishment through. Because Dain was an honorable man.

He was.

A man honorable in the little things would be honorable in the big ones.

Certainty blasted through her like a cold wind, so overwhelming that she closed her eyes. He hadn't been part of the plan to murder her.

He was head of the enforcers, yes, but he couldn't have known about the plot or he'd not have allowed it to happen. He'd met with Nathan and the enforcers, but she must have misinterpreted their being friends.

Oh Prophet, Dain. She'd been an idiot. Nathan's betrayal had shaken her so badly, she hadn't trusted her own senses.

That meant she could tell Dain her identity. She laced her hands tightly together. Would he help her get justice? Keep her safe? Her heart began to hammer as other questions whispered in her mind like a song. Would he forgive her and take her back?

She ran to the door of the cell, staying clear of the restraint field, and yelled to the attendant down the hall. "I need to make a comcall. To report a crime. Can I use a comunit?"

He eyed her for a minute and then nodded. "We allow calls to the Port City area. Nowhere else." He brought her a comunit off the desk. "Who to?"

"Dain." *Dain what? Oh dear.* "He's high up in the enforcer stuff, and…um…" Her brain went blank. What was his clan name?

The guard snorted. "You're the Earther, aren't you? Happens Nexans only have one name to a person. It's unique; there's only one Dain on the planet. But don't think to call him as a joke. He's General Dain, head of Planetary Security, and he has the sense of humor of an irritated regstal."

"That's him."

"Good luck, Earther." He punched in the number, handed her the comunit, and moseyed back to his desk, shaking his head.

"General Dain's office," a woman answered, and Mella felt like crying. She wanted to hear Dain's voice so badly. Was this his secretary?

"I-I need to speak with General Dain, please." Her certainty eroded away by the second. What if he refused to talk to her?

"He's in a meeting. May I take a message?"

Heavens. She sucked in a breath and searched for self-assurance. "Yes. P-please." Her voice wavered, and she tried to firm it up. She didn't succeed. "W-would you tell him Mella called and…" What could she say? "Um, tell him I'm sorry, and I trust him, and my name is Armelina Archer."

She heard the secretary's gasp, ignored it, and doggedly continued. "And that I'm not dead."

Chapter Nineteen

N ILARD AND HANWELL entered Dain's office together, big men in black uniforms with zappers on their belts. Sitting at his desk, Dain eyed his two enforcers and suppressed a growl. Now he looked closer, the signs of uneasiness were easy to read—tighter muscles around eyes and mouth, slightly wary posture. He pointed to the two chairs in front of his desk. To the right of Dain's chair, Srinda sat quietly. On the left, Tech Gregior leafed through the papers on his lap.

"Enforcers," Dain said, tipping his head. "I have a few questions about some discrepancies in your investigation." He had a growing fear that the two hadn't just taken a bribe to overlook the bombing but had done the murder themselves.

"Gregior, explain what you found on the tape."

From the technology-oriented Falconior kinline, the young tech enforcer possessed an almost mystical talent with vids and infounits. He stepped over to Dain's infounit to project a security vid of the spaceport onto the far wall. As they watched, the man designated as the stalker appeared and walked down the dock.

"That's the person who blew up the singer's ship." Hanwell frowned. "We know this already, so—"

Gregior interrupted him. "The problem is here." He repeated the segment in extreme slow motion. Right before the stalker appeared, the picture fuzzed. "See that? Someone edited the vid. They did it neatly, but it's definitely edited."

Dain leaned back, his gaze on Hanwell and Nilard. Frowning at the vid, Nilard ran a hand up and down his thigh. The more technologically oriented of the partners, he had the skills to corrupt the vid. "Nilard," Dain said. "Did you edit this vid?"

"No, of course not." Nilard shot Dain a shocked look.

"Lie," Srinda murmured.

From the dismayed looks on the two men's faces, they'd just caught the intention behind her presence—that this was an interrogation with *them* as the suspects.

"Hanwell, did you plant bombs on the ship?"

"No." The man's face grayed, and beads of sweat appeared on his brow.

Dain couldn't read him at all. Apparently, the enforcer possessed enough talent to block Dain's limited strength. Unfortunately for Hanwell, judges could penetrate any barrier.

"Lie." Srinda sighed and rubbed her forehead. Dain squeezed her shoulder. The concentration required to pierce a mind-block took its toll with headaches and nausea.

"Hanwell, did Nathan Hamilton hire you to kill his wife?" Dain continued.

The enforcer opened his mouth, and then his gaze shifted to Srinda.

She waited. Dain waited.

Hanwell's shoulders slumped. "Yes. Herina help me, but he offered so much money. Enough that we'd be wealthy. And it seemed so simple." He looked at Dain. "Dain, I'm—"

Years ago, when Dain transferred from the militia into security, Hanwell had been the first enforcer he'd hired. Dain met his eyes.

Hanwell flinched and dropped his gaze.

"Gregior, show them the other vid," Dain said.

The display changed to later in the evening. The flow of people in the spaceport had markedly increased. Firefighters and enforcers outnumbered the others. When a short, curvy woman followed a firefighter out the exit, Gregior stopped the vid.

"Is that the singer? Armelina Archer?" Dain asked, staring at the hologram of Mella. She had a cut on one cheek, dirt and blood streaked her clothing, and terror swam in her eyes. He pulled in a slow breath, trying to control the fury searing his gut.

"By Cernun, she's alive?" Nilard stared. "How did she escape?"

"Good question." Dain's jaw tightened. So the enforcers hadn't known she survived. "Gregior, send a squad to the Felin's Rest Hotel to arrest Nathan Hamilton. Then go pick up an unshuline named Mella from the Indenture Hall and bring her here."

Dain steepled his fingers and stared at the two enforcers. They'd betrayed him, their clans, and the Nexan people. For *money*. "Hanwell, start at the beginning and tell me everything."

When the man's mouth closed in unspoken refusal, Dain let his anger show. "You two might recall that if a judge endorses that you committed a crime involving injury or murder, I am permitted to interrogate you using *stadilaig*." Dain rose, planted his hands on his desk, and leaned forward. "If you do not start talking right now, you will be in the medroom within five minutes, and I will ask you questions until you are drooling idiots. I might even enjoy the sight."

"Truth," Srinda murmured, and both men went white. Stadilaig often left just a husk of a person after use. Since it was only used on endorsed uncooperative criminals, no one particularly cared about the drug's adverse effects.

Hands trembling like leaves in a high wind, Hanwell cleared his throat. "A man approached us two months ago…

THERE WERE EXACTLY eight steps from one side of her cell to the other. After going back and forth several dozen times, Mella started humming old marching songs to go with her pacing. Earth had a lot of military tunes.

Had that secretary forgotten her message?

Maybe Dain just didn't want to see her. Or thought she was a crackpot. She turned and paced back, this time to an even older Earth song "The Battle Hymn of the Republic." Perhaps rather bloodthirsty for a hymn, but it had a fine martial melody.

Behind her, the hum of the restraint field died. She spun around. Dain had come? *Thank you, god. Or goddess.*

A hooded man stood in the doorway, slapping a z-rod in his palm. "Well, hello, Armelina. Apparently the reports of your demise were greatly exaggerated."

Her breath caught, and she jerked backward. *That voice.* Terror flooded through her so hard, she felt her body shake. She forced herself to inhale. "Nathan."

"Very good." He bowed slightly. "Come along now."

"No. I'm not going anywhere with you." She eyed the z-rod. Did he know how to turn it on?

A slight hum answered her. He motioned with the rod. "Out, or I'll zap you so hard, you'll never wake up."

Screaming wouldn't work. Shrieking slaves were common in this place; no one paid attention. She edged past Nathan and out into the corridor. The guard at the far end was sprawled on the floor, his head in a pool of blood.

"I hit him harder than I'd planned," Nathan said as coolly as if he'd confessed to using a swear word. He pointed down the hall. "We'll go out the back door."

With Nathan behind her, Mella stepped around the guard's body. Her stomach twisted at the blank, staring eyes. Dead.

Like her, if she left with Nathan.

Just past the desk, she jerked back and snatched up the guard's wooden chair. She whirled, holding it up.

Nathan swung the z-rod. She blocked it with the chair, knocked away another attempt, then jabbed the wooden legs toward his face.

He jumped back. "Damn you, you worthless—"

"Mella!" Canna burst through the door from the reception area. "Mama's giving the man your clo—" She skidded to a halt beside Nathan, staring at the blood and the guard.

Prophet no! "Canna, run!" Mella yelled, lunging forward with the chair.

Nathan sidestepped and grabbed Canna by her hair. "Stop, Armelina, or she's dead." He held the z-rod against the girl's cheek.

Terror for the child blasted through Mella. She froze.

Body stiff with fear, Canna stood unmoving, her eyes wide and her little face terrified.

"I set the rod on high. The charge will kill her, Armelina." Nathan's thin lips twisted into a smile. "Put the chair down, and come here like an obedient wife."

The doors were closed—no help in sight. "Let her go, Nathan," Mella whispered.

"Throw it over there, and I won't stun her."

No choice. Mella tossed the chair into the corner behind her.

With a high laugh, Nathan clicked something on the z-rod and slapped it against Canna's side. The girl dropped without a sound.

Canna. For a second Mella couldn't move, staring at the little body on the floor. "You promised!" She charged.

Nathan slammed the metal rod into her neck. Fire burst through her as every nerve short-circuited and spasmed. *Oh Prophet, the pain!* She went rigid, then collapsed when he pulled it away.

He caught her in his arms and put her over his shoulder. Hauling her like a dead bundle, he carried her out the back way to the access road behind the hall. A solacar waited there, engine humming.

As the car door slid open, Mella screamed and screamed, but not a sound escaped her frozen throat.

DAIN STOOD IN his outer office, listening to his secretary.

"That's the message from Armelina Archer, General," Esosha finished and folded her hands on her desk, waiting for orders.

"Thank you," Dain said. With an eidetic memory and an unsurpassed talent for organization, the secretary was worth her weight in gold. Especially now. She'd even included Mella's *ums* and hesitations.

Despite the mess he had on his hands, Dain smiled. As he rubbed his aching neck, he thought how much he wanted the little Earther back in his arms. By Cernun's spear, Mella had good reason not to trust him, considering what Hanwell and Nilard had said. She'd watched the enforcers—*his* enforcers—kill her friends and blow up her ship.

Thank Herina that she had escaped the explosion, however she managed it. He headed back into his office and sat behind his desk.

A soft chime. Then Esosha's voice said, "General, *Lefnant* Olanard is reporting."

"Put him through." Dain waited until the enforcer appeared on-screen. "Do you have Nathan Hamilton in custody?"

"No, sir." Rigidly at attention, the lefnant stared at a place past Dain's shoulder, his customary casual stance missing.

Dain's jaw tightened. Nilard had not only betrayed the enforcers, but also his Milianard kinline, where the majority of members served in law enforcement and security. His kin would feel disgraced. Young Olanard felt disgraced.

As the Arewell kinline would be shamed by Hanwell's treachery. Blackwell would be furious. "What's the problem?"

"Nathan Hamilton checked out of the hotel earlier. I've put out an alert for the solacar he rented."

By Cernun, what else could go wrong? "Send enforcers to the spaceport to ensure he doesn't leave the planet."

"Yes, sir." Olanard's face blinked out.

"General, I have Gregior also," Esosha called through the open door.

"Go ahead." Dain waited until Gregior's face appeared, the Indenture Hall behind him. No one standing beside him. "Gregior, where's Mella?"

"She's not here, sir."

"Did Blackwell pick her up?"

Gregior shook his head.

Rising, Dain gripped the edge of his desk and growled, "Where is she?"

Despite being at least a mile away, Gregior took a step back. "Sir, I'm trying to find out. She's not in her cell. An attendant's been murdered, and the admin people are—"

"Be that your boss?" A man appeared beside Gregior, his back-country accent thick as he said, "I be Handler, head of processing. A man with hood over his face removed the slave named Mella. The security vid shows him carrying her out the back exit. She be unconscious. He killed a guard and stunned a child. Tracking on the unshuline be instituted right now. Do you wish the data uploaded to your unit there?"

The husband had her. Dain's hands tightened, and the edge of the desk crumbled. "Upload to here and to the city units also. Make tracking the unshuline a priority. We need to get this murderer before he kills again."

"May he burn on Ekatae's sands." Handler bowed. "All shall be as you say."

As Handler hurried away, shouting orders, Gregior waited. "Sir, what are—"

Dain held up a hand. Visions of Mella covered in blood—dead—vied with his control. He smothered the fear, iced the fury, and forced his mind to work. The insane Earther had Mella in a solacar, so he could easily cut her throat and toss her out.

But her body would be found and identified, revealing that she hadn't died in the ship explosion, but later. Hamilton must know he'd be the first suspect. Even if he managed to escape Nexan justice, the questions would tie up his inheritance on Earth for years.

Hamilton wouldn't have access to explosives. Burning a corpse left teeth behind. Dain flinched at the thought.

He took a breath. That cold, calculating Earther must know his freedom depended on getting rid of his wife without leaving a body. The only sure way to accomplish that expeditiously would be to leave the planet.

Dain exhaled, his muscles easing. Hamilton wouldn't realize Archer's survival had emerged—or that anyone other than him had discovered Mella's identity. He would realize no one searched very hard for escaped unshulines. Without a positive ID on the murderer, they couldn't extradite Hamilton from Earth for the guard's murder.

"He's going to head for the spaceport, Gregior. Order his ship held."

"Yes, sir."

MELLA'S ARMS AND legs felt as if a million pins poked into them. She hung limply over Nathan's shoulder as he threaded through the crowd at the spaceport. Shouting and cursing, people pushed to get to the docking gates. The place seemed incredibly busy. After a minute, she remembered—Artema's festival days had ended last night. The Nexans and off-worlders who'd come for the celebrations would leave today. Apparently, a lot of people showed up for the five days of festivities, even though only Nexans—*and me*—took part in the Starlight Rites.

A huge man slammed into Nathan, knocking Mella off his shoulder. Like a rag doll, she landed heavily on the concrete, unable to move to break her fall. Pain exploded in her ankle and shot up her leg. *Oh Prophet.*

Cursing foully, Nathan grabbed her arm and dragged her to a corner out of the flow of traffic. Face streaming with sweat, he bent, hands on knees, breath heaving like a bagpipe.

Surreptitiously, Mella massaged her arms and legs. If only she could get them to work…

Eventually, he straightened and glared down the people-clogged concourse, then at her. As if she was causing him trouble.

She smothered a bitter laugh and cleared her throat, surprised that her voice worked. "You know, your contacts here or on Earth can't help you if you murder me now. Even this backward planet can identify bodies."

He wiped his face with a white handkerchief. "I'm not stupid, Armelina. I'm going to cycle you out the air lock somewhere between the stars."

She stared at him, and a chill crept up her spine. His plan could very well work. Everyone thought she'd died in the explosion. After her phone call, Dain might believe her, but with no ID scans, they'd have no legal proof she'd survived the explosion. Without a corpse... Muscles tightening, Mella eyed the crowd around her.

"Going to try to run?" Nathan gave her a thin smile. "Go ahead. Then I'll have a good reason to beat you. On this fucking planet, no one cares if a slave gets whipped." His hands closed into fists. "You've caused me a lot of trouble. I'm going to enjoy hurting you, Armelina, before you die."

The gloating satisfaction in his voice turned her stomach, and she swallowed against the roiling bitterness. He was insane. *Evil.*

He tucked his handkerchief into a pocket, then yanked her to her feet. She stood, wobbling. The numbness had disappeared, but her injured ankle burned like fire. She staggered and almost fell when she put weight on it.

Wrapping his arm around her, Nathan held her up. "Better walk, Armelina. If you fall, I'll drag you by your hair."

Chapter Twenty

THE SIREN CLEARED a path for Dain's solacar. He'd almost reached the spaceport when his comunit beeped. "This is Dain."

"Handler here. The unshuline be at the port. Direction she heads is toward the south end."

"Thank you, Handler. Inform me if her course changes." He'd guessed correctly.

"Yes, General."

Dain abandoned the solacar at the massive arches and headed for the public concourse at a dead run. His comunit beeped, and he flipped it on, only to receive static. He veered toward a wall with a transmission node. "This is Dain."

"This is Gregior. I'm at the port, but I can't lock down Hamilton's ship. It's already cleared and sitting on a fastpad."

"Scorch him!" Dain shoved people out of the way, fighting against the crowd. "Cordon off the ship so he can't reach it."

"I'm trying, sir, but port security is assigned to the gates. My men are caught about halfway down the concourse. There's no getting through this mess quickly."

Dain shouldered his way another few steps. A woman fell in front of him. He pulled her to her feet and moved on without pausing. "Do your best, Gregior. If that ship lifts, the singer is dead."

"Yes, sir." The comunit clicked off.

+ + +

I'LL BE DEAD if he gets me to the ship. The thought echoed in Mella's head as Nathan half dragged her through the crowd. Her ankle wouldn't support her weight, so she had to lean on him, although his touch made her skin crawl.

To speed up their progress, he veered out of the packed center of the concourse and closer to the vendors by the walls. They passed a drink booth and a familiar popcorn stand; the crunchy kernels were sold on every planet with humans. She caught the scent of the spicy meat ubiquitous on Nexus.

A strain of lively music drifted over the noise of the crowd like a clean mountain wind.

Mella lifted her head to see where the music was coming from. Unthinking, she set her weight on her bad ankle. Pain ripped through her, and her leg buckled. Nathan's grip failed, and she fell hard onto her knees on the cold concrete. Her ankle throbbed as if squeezed in a vise, and she rocked against the agony.

Nathan gave a nasty laugh and backhanded her, knocking her sprawling. "Nice try."

Blinking back tears, she pressed a hand to her stinging cheek. What she'd give to be big and strong. He'd die for what he'd done to her friends. *To Canna.*

He yanked her to her feet. "You pull that again, and I'll kick your teeth out."

He would too.

An arm around her, he set out. Each touch of her foot on the ground felt like knives stabbed through her ankle. Tears pooled in her eyes, then spilled over.

The bouncy music grew louder, and Mella spotted the source. In a backwash of a jutting corner, some itinerant musicians had set up, playing a guitar and pianete. They had a decent sound system, enough to reach quite a ways through the crowd, and the bored people waiting for admission to the reserved fastpad area were tossing royals onto the makeshift stage.

Thinking only of his destination, Nathan headed right for the fastpad gate. Mella clenched her teeth. He'd bribe the guards, go to the head of the line and straight to the ship. Her chance at avenging Cap and Pard and Johnnie and Canna would vanish.

And she'd die.

Bitterness churned inside her. How funny that everybody in the galaxy thought Armelina Archer was already dead. Like that vid she'd seen showing an altar holding her name and a miniature harp. Flower bouquets had spread like a garden around the little memorial. If they only knew...

Mella sucked in a breath. *If they knew...*

She and Nathan stood only a few feet from the two musicians. Both male. She was female, and some Nexan men considered her exotic. Would the musicians think so?

What can I lose?

Twisting in Nathan's grip, she jammed her knee right into his private parts.

With a horrible low sound, he released her, his legs buckling. He curled around himself, covering his groin.

Left without support, Mella staggered, and agony seared through her ankle. She couldn't even walk; fleeing wouldn't work. The musicians were her only hope. She threw herself on the plank stage.

The singing stopped abruptly. "Sands, Miss. Are you hurt?" The younger one, barely into his twenties, helped her onto his stool.

"By Mardun's sword, she's a slave, Caratill." The other young man had a scraggly beard and worried brown eyes. "We'll get in trouble if we help her, Brother."

Her helper took a step back, and she gave him a meltingly sweet smile, even as terror fizzed through her stomach. If Nathan got up, if he said she was trying to escape... *Hurry, hurry, hurry.* "I wanted to ask if I could sing. Just one song with you."

The brothers glanced at each other. "That be a different request," said the older one, and then he shrugged. "What do you want to sing?"

"'Lament for a Lost Spring.'" Gratitude at such kindness almost brought tears to her eyes. She glanced over to where Nathan had started to move. "I wrote it when my sister died."

Ignoring their look of *this woman is crazy; she thinks she composed Archer's song*, Mella set her fingers on the pianete's keyboard. She closed her eyes. Took a breath. Pulling up the music in her mind, she let it flow down her arms. The opening strains—bouncy like Kalie's attitude, then turning somber as the young life was snuffed out before truly being lived.

Without having to think, she raised her voice in the song as sadness twined around her like a vine in winter, the shriveled leaves falling to a cold ground.

As the noise of the crowd slowly died, Mella opened her eyes. She saw the people's shock as they realized who she was—that Armelina Archer truly lived. She felt their joy. Her song, what she'd considered her present to the world, flowed back, transformed by their love into a gift for her in turn.

When she slowed into the final strains, she realized there was more to say. She needed to tell what Dain had taught her, so she continued on, adding what she had so recently learned: *There is life after death and love after mourning.*

Tears glittered on the faces of the people gathered near the platform, and her own cheeks were wet. "Thank you," she whispered to those who had listened. Even if she died now...

Arms came around her from behind, and she jolted, yet the embrace was gentle, and then Dain's cheek pressed against hers. "I think you ripped my heart out with that one," he murmured in her ear.

She saw Nathan being yanked to his feet by enforcers. He glared at her, and she didn't care. She turned her face to Dain, feeling the strands of her soul return from the music, rewoven into something new.

Dain tightened his arms around her.

Here was her anchor, her safe place in the universe. *Her home.*

✦   ✦   ✦

THAT EVENING, MELLA stood beside the refresher at the enclave. After sending Nathan off with his enforcers, he'd tucked Mella into his solacar. He hadn't wanted to talk about anything. Said they'd discuss it all later. His face had been hard and cold, his hands gripping the wheel so tightly, his knuckles turned white.

And then he insisted on showers for both of them and carried her here into his refresher without listening to her protests. Apparently, she might be Armelina Archer, but she was still his unshuline.

Of course, he dominated just about everyone this way. On Earth, they'd call him the alpha of the pack.

Silently, he stripped and stepped into the shower. After adjusting the settings, he picked her up and set her beside him. "Brace yourself, laria."

"Why?" The warm water hit her bottom. "Ow!" *Ow, ow, ow.* Every welt he'd given her last night burned like fire. He'd known how much it would hurt. She glared at him.

His cheek creased, and the chill in his eyes lightened with his amusement, but his hands were very gentle as he washed her with cleansing gel. Gentle, but also thorough, and a little more intimate than she'd anticipated. When he helped her into the drying stall, her butt hurt, her nipples tight, and her pussy throbbed.

After the jets dried her off, she paused. What should she do now? Return to her room? She had no nightgown. And she couldn't walk.

He stepped up beside her, finished drying, and carried her to the bed. "Lie on your stomach."

She gave him a suspicious look. "Why."

His voice deepened. "Now, Mella."

She rolled over before she could stop herself and then craned her neck to see behind her.

He squirted something in his hand and applied it to her bottom.

She yelped at the searing pain. When she tried to squirm away, he put his knee down on her lower back and held her in place as his fingers rubbed cool lotion into the welts. Her hands were fisted by the time he had finished.

"Sorry, laria, but your pretty set of stripes will heal faster this way."

Fine, but she might die from his healing techniques. He moved to straddle her, and his balls brushed tantalizingly against the backs of her thighs. He picked up a bottle off the nightstand.

"No," she said. "No more. Please."

He chuckled. "This won't hurt. Your body isn't used to being restrained like you were last night." Lotion drizzled over her back, making her jump, and then he firmly stroked the silky liquid in and her tenseness out. When his hard fingers massaged the knotted muscles in her shoulders, her eyes almost crossed. He knew just how much to press, right to the edge of pain, and then he would ease, letting blood rush into the loosened muscles.

The bed became fluffy clouds, and she sank down through them, and she didn't care, her mind drifting in pure enjoyment.

Halfway to sleep, she felt herself being turned over, and her eyes popped open. "Hey."

She lifted her hands to protest and looked straight into dark, disapproving eyes. "I will do the front now, and I want your hands at your sides. Can you keep them there, little thief, or do you need help?"

Prophet, when he talked to her like that, her insides quivered. "I-I won't move."

His eyes crinkled.

She relaxed as he massaged more lotion into the front of her shoulders. His strong hands circled her arm and squeezed the tension out of those muscles. He did the other arm, the top of her chest, and then, with a faint smile, he squirted lotion right onto her breasts.

She squeaked. "I don't think those have muscles."

"Ah, laria, look how tight your nipples are." His lotion-covered finger circled one jutting tip, then the other, sending heat lancing through her. Watching her through half-lidded eyes, he massaged her breasts, then returned to the jutting peaks, rolling each one between his fingers until she arched up.

She was still tender from her use at the party, and his calculated touch poised her on the edge of pain and pleasure.

By the time he moved down her body, her breasts felt swollen and too tight, and her nipples throbbed. More lotion drizzled onto her stomach, accompanied by teasingly soft touches that moved lower and lower, until her pussy burned in anticipation.

"Spread your legs for me." His gaze on her face, he waited.

She wanted him, wanted his touch, but somehow this seemed so much more intimate than it had before. She knew more of him, but mostly...he knew who she was now. He realized she wasn't a real unshuline, but he hadn't changed how he treated her.

As if he read her thoughts, his lips curved, and a firm hand closed on her uninjured ankle in an unmistakable warning. Either she followed his command, or he would tie her legs open. As he'd done before.

She parted her legs, and he lay down on the bed between her knees, his broad shoulders pushing her even farther open. She could feel how wet she had grown, and a second later, so could he as he touched her intimately.

She gasped. After the long night, her labia were exquisitely sensitive, and if he—

"Ah!" Her hips jerked as his finger stroked over her clit. Just the flickering touch sent sizzles of electricity through her body.

His laugh was deep. "My fingers are too rough? All right, then."

His mouth engulfed her clit in heat, and she moaned at the exquisite sensation. His tongue circled her, teasing the ridges of the hood, barely brushing the acutely tender clit itself. Her hips wiggled, and his arm settled on her stomach, pressing her into the mattress as his tongue continued its leisurely movement.

He drove her higher, until her eyes squeezed shut, until only his touch remained, until she panted with burning need.

Then she felt his finger pushing her swollen tissues aside and sliding into her, awakening nerves deeper in her body. The incoming sensations ricocheted back and forth between his tongue on her clit and his finger inside, merging into an aching, craving whole. Each stroke he gave her was deliberately, agonizingly slow, and her vagina tightened around him in desperation. She tried to lift her hips and couldn't.

He slowed even further. As her breathing stopped, he kept her poised at the pinnacle, straining. And finally, finally, his tongue rubbed hard right on top, and his finger pressed deeper.

Everything in her exploded, and devastating pleasure cascaded through her. With each wave of ecstasy, she could feel the hard pulsing of her insides around the thick intrusion.

Before the convulsions stopped, he rolled her over with firm hands and pulled her back onto her knees, lifting her bottom high. His hand between her legs made her moan, and then his thick shaft pressed against her and slid into her still-spasming vagina. Her oversensitive, swollen tissues stretched around him until his cock filled her completely.

She moaned as the intense pleasure smothered the discomfort, and the knowledge he was taking her for his own satisfaction excited her even more. He kneed her legs farther apart, the position allowing him deeper inside her body.

Her breath came in hard gasps. He gripped her hips, holding her, anchoring her in place. Her hands fisted on the covers as he moved inside her, withdrawing, sliding in. Gradually his speed increased, and he set an erratic rhythm she couldn't predict.

A burn flickered to life and spread through her entire lower half.

THE LITTLE EARTHER moaned, long and low, her husky voice turning the sound into a song of pleasure.

The joy of being inside her was like nothing Dain had ever felt before. That she finally, *finally* trusted him added another layer of satisfaction.

He hadn't planned on taking her, not after what she'd experienced, but he wanted—needed—to mark her as his. Knowing Hamilton had touched her… The compulsion drove him to possess her, brand her, so no one could steal her away again.

He dug his hands into her hips, and she tightened around him as she neared release. *Not yet, little thief.* She wouldn't rob him of a long ride. He slowed, withdrew until only the crown of his shultor bobbed in and out of her. Her thighs, held wide by his, quivered as she strained to push her hips back, to shove her maline onto his cock.

"Soon, little one, soon," he said, and her inmaline clenched at just the sound of his voice. By Cernun's spear, how could he let her go? Yet his barely formulated plans to keep his unshuline after her indenture had fallen into dust today. She wasn't an unknown thief, but the most renowned singer in the galaxy.

Smoothly he plunged back in, hammering in short, fast strokes that would take them both to the top. Reaching down, he slid his fingers through her wetness and over her clit.

"Sing for me, sweet Armelina," he murmured as her whimpers changed to moans and then a lovely set of high cries as she came, hard and fast.

He rode her through her orgasm, the milking sensation on his shultor adding to his enjoyment. As the need became overwhelming, he pressed so far into her that he touched her womb, and finally let himself go. His release seemed to start in his toes, moving up and squeezing his globes and then bursting into sharp jerks of pleasure.

Still firmly encased in her center, he rolled to one side, pulling her back against his chest, and wrapped his arms around her. Tonight they would sleep joined together as deeply as any couple could.

And tomorrow he would release her from being his unshuline.

Chapter Twenty-one

*B*LOOD COVERED THE *walls and the floor in ghastly pools of red. It dripped from the lamps. Red everywhere. Her hands were sticky. Thick, hot rivulets ran down her face.*

"You're next." Nathan stepped into her hotel room, gripping a knife. "I've come—"

Her own scream woke her. Mella shuddered, scrambling upright in her bed. She slept with the bedside lamp on these days, and now she stared around the room. *No red.* She rubbed at her perfectly clean hands, where the obscene feel of the blood lingered. After sliding out of bed, she hurried over to check the door.

Locked. Chained. Chair wedged under the handle.

And still she had to look under the bed and in the closet before her heart would stop pounding.

Pushing sweat-dampened hair back from her forehead, she glanced at the shower. No, she couldn't. Not yet. Later, when she wouldn't spend the entire time listening for footsteps over the sound of the water.

She sank onto the bed with a hopeless groan. *What am I going to do?* When she slept, the nightmares came. Every single night—except the one she'd spent in Dain's arms.

Tears stung her eyes. Why had he released her? Hadn't she shown him that she loved being his unshuline?

What did I do wrong?

But she knew. The day after the incident at the spaceport, Dain had answered the house comunit, and his grandfather had seized the opportunity to speak to her. "*Cowardly Earther, you almost cost me a great-grandchild. She still can't talk.*" He'd spit on the floor and walked away.

Coward. Little. Fat. Not a leader or strong or anything else that Dain's kinline required in a mate. Just as well she'd let her staff carry her off to the hotel. At least with the trials and finances and all the details involved in coming back from the dead, she only missed Dain, oh, maybe half of every minute.

She scrubbed her hands over her face, feeling the dampness. Crying again. This was pitiful. *She* was pitiful.

But why, why *couldn't he have loved me?*

He hadn't even come to see her. Or called.

All that wonderful night, she'd just known he'd keep her. He'd been so loving. Caring. She rubbed her chest. Every day the lump in there got bigger. Heavier. Someday it would take over, and all that would remain would be pain and nightmares of blood.

It was time to go home. To Earth.

DAIN STABBED THE comunit off and stared at the blank wall of his office. Once again Mella's lackeys had turned him away. As if he stood on Ekatae's burning sands, anger heated his blood. He rose to pace across the room.

He'd just discovered that she'd booked passage on a starship leaving tomorrow. *Tomorrow.*

By Cernun's spear, he'd been a fool. He'd wanted to give her time to recover and get her life back on solid footing before he talked to her. He thought maybe…maybe they might have a chance together. But as her people from Earth arrived, she'd disappeared behind vast layers of protection. They knew that he no longer needed to see her in an official capacity, and in their narrow-minded Earth mentalities, Armelina Archer couldn't possibly need to speak to a Nexan, so they never let his calls through.

In fact, she might not even know of his calls. At that thought, his fury boiled over. He slung on his enforcer belt and loaded it as if he were going patrolling for regstal. Pausing at Esosha's desk, he said, "I'll return tomorrow. Handle everything."

Her mouth dropped open. "But your appointment with the council and—"

The rest of her complaint faded away when he walked out the door.

He left the solacar in front of the hotel with the enforcer lights running to keep the doorman at bay. In the lobby, he ignored the line and stalked right up to the reception desk. "What room is Armelina Archer in?"

The thin clerk gaped at him. "I'm sorry, sir, but I cannot—"

Dain dropped one hand to rest on his holstered zapper.

"Six fifteen," the young man blurted.

"Thank you."

He made it past the guard at the entrance to the hallway, then pushed aside the admin type who opened the door to the suite that apparently served as an office. Mella's bedroom must be on the far side. He eyed the short, pinch-faced woman who planted herself in front of him, as feral as a hungry relix. She reminded him of a miniature Arewell female; no back-down at all.

With a grunt of annoyance, he grasped her around the waist and tossed her onto the couch. They could probably hear her shriek of anger all the way at the port.

The door to the bedroom suite opened, and Mella appeared. "Cynthie, are you all—" When she saw Dain, her face drained to white; the only remaining color, her jewel green eyes. "Dain?"

He crossed the room—*to the sands with proper etiquette*—and pulled her into his arms.

Far from protesting, she burrowed closer, like a canin pup. Soft, round, warm. *Mine.*

HIS CLEAN, MASCULINE scent engulfed her, and she couldn't seem to get close enough. When his arms tightened around her as if in response to her thought, she sighed.

After a time, perhaps a long time—had Cynthie tried to talk to her?—she finally pulled back. He released her immediately.

Her heart pounded so loudly; surely he must hear it. But he couldn't want her clinging to him.

She had a vision of him trying to leave and how she'd clench his ankle so hard he'd drag her with each step. *I have more dignity than that...don't I?* She cleared her throat, but her voice still came out husky. "Did you come to say good-bye?"

He didn't answer, just regarded her for a long minute. His eyes narrowed, and then he walked around her as if she stood on the auction stand.

"Dain?"

He actually growled. Taking her chin in his hand, he turned her face from one side to the other. "Have you slept at all since you left me?"

The unexpectedness of the question made her blink. He released her only to grasp her upper arms and squeeze. "Have you eaten anything?" His voice was low. Harsh. His gray eyes looked even angrier than when she'd lied to him—not cold, but blazing hot.

"I—"

Three men burst in the door, followed by Cynthie. "There he is. Remove him at once."

The security guards got two steps before Dain turned his furious gaze on them. They stopped so suddenly that one bumped into the other.

Dain didn't move. "If you annoy me, you'll see the inside of a Nexan prison within an hour."

Mella could see the moment his enforcer uniform registered. That and the menace in his voice finished off the guards.

"Uh. Sorry, sir." They tumbled back out the door posthaste, one whispering to Cynthie, "Crap, woman, that's an enforcer. Do you know what they do to criminals here?"

Cynthie glared after them before turning to Dain. "Listen, you, I—"

"What kind of care have you taken of your mistress?" His tone was just one note away from a snarl. "Look at her."

Cynthie bit back an answer. Her muddy brown eyes raked over Mella and widened. "Armelina, you look horrible."

"Well, thank you." Nothing like feeling ugly to improve a nice good-bye. Mella averted her face to hide the dampness in her eyes. Maybe he wouldn't notice.

"Laria, do not cry," he murmured. "You'll break what's left of my heart." Picking her up like a baby, he cradled her in his arms.

He gave Cynthie a steely glare. "You may escort us to the exit so that your massively incompetent staff allows us to leave."

He was going to take her with him…because he felt sorry for her? She pushed against his chest, which only made his arms tighten more. "Dain, I can't go home with you. I'm leaving tomorrow."

The look he gave her was one she recognized all too well from their times in the bedroom. "You can, and you will, little Earther," he said evenly. "You will eat. You will sleep in my arms tonight.

"And we will talk."

WHEN THEY REACHED the enclave, the joyous sensation of coming home terrified her. *The ship leaves tomorrow.* And she still felt contentment fill her just from being enclosed within the massive adobe walls. Dain's embrace gave her exactly the same feeling. *Prophet help me, I'm a mess.*

He parked the solacar at the back, and as they walked across the lawn, Quenoll appeared. The old gardener didn't speak, but his pleased smile and the blue *toriday* flower he handed her needed no words.

"Thank you," she said, her voice only a whisper of sound.

Dain tucked an arm around her and pulled her into the house. "Do you want to see Cannalaina before I feed you?"

"May I?" Mella gripped his arm as hope rose in her. "Really?" She'd wanted to see the girl so badly, but after the clanae's words and Dain's good-bye, she'd known she wasn't welcome at the enclave any longer.

A frown flickered over his face. "Of course, laria. Why would you not?" His fingers curled warmly around the back of her neck. "Canna's asked about you every day. So you go on in. I'm going to tell Ida that you need to be fed up."

Canna and Reblaini and Felaina sat in the clan family room, working on an intricately carved wooden puzzle. Mella was at the table before they saw her.

"Mella!"

"Mella!"

The two children slammed into her, knocking her back a step with their enthusiastic hugs.

After bestowing a multitude of kisses, tiny Rebli crossed her arms over her chest and frowned at Mella. "Where have you been?"

Mella ran a fingertip over the black brows. So like Dain's, even to the crease between them. Her heart squeezed painfully. "I had lots of business things to take care of, sweetie. I thought of you often." So often that her finance man had decided she had the concentration of a gnat.

"Oh."

"Canna, are you all right?" Mella asked and braced herself for the child's answer. She'd searched the infonet and discovered that the side effects of the z-rod included paralysis, nerve damage, and even brain dysfunction. Each article had deepened her shame. If it weren't for her, Canna wouldn't have been hurt.

"Sure, I'm fine," Canna said. "Mama made me stay in bed for a day." She scowled at her mother. "And I missed Lisadona's party."

"You're all right? Really?" Hope rose like a swelling tide. Mella looked at Felaina for confirmation.

"Really. One day of being unhappy and that's it." Still sitting, Felaina pulled her daughter back and squeezed her tightly. "She's a lucky girl. And she'll never do something like that again, will she?"

"No, Mama." Canna squirmed.

Mella leaned against the arm of a chair. "Why was she in the Indenture Hall, anyway?"

"Dain had asked me to take your clothes to the hall so you'd at least receive them when your indenture ended." Felaina tugged her daughter's hair. "While I talked to the manager, this little felin decided she'd find you. She sneaked into the hallway at just the wrong time."

Tears filled Canna's eyes, and she came to stand in front of Mella. "I'm sorry for my—what I did. You got hurt because I didn't mind Mama."

"Heavens." Mella's eyes puddled up too. "You got hurt because of me, Canna. It's my fault."

Felaina snorted. "If anyone asked me for my opinion, I'd say we should blame the unbred regstal who held the z-rod." She rose. "Now, my little babies, let's get cleaned up for lastmeal." She shooed the children out the door and stopped long enough to give Mella a hug and whisper, "I've missed you."

Mella cried for a good five minutes after that, and it took a while for her to put her composure back in order. Honestly, she'd turned into an emotional faucet. Now she had red, puffy eyes, and Dain had already mentioned she looked horrible.

Just the thought of him sent her heart racing and gave her prickles all over her skin. One more day with him. *One more day.* Pain and joy mixed in a disharmonic tune inside her as she stepped into the hallway—

And ran right into Dain's grandfather. "Heavens, I'm sorry." Not that she'd hurt him any. Hitting that old man had felt like bumping into a tree. "I'm just on my way to find Dain." She tried to step around him.

He stepped in front of her, blocking her way. His mouth was tight, and his eyes had turned blacker than night in the dim hallway. He looked her up and down, making her acutely conscious of being short. And round. And cowardly.

Her hands fisted at her sides, but she straightened and lifted her chin. *Do your worst, old man.* Her ship left tomorrow, and nothing he said could hurt as much as leaving Dain would.

"Canna said you would have gotten away if she hadn't arrived," he stated, not asking a question.

She answered anyway. "Perhaps. Perhaps not."

"You let him capture you to keep her from being hurt."

Mella's eyes filled. "It didn't work, did it? He still stunned her."

"But not on the full charge."

She shrugged. "I don't know why he switched it."

"I do." The clanae's lips curved slightly as he crossed his arms over his chest. "He feared your reaction if he murdered her in front of you."

Nathan. Threatening to kill Canna. Fury surged through Mella, tingeing the walls with red streaks. She snarled under her breath, "I would have killed him. Killed him and—"

A deep chuckle from the old man startled her, and she shook her head to loosen the tightness around her skull. What in the world was wrong with her? "Um, sorry, sir." She edged sideways.

"Your method of escape by singing was rather unique," he said, moving to block her again. "Of course, a Zarain woman would have flattened him and not had to resort to such silliness."

Her mouth tightened, and she forced herself to keep her chin up. What she wouldn't give to transform into someone tall and brave and strong. Someone worthy of Dain's attention.

"But you didn't panic. You took advantage of the opportunity presented." A corner of his mouth curved upward. "Your actions were intelligent and brave. And loyal."

Her mouth dropped open. *A compliment?*

"You will take fighting lessons." With a firm nod, he stepped around her and continued down the hall, leaving her staring after him.

+   +   +

SHE'D EATEN WELL, and Dain smiled to see some of the haunted look disappear. He put his arm behind his head and studied her for a moment.

The little thief had obviously suffered over the past days. The trial of Nathan Hamilton had been the worst media circus Dain had ever seen. The rude Earther reporters who'd flooded the city hadn't bothered to learn Nexan laws or courtesies. Their judgment improved radically after a pair of enforcers took the forbidden vid-cameras and tossed them into recycle bins. Dain had ordered a bonus for his two men.

The Earthers had expressed their disbelief in the Nexan truth-readers, and the relationship between the two planets might have suffered, but then Mella had given the judge a holocard. Two worlds watched in fascinated horror when the judge played the hologram and Hamilton convicted himself with his boasting.

Dain's mouth tightened, thinking of what Mella had suffered. The murdered crew had been her friends. She'd been alone. Terrified. No wonder she'd been forced to steal, tried to escape. If he'd only known...

But, he hadn't. He'd have to burn away his guilt and regret by ensuring that Mella was never, ever afraid again.

By the end of the trial, Mella's ex-husband knew he'd attempted murder on the wrong planet. His money and power had proved useless on Nexus, and any obligations others owed to him—including marriage—were severed with his conviction. His shoulders had been hunched, his face drawn tight with fear by the end of the speedy trial.

The sentencing had been fast and brutal. Hamilton, Nilard, Hanwell would spend the remainder of their short, painful lives in the mines.

Of course, the man's life had almost ended in the spaceport. Dain had never been so close to abandoning his vows as when he'd caught up to Hamilton in the port concourse. One blow and Mella's ex-husband would have died with a broken neck. Thank Cernun's justice that Gregior had arrived to take custody and...

"Dain?"

"Sorry, Iaria. I was remembering last week at the port." Dain shook his head and returned his attention to the moment at hand. And a very lovely moment it was.

She started to lean forward.

"Do not move."

She hesitated. Balancing on her knees on the mattress, the little Earther straddled his hips, his shultor deep inside her. Face flushed with arousal, she quivered when he gripped her buttocks to hold her still.

"But—"

"You do not have permission to speak," he warned. Smothering his smile, he stroked his fingers over her lush breasts, pinching the nipples into peaks. Her arms moved, and he gave her a look that kept her hands laced behind her back. "You're a beautiful woman, little Earther," he murmured.

Her only answer was a whimper. She hovered very close to her release—and that precipice was right where he wanted her.

"I thought perhaps the time had come for us to talk."

Her eyes widened, and she gave a tiny bounce as if to say *get on with the business at hand*. But that wouldn't happen until he asked his question. And received the correct answer.

"All your legal and financial problems are concluded, I believe," he said.

Her eyes darkened, so he pressed upward with his shultor to remind her of her immediate concerns. Her sharply inhaled breath pleased him.

Her singing pleased him even more. Earlier, he'd heard her singing in the hallway, and then in the shower, and later when she'd strolled in the shade garden at dusk. Her heart had healed, and now music trailed after her like a canin pup on a leash.

"You plan to leave tomorrow," he continued.

Her head bowed. "Yes."

He could feel the sadness well up in her, and he wanted to hit himself. As much experience as he'd had with women, he'd been blind when it came to her. Blinded by his own desires.

She doesn't want to leave me.

His hand traced down her soft stomach to the engorged, glistening somaline just above where his flesh joined with hers. When he slid his finger over the wet nub, she tightened around him. "Stay here, Mella. Stay as my wife."

HIS WORDS MERGED with the coiling tightness in her, merged with his stroking finger, and burst into an overwhelming orgasm, shaking her from the inside with the intensity. Her cries echoed through the room.

She heard his deep laugh, and then his hands gripped her hips tightly as he moved her up and down on his shaft, sending more exquisite sensations through her. Hard and fast. He groaned, and she could feel him pour into her as if giving his very essence into her keeping.

With firm hands, he unlaced her fingers, bringing her hands forward, and then he rolled them over. His weight came down on her, and he remained deep within her. She wrapped her arms around him, feeling the contoured muscles of his back. *Never let go.*

He braced his hands on each side of her face, forcing her to look into his dark eyes. "Answer my question, Armelina."

Hearing her real name from him still had the power to thrill her. *He wants me to stay.* Joy washed through her until she could hardly contain it. She smiled at him, pushing the sensations back, striving for some control. "You didn't ask a question, now did you?" she asked, daring to tease him. *I'm Armelina, not just an unshuline.*

His gray eyes were intense as he searched her face. "Will you be my wife?"

The clanae had shown his approval at supper. Afterward, Dain's mother had caught her in the gardens to discuss kinline colors and how she should properly display them on her gowns.

Then Dain's sister had dragged Mella off to feed the tiny green fish in the courtyard pond, gifting Mella with stories of Dain and how stubborn and dominant he'd been even as a child. When Felaina warned that his children would be the same, Mella's knees had wobbled. Have Dain's children? And then she had remembered. "*I can't have children. I'm barren.*"

Felaina had frowned at her. "*No, the Indenture Hall doctor would have noted that on your papers. Just like they did for that murderous agrustal. He's the infertile one.*" She had sniffed in disgust. "*Did he try to blame you?*"

Not barren? He'd lied? The anger had given way to the joy welling up inside. She could—really could—have Dain's children.

Felaina had laughed and then kissed Mella's cheek, saying, "*He's an overbearing, bossy man, but you will always feel safe. And very loved.*"

Looking up at him now, she could see that love. And what she could give him in return. He had a dark job, and he needed her joy and lightness as much as she needed his strength.

Her lips curved. "Well, if you'd asked me a minute ago, I would have agreed to anything." In the past two hours, he'd brought her to the edge of coming over and over again, damn him. "But now—"

He growled and took her lips, plunging deeply inside as if to establish his territory. She gave back equally, feeling her body tighten around his shaft as he brought her to arousal again. She began to burn.

Lifting his head, he traced her lips with his tongue. "Little thief, you've stolen my heart," he murmured, and then his gray eyes trapped hers. "Now give me an answer."

"Well, I don't know. Can I keep singing?"

A crease appeared in his cheek as he recognized her teasing tactics. But his reply took her breath away. "Of course. And with the excessive security here at the enclave and in Port City, you can sing for an audience if you wish."

He would keep her safe. She had no fears when he was near. And she remembered the feeling, the bond between her and the people in the port, the flow of energy streaming from them, changing her song, changing her. Her heart gave a hard *thump*. "Oh, Dain, yes."

He knew how she had wanted an audience. Just as he knew how to touch her. Or when she needed a hug, or even when she liked to be ordered around. He gave her so much, but…she could give him much in return.

"Will we have children?" She stroked his cheek, touched the scar over his eyebrow. Didn't dodge a knife fast enough, he'd told her with a shrug. From saving Blackwell, she knew. Tough, stubborn man. Dedicated man.

"As many as your heart can hold." His eyes darkened. "As long as your heart holds me also."

She studied the deeper lines bracketing his mouth. The betrayal of his enforcers had hurt him. She ran her finger over his firm lips, those demanding lips that never lied. Pressing her hand to his chest, she felt the steady, unwavering beat, and she whispered, "You already live in my heart; didn't you know?"

Even as he smiled and took her lips in a kiss, the seed of a new song, one of love and belonging, took root within her and gently bloomed.

~ The End ~

Want to be notified of the next release by Cherise Sinclair?

Sent only on release day, Cherise's newsletters contain freebies, excerpts, and articles.

Sign up at:

http://www.CheriseSinclair.com/NewsletterForm

Nexan Glossary

agrustal: four-legged, wolf-sized, omnivorous amphibian that comes out of the ocean to breed during the rainy season.

aphrodica: drug to create need for sex.

Artema: daughter goddess who reigns over spring, mercy, and charity.

backcountry: less-populated and -civilized parts.

berstal: flying carnivorous reptile with a spring and fall migratory pattern.

canin: dog.

Cernun: father god who reigns over winter, law, learning, and government.

cherly: small red fruit.

clanae: head of clan which is made up of several kinlines.

comunit: any communication device.

deerlet: small deerlike creature with horns curving back over its head, very fast.

doshuline: brothel slave.

Ekatae: one of the gods, but considered outside the world and the pantheon; crone goddess of death; carrion-eater animals (buzarn and jackals) are associated with her. Upon death, a mortal walks her desert sands until the cares of the world are burned away.

enforcers: police serving in the Planetary Security force.

felin: knee-sized, sleek, multicolored cats.

flutter: dragonfly type insect.

globes: testicles.

greiet: large, furry, timid rodent with short, round ears. Turns white in the winter months.

Herina: mother goddess who reigns over summer, home and hearth, and children.

hovercar: antigravity vehicle used on Earth.

infounit: computer.

inmaline: vagina.

kinae: head of a kinline.

laria: sweetheart.

larrien: tall bushes used for hedges.

lefnant: officer rank used for enforcers and militia.

maline: pussy.

Mardun: son and warrior god who reigns over fall and war.

mounut: mouse; a small, cowardly rodent.

panthat: cousin, loved relative, or friend.

parogan: tiny yellow bird that likes water.

pianete: musical instrument similar to an Earth piano.

podnat: an ocean polyp similar to anemone that moves across the ocean bottom to eat. Only able to move and eat. Brainless.

pyr: large guard dog, often used to tend livestock.

r-pen: restraint pen that delivers a shock when force lines are crossed.

regstal: seven-feet-tall, carnivorous reptile with a seasonal migration pattern.

relix: cat-sized lizard that eats insects. Snakelike neck and very fast strike.

ronves: small, fragrant, flowering bushes.

shulin: the act of sexual intercourse.

shultor: cock.

solacar: Nexan vehicle with antigravity, usually heavily armored.

somaline: clit.

stadilaig: truth drug with the possible side effect of damaging the mind.

The four gods: Cernun, Herina, Mardun, Artema, Ekatae is considered outside the world and the pantheon.

toriday: blue flowering plant.

truth-reader: one who can determine if a person is telling a lie; all judges on Nexus are truth-readers.

truth-say: the act of truth-reading.

unshuline: sex slave for one person.

vid: television equivalent, sometimes with holographic capabilities.

wulkor: large, feral canine.

x-scan: medical X-ray.

z-rod: electric shock device with different settings.

zapper: weapon used to stun, only holds one charge.

Preview of
The Wild Hunt Legacy: Book 1
Hour of the Lion

Readers prepare to be swept away by this amazing tale! Author Cherise Sinclair has another winner with Hour of the Lion!

~ Shannon The Romance Studio

Erotic paranormal ménage romance

FIRST A MARINE, then a black ops agent, Victoria Morgan knows the military is where she belongs...until a sniper's bullet changes her life. Trying to prove she's not washed up, she rescues a young man from kidnappers. When the dying boy transforms into a cougar—and bites her—she learns of an entire hidden society. He begs her to inform his grandfather of his death and to keep the secret of the shifters' existence. She can't refuse, but what if the creatures pose a danger to the country she swore to protect?

As guardian of the shifter territory, Calum McGregor wields the power of life and death over his people. When a pretty human female arrives in their wilderness town, he and his littermate become increasingly concerned. Not only is the little female hiding something, but she is far more appealing than any human should be.

While investigating the shifters, Victoria begins to fall in love with the werecat brothers and the town as well. For the first time in her life, she might have a real home. Her hopes are crushed when a deadly enemy follows her from the city, and the shifters discover she knows their secret. Now nobody is safe—least of all Victoria.

Excerpt from Hour of the Lion

"WHERE ELSE ARE you hurt?"

Why would the big sheriff ask that? Vic wondered, feeling a chill. She'd covered the blood and bruises adequately. Had her description and injuries been on an APB?

Dammit, he'd already given her one scare. For a nasty moment, she'd thought Swane had hired him until it became obvious he was just a small-town cop having himself a good time.

"Don't be silly," she said, deliberately misunderstanding. "A little nail scrape doesn't warrant all this concern."

Nudging his arm away, she shook hands with the realtor. "Ms. Golden, nice to meet you."

"Just call me Amanda." Tall, blonde, wearing silky black pants with matching jacket, she was the epitome of a refined style that Vic had never mastered. After giving Vic's hand a firm shake, the realtor frowned at the cop. "Is there a problem?"

"You got here just in time," Vic said. "Your policeman was about to arrest me and haul me away."

Amanda's snicker wasn't at all businesslike. "Ah, yes. If his jail's not overflowing with criminals, Alec feels he's not doing his job." She leaned forward and whispered loudly, "Of course, it's only a two-cell jailhouse."

Vic smiled and glanced over her shoulder to see how the sheriff took being taunted. With one hip propped on the railing and a lazy grin on his tanned face, he didn't look too upset.

When his focus shifted from Amanda to Vic, his gaze intensified, as if he were trying to see inside her. She felt a quiver low in her belly, but from worry or attraction—she wasn't sure. Probably worry.

Towering six feet five or so with appallingly broad shoulders that narrowed to a trim waist, the man moved like a trained fighter. Not all spit and polish like a soldier though. His golden-brown hair brushed the collar of his khaki-uniform, and he'd rolled his sleeves up, revealing corded wrists and muscular forearms. She remembered how easily he'd lifted her, how those big hands had wrapped around her. He was damned powerful, despite the easy-going manner.

Yeah, the quiver was definitely from worry.

But then he smiled at the realtor, and a dimple appeared at one corner of his mouth. The laugh lines around his eyes emphasized a thin blue-tinted scar that angled across his left cheekbone as if someone had marked him with a pen. His voice was deep and smooth and slow as warm honey, and she felt her muscles relax. "You have a mean streak, Amanda," he was saying. "I'll have to warn Jonah."

"He wouldn't believe you," the realtor said as she worked on unlocking the front door.

The sheriff turned, letting that should-be-a-registered-weapon grin loose on Vic, and her temperature rose. "So," he said, "Ms. Waverly, will you be staying in Cold Creek?"

He was gorgeous, and he looked at her as if she was something tasty. "Um…" she said and his smile increased a fraction, just enough that she realized what an idiot she was. *You're losing it, Sergeant.* She scowled at him. "A while."

And the sooner she left this damn town, the better.

The breeze whipped his shaggy hair "Well, while you're here—" he started.

"I need to get my stuff," she interrupted. Anything to escape. Odd how the scare from the sheriff's appearance had wiped out her need to pee.

To her annoyance, he followed her down the steps. "You're going to enjoy Cold Creek," he said. Before she could dodge, he slung an arm around her shoulders, and she felt his fingers trace the thick gauze dressing covering the cat-bite.

"Thank you, but I can manage," she said, smoothly enough despite the way her heart was pounding. Then she looked up.

Dark green eyes the color of the mountain forests narrowed, and he studied her as if she were a puzzle to be solved. A quiver ran up her spine as she realized the laidback manner and slow voice camouflaged a razor-sharp intelligence. Knives tended to come at a person in two ways: dark and hidden, or out in the open, all bright and shiny. A bright and shiny blade could still leave you bleeding on the sands.

She pulled away. "I'll be fine."

"Well then, I'll take myself off so you can get settled in." He waved at Amanda Golden and smiled at Vic, but this time the smile didn't touch his eyes. "I'm sure we'll run into each other again, Ms. Waverly. Cold Creek's a small town."

Cordial, polite. And Vic heard the threat underneath.

✦　✦　✦

Want to be notified of the next release?

Sent only on release day, Cherise's newsletters contain freebies, excerpts, and articles.

Sign up at:

http://www.CheriseSinclair.com/NewsletterForm

Also from Cherise Sinclair

About Cherise Sinclair

Authors often say their characters argue with them. Unfortunately, since Cherise Sinclair's heroes are Doms, she never, ever wins.

A *USA Today* Bestselling Author, she's renowned for writing heart-wrenching romances with laugh-out-loud dialogue, devastating Dominants, and absolutely sizzling sex. Some of her many awards include a National Leather Award, *Romantic Times* Reviewer's Choice nomination, and Best Author of the Year from the Goodreads BDSM group.

Fledglings having flown the nest, Cherise, her beloved husband, and one fussy feline are experimenting with apartment living. Suffering from gardening withdrawals, Cherise has filled their minuscule balcony with plants, plants…and more plants.

Connect with Cherise in the following places:

Website:
http://CheriseSinclair.com

Facebook:
https://www.facebook.com/CheriseSinclairAuthor

Facebook Discussion Group:
http://CheriseSinclair.com/Facebook-Discussion-Group

Want to be notified of the next release?

Sent only on release day, Cherise's newsletters contain freebies, excerpts, and articles.
Sign up at:
http://www.CheriseSinclair.com/NewsletterForm

Printed in Great Britain
by Amazon

33585767R00131